To Kam,
tai chi buddy
Chuck

# WILHELM'S WAR

# Wilhelm's War

## A Novel

### Charles H. Stammer

iUniverse, Inc.

New York Lincoln Shanghai

# Wilhelm's War
## A Novel

Copyright © 2004 by Charles H. Stammer

iUniverse books may be ordered through booksellers or by contacting:

iUniverse
2021 Pine Lake Road, Suite 100
Lincoln, NE 68512
www.iuniverse.com
1-800-Authors (1-800-288-4677)

ISBN: 0-595-33609-4

Printed in the United States of America

To my wife, Shirley, and to my

children, David and Nancy,

with whom I have spent

the best part of my life.

# CONTENTS

▼

# Acknowledgments

My sincere thanks go to the members of the Athens, GA, Third Wednesday Writers Group, who have listened to and patiently critiqued this manuscript many times over. I am grateful to the late Professor James Kilgo, who allowed me to take part in his classes, as well as to Professor Emeritus Charles Beaumont, both of the Department of English, University of Georgia. Thanks as well go to Vicki Bauer for strong encouragement and to Jennifer Patrick for editorial evaluations and especially to Mary O'Briant for volunteering to copyedit the manuscript and to Walter O'Briant for formatting assistance.

# Foreword

When my neighbor, Charles Stammer, casually mentioned over the back fence one day that he had written a book about his experiences as a POW in World War II, I thought the manuscript might be interesting to read. But since I knew him not as a writer but as a professor of organic chemistry at the University of Georgia, I also thought it a bit unusual. My experience as a copyeditor didn't suggest that a scientist accustomed to writing grant proposals and scientific articles might produce a literary work of any special value. Intrigued, however, I promised to look the manuscript over for him when time permitted.

Several weeks later, *Wilhelm's War* appeared at my doorstep and, well, was I surprised! Once started, I had to read on to the finish. Professor Stammer has written a compelling novel, based on his own and others' experience of being captured in the so-called "Battle of the Bulge" and subsequent imprisonment by the Germans.

Technically, this book falls into the "creative nonfiction" genre, because Stammer has told his story through the words and actions of a fictional character, Jimmy Wilhelm. He has combined and embroidered the basic facts of Wilhelm's experience to make the narrative more gripping than a day-to-day account might have been. The story represents real life during a dark time in Stammer's own young life—he was just nineteen at the time—and, through the skillful use of dialogue, he draws his readers into the misery that he and his buddies experienced during the terrible winter of 1944–45.

As Stammer's story unfolds, it becomes clear that his misery was compounded by the fact that he came from a German family. He grew up enjoying traditional German holiday food and songs. So when he found himself under orders to kill German soldiers, the ambivalence many soldiers feel about killing was compounded by his fear of killing a relative.

In this time of renewed appreciation for men of the "Greatest Generation," many books about life in POW camps have appeared. But Stammer's account differs dramatically from others I have read. Most important is its readability and the sense the reader gets of Wilhelm's real-time thoughts—the thoughts of a boy who belonged in school but found himself in a war he didn't fully comprehend. Although Stammer wrote *Wilhelm's War* later in life, from a mature person's perspective, he captured his subject's youthful, somewhat nerdy naïveté. For example, he writes in an amusing way about Jimmy Wilhelm's efforts to read an organic chemistry textbook during lulls in the fighting.

I found *Wilhelm's War* to be an easy and fascinating read but, beyond that, a source of deep insight into what life was really like—and in some universal sense what life is always like—in war. Wars are fought by young men on the ground in freezing rain, or snow and ice, or under a blazing sun, knowing their chances of survival are problematic. Yet they persevere, and in the end, if their luck holds and they come home safely, they carry on, perhaps enjoying a life that they, better than many of us, know is truly dear.

Mary O'Briant
October 2004

# CHAPTER 1

▼

# BORN AGAIN

"God, that air smells good," Jimmy Wilhelm mumbled as the three-quarter-ton truck dropped off the ramp and splashed up the embankment into the little town. A cold December wind blew through the open cab as thoughts of the clear spring air back in Indianapolis filled Wilhelm's head. Spring's a long way off, he thought, a helluva long way off.

Double-clutching into second gear, he turned to the stocky soldier seated beside him. "That diesel-oil stink on those ships really gets to me, Sarge. Bother you much?"

"Some." Cradling the submachine gun on his lap, Steve Dolan thought not about diesel oil and spring air but about whether the three rookies he'd been stuck with could be made into a real radio team before the shit hit the fan. Squinting at the wisps of smoke rising from a burnt-out tank in the cobblestone gutter, he doubted it.

"I was sicker'n a dog last night. That damn LST comin' across the Channel was worse than the ship comin' over."

Wilhelm kept his eyes on the truck in front.

The sergeant turned and stared, but said nothing.

Wilhelm hesitated, then tried again. "Sorta like bein' born again, ain't it, Sarge? Comin' up outta that big hole in the nose of the ship?"

Wilhelm grinned, hoping to get a smile out of the old-looking guy next to him. The wrinkles around Dolan's eyes and the gray stubble next to his ears augmented Wilhelm's thought. Still a mystery to the nineteen-year-old, the sergeant had come to the Signal Company only a few days before the division had left England. He'd heard Dolan was a high-voltage lineman at P.G.&E. back in California before the war. He's got to be one tough guy to climb around on those high-tension wires all the time, Wilhelm decided. Sorta like my dad, the ex-Marine sergeant—you don't want to make him mad.

"If you say so," Dolan finally responded.

Got more'n three words out of him that time, Wilhelm mused. More'n the whole time crossing the channel. He shifted into third gear and pulled the truck closer to the two-and-a-half ton on the road in front of them. Staring at the men jammed into the back of the big truck, he thought again how lucky he was to be a radio operator, not an infantryman. Basic training at The Infantry School in dear ole Fo't Bennin' GA was bad enough. A lot of those dogfaces in that truck up there won't make it back. But I will. I'm going to school. I got *things* to do.

Seeing conversation was hopeless, Wilhelm looked around at the rubble and smoldering buildings along the street. He decided the town had probably looked a lot like the little English villages they'd passed through on the way to Portsmouth. But they didn't look anything like the small towns in good ole Hoosierland.

The scene changed as the truck convoy rolled deeper into the town, a few businesses open, others under repair. "Not too bad here, is it? Must notta been too much shootin' along here."

Dolan swung around. "You ever been in a firefight, Wilhelm?"

"Uhh, no, I guess I...."

"Well, then, don't be sayin' what's bad and what ain't. You don't know shit about it."

Wilhelm looked away. Jeez, I gotta watch what I say to this guy. Damn sergeants are all alike. Think they're God's gift to mankind, or something. He felt suddenly light-headed, like back on the LST watching the puke slosh back forth in the piss trough, or breathing the stink of the swabbies' food in the chow line.

But maybe he was just afraid of the big fight that was coming. He'd always avoided fights, except with the redheaded preacher's kid across the street, and now here was the big fight—*the war*—the battle he'd spent the last fifteen months training for. He didn't really want to kill Germans. He came from German stock. He liked Germans. Hell, he thought, I might kill a Wilhelm, a cousin or an uncle, or something. I don't want to do that.

"C'mon, kid, quit dreamin' and move up! The convoy's pullin' away!" Dolan's steel gray eyes stared ahead.

Wilhelm double-clutched into third and gunned the engine, the rear wheels spinning, backend fishtailing.

"Sorry, Sarge." He wished he hadn't said that. "Never make excuses, Jimmy," his dad always said. "Just keep your mouth shut and do what you're told."

"You been in France before, Sarge?" Dammit! It just popped out. Why don't I keep my mouth shut?

"Yeah. Took a bullet on the beach. Spent some time in rehab."

"Oh." Wilhelm blinked. "Not too crazy 'bout comin' back then, I guess, huh?"

"Oh, yeah. I'm nuts about it." Dolan almost grinned. His voice dropped a notch. "You guys just do your job, I'll be okay." Dolan shifted his chaw and spat into the ditch along the road. "You know the guys in back?"

"Charko and Goldman? 'Bout as well as you do, Sarge. They came to the Company just before you did."

Dolan nodded and went back to watching the road. The town gave way to trees and bushes, broken hedgerows, pock-marked fields, and the bent-iron debris of war. The two men sat in the freezing wind, watching the sleepy-eyed men, bouncing and swaying in the truck ahead. Wilhelm was wondering why they never told them anything, where they were going, what they would do when they got there. "How long you think it'll take us to get where we're goin'?" Wilhelm shouted above the roar of the engine.

"We don't run into some kinda trouble, we oughtta be in Belgium by tomorrow. Or the next day." Dolan leaned out and decorated a snowdrift with his own brand of tobacco juice. "Just watch the ruts and keep this crate on the road, kid. We'll make it okay."

Kid. So now I'm a kid. Well, *Mister* Dolan, I don't need driving lessons from you or anybody else! My dad drives a fire truck, and he taught me all I'll ever need to know about driving. Wilhelm grinned. The old blue Plymouth bucking to a stop, his dad shouting, "Kick the clutch out! Kick the clutch out!" popped into his mind. His first driving lesson was the day the war started, he remembered. They had just come home when they heard the old Atwater-Kent radio in the living room shout, "The German Army has just attacked Poland." All that killing on such a hot, sunny Hoosier day. Five years ago, now. My God, how time flies.

A boreal wind, quick and cold, whistled through the open cab, bringing a thin, icy rain with it. Wilhelm's left arm already felt wet, the rain soaking through his overcoat and field jacket. Shoulders hunched and collar up, he stopped making conversation and concentrated on the narrow, winding strip of road before him. He had double-clutched and shifted gears so many times by now, his left calf and right arm ached.

Just after dark, the convoy stopped along the side of the road. The men got out, relieved themselves, and headed up the convoy to find some chow. Wilhelm broke out his raincoat and mess gear and joined them. Dolan stayed behind, waiting, apparently, until the others were fed. Coffee slopping, dehydrated potatoes, corn, and slimy limas cooling fast, Wilhelm trotted back to the truck and dropped into his seat. The aluminum cup scorched his lips, but the strong, bitter coffee warmed him. Head resting against the wall behind the seat, he closed his eyes and listened to the soft patter of rain on the canvas overhead. Back home, he'd kept his bedroom window open at night to listen to the rain. Even French rain made him sleepy.

Dolan returned with a full mess kit and began to eat. Wilhelm yawned. "Where we sleepin' tonight, Sarge? In the back?"

Finished eating some minutes later, Dolan stuffed a fresh wad of Red Man in his mouth and worked it around. "The back'll only sleep three, two on the benches and one on the floor. Somebody'll either hafta sleep up here or up top."

Wilhelm's forehead wrinkled. For sure, Sarge ain't sleeping up top, and I ain't either. Not if I can help it.

"You got a sleepin' bag, ain't you?"

"Yeah. But I don't think it'll fit around this gearshift up here." Wilhelm grinned hopefully.

"Waterproof, though, ain't it?"

"Well, yeah, it's s'posed to be. But it's brand new and I ain't never…."

"Okay. You sleep up top. Find out if your new bag is waterproof." Dolan almost chuckled.

Well, shit, I sure stepped into that one. "Awright, Sarge, if I hafta." Hell, I shoulda left the damn thing home. I'll be sleepin' out in the cold and wet the whole time we're over here, while the other guys're sleepin' inside. Lips pursed, he dropped out into the road, walked around back, and pushed open the overhead door. He yanked his duffle bag out and, rain dripping off his steel helmet onto his hands, undid and opened it.

"Whacha doin' there, Wilhelm?" Grinning big, Corporal Izzy Goldman dropped into the road next to the driver and looked down into Wilhelm's bag.

"Dammit, Goldman, back off, will ya! You're runnin' water into my stuff!" Wilhelm pulled out his raincoat and put it on, found his sleeping bag and flung it up on top of the truck.

"What the hell's that?" Both men knew what it was. Goldman's grin became a snicker. "Hey, it's a sleepin' bag, ain't it?" The small soldier stuck his head back into the truck. "Hey, Blackie, look at this!"

Corporal Charko, the fourth and arguably the best radio operator among them, hung over the tailgate. A dark, heavy-set fellow from Chicago, he had washed out of the Air Corps radio school and had been assigned to the 106th Signal Company with several others.

"I'm sleepin' up top tonight 'cause I wanna get as far away from you guys as I can." Wilhelm kept a straight face.

Blackie nodded. "That means me and you'll be sleepin' in here tonight, don't it Goldman." They smiled at each other.

"Yeah, but the Sarge," Goldman's eyes flashed around the edge of the truck, "will be back here with us, buddy. We'll be dry and warm, though, won't we, Blackie? Dry and warm!"

Eyes narrow, Goldman turned to Wilhelm. "Sarge put you up there on account a you got a sleepin' bag, didn't he?" He laughed long and low. "You got a real ass-soakin' comin,' buddy. Ain't no way that thing's waterproof."

"Well, thanks a lot, Goldman. I didn't know you were an expert on sleepin' bags. Like always, I treasure your opinion." For ten days, Goldman had shared a double-decker bed with Wilhelm in the midlands of Merry Old England. They knew each other only too well.

Wilhelm closed his duffle bag. By way of the tailgate, he hoisted it and himself onto the top of the truck and laid out the sleeping bag—a gift from his dad before he shipped out. Water's beading up nice, he mused. Very good. The plywood beneath the canvas creaked as he stepped around his new bed.

Wilhelm flinched when three more duffle bags came flying up and dropped next to him. Then Charko appeared with a roll of black, waterproof paper, left over from that used to encase the plywood roof and walls of the back of the truck. "I got an idea, Wilhelm," he said, "how we can fix you up real good."

Wilhelm grinned at the dark-eyed, chubby fellow, the last to join the team and still pretty much a stranger. Catching on to Charko's plan, he helped him stretch the paper over the sleeping bag and tuck it under the duffle bags laid out on either side. "There you are, buddy! Your own personal pup tent. Gonna be dry as shit in the Sahara up here." Charko's tobacco-stained teeth flashed in the growing darkness.

"Well, thanks a lot, Blackie. It looks good. Real good." Maybe I oughtta get to know this guy, Wilhelm told himself. He's a strange one, though.

Some time in the middle of the night, a trickle of cold water on his toes woke Wilhelm. He reared up and found the waterproof paper gone, his sleeping bag amid a teeming lake the size of Garfield Park. He pulled the flap back over his head and looked around. His shorts, long-johns and pants were wet. Longjohns and pants must be wet too, he decided. This is bad. Real bad. The worst thing that can happen when you're out in the middle of nowhere. Go down and climb inside? Hell, there's no place for me in there. Already wet. Might's well stay here. He stuck his head out and squinted up into the rain. "Damn you! How'm I ever gonna get dry after you drowned me like this?" The wind whispered, "How, indeed?"

*       *       *       *

Three days later, Wilhelm was driving down a narrow road, painstakingly following a pair of deep, white ruts through a long, dark tunnel. Belgian pines, their limbs knitted together above the road, hung low beneath a cloud-laden sky. Snow swirled down slim, white corridors between the snow-laden pines. The sporadic roar of cannons and the ticky-tick of machine gun and rifle fire came from somewhere up ahead.

"Finally get your stuff dried out, Wilhelm?" Dolan blew a wad of tobacco into a passing snowdrift and stuffed a fresh lump in his mouth.

"Yeah, just about. First Sergeant let me hang my blankets and bag in front of the power generator's fan. Bag's still damp, but it's okay."

"Good." Dolan rolled his chaw from cheek to cheek and squinted ahead. "Keep your eyes peeled, now, kid. We oughtta be comin' to this here coffin corner pretty quick." Dolan's gloved finger rested on the map in his lap.

The hair on the back of Wilhelm's neck came to attention. "The *coffin corner,* Sarge? What's that?" "Yours is not to question why, yours is but to do and die," flashed across his mind, followed by, Who the hell said that, anyway?

Dolan frowned. "That's what the Capt'n called this open spot on the mountain up ahead. Not far from the Siegfried Line. Kraut 88s got it zeroed in." He grinned at his driver. "Don't sweat it. Just drive easy, kid, and let me do the worryin'."

"Yeah, okay, Sarge. Okay." The burnt-out trucks and tanks he'd seen back in France flashed across Wilhelm's mind. The captain must be nuts, sending us this way. Back in basic, they told us officers always looked out for their men. GI bullshit, I guess.

"Watch it here." Dolan shouted. "Looks like we're comin' to the end of the...." The truck bounced wildly and veered to the right, as the ruts ahead became a sea of mud. The woods on the left dropped away into a ravine, while a towering cliff dotted with boulders and twisted pines shot straight up on the right. Goldman and Charko in the back, their helmets cracking against the truck's plywood top, began to yell.

Suddenly, a salvo of shells slammed across the road and up the cliff. Mud, rocks, and limbs rained down. Stunned, Wilhelm floored the accelerator and tried simultaneously to shift into second gear. The engine died, and the truck slid to a stop at the edge of the ravine. The "kid" looked down at the twisted wrecks below and froze.

"Dammit, Wilhelm! C'mon! Get goin'! Get goin'! The bastards are reloadin'! C'mon!" Gasoline fumes blew in their faces. "You got the fuckin' thing flooded, boy! Pump it! Pump it!"

Wilhelm shoved the gearshift in neutral, pumped the accelerator with his left foot, and hit the starter rod with his right. "C'mon, baby! C'mon! C'mon!" he cried, bouncing back and forth in his seat. A second salvo of 88s screamed over and into the face of the mountain, mud and rocks again raining down. The engine ground and whirred and finally caught. The wheels spun and, just as a third salvo roared in, the truck tore around the mountain to safety.

"God damn!" Wilhelm shouted. "God damn!"

▼

# CHAPTER 2

# THE FIRST ONE IS ALWAYS THE WORST

Knees weak and mind still spinning, Wilhelm rested his helmet against the truck's warm hood, his belly cold against the left front fender. Stalled her right in the middle of the Krauts' favorite target. Damn near got us all killed on the first day! Screwed up royally. Whole damn mountain like to fell on us. On the Sarge's shit list from now on.

Wilhelm lifted his head and peeked across the yard at Dolan, Charko, and Goldman, standing before the little gray farm house. The sergeant looked straight at him, his face hard.

God, I hate those two guys. Goldman's a pain in the ass. Charko'd be okay, if he'd quit grinning all the time and wipe the spit out of the corners of his mouth. I have to spend the rest of the war with those two, I'll go nuts.

Hand shaking in his thick "driver's glove," he finished wiping the mud off the windshield, picked his carbine off the wall behind the driver's seat, and started for the house. The word KRATUS smeared white on the olive-drab side of the truck caught his eye. One of Al Hopper's double-talk words. "Kratus! The Greek Goddess of Victory!" Al had yelled at them as they had pulled out of the English midlands. "It'll bring you guys good luck wherever you go."

A funny guy, Al was, always acted like the war was some kind of game. *I wish to hell it was.*

"The truck okay?" Dolan squinted as Wilhelm arrived at the house.

"Yeah, she's okay. A few dents, but she's okay."

"How 'bout the radio?"

"Oh, uhhh, hell, I didn't think to…I'll go back and…."

"Nah. We'll check it out when we move it inside. Right now we gotta clear this house and get on the air." Dolan swung his machine gun—a 45-caliber weapon the GIs called a grease gun—off his shoulder, hawked, and spat.

"I know you guys ain't been at the front before." His eyes swung across to each man. Charko took a drag on his Lucky Strike and looked away; Goldman's cheek twitched more than usual. "So let's go over some things you maybe forgot about since basic: first, the Krauts don't give a shit whether you operate a radio or drive a tank, you're just another fuckin' dogface to them." He spat, letting his words sink in. "Killin' GIs is what they do for a *livin'*. So don't forget it."

An old speech, Wilhelm decided, probably gave it to his boys before they hit the beach back in June.

"Okay, now," Dolan continued, "don't touch *nothin'* in the house till you check it out. Could be booby-trapped. Keep your eyes peeled and your ears open, and you'll be with us tomorrow. Maybe even the next day."

Goldman, his cheek knotting, raised his carbine and stepped toward the big front door. The back of Dolan's hand caught him flat across the chest.

"Hold it!" the sergeant growled. "You don't move till I say 'Move'! You don't do *nothin'* till I say to! You got that, soldier? You got it?" Stepping back into his tracks, Goldman nodded slightly, his weapon still pointing at the door.

"Okay, now, let's go on in. Charko, you take the point."

The fat soldier blinked, rolled his eyes, stepped in and punched the door open with the butt of his carbine. The door banged into the inside wall and bounced back.

"For chrissake, Charko, why don't you just tell ever'body we're here?" Dolan hissed. "Keep it *down,* will ya?"

"Hell, Sarge," Charko mumbled, stepping over the high stone threshold, "anybody don't know we're here must be deef as a hole." The sergeant ignored him.

Goldman and Wilhelm followed Charko inside; Dolan, Janus-like, stopped on the threshold, looking both inside and out.

"God! What's that stink?" Wilhelm's nose wrinkled.

"That's shit, Wilhelm! You don't rec-a-nize it?" Goldman chuckled.

"Damn. We gonna stay in this dump, Sarge?" Charko held his nose and turned back to the door.

"Awright, forget the shit and stay on your toes." Dolan stepped inside and looked around. The foyer, lighted only by pale snow-light coming through the open door, went all the way to the back wall, where a stairway, looping back over their heads, rose to the second floor. On their right, under the stairs, a half-open door led to the living quarters, while to the left, a wall, damp and peeling, held a large wooden door. A shuffling sound behind it brought Goldman and Wilhelm around, their weapons leveled. Charko, carbine across his chest, backed up the stairs onto a small landing.

"Wilhelm, make sure there ain't nobody behind you in there." Dolan's head indicated the living quarters. "Be quick about it."

The heft of the carbine always made Wilhelm feel strong, invincible. Carefully, he pushed the parlor door all the way open and stuck his head inside. "Looks clear in here, Sarge," he said, softly, turning back into the foyer.

"Okay, you guys don't do *nothin'* till I get back! Charko, let's check out that noise."

After Charko had passed through the outer door, Dolan turned back. "You guys don't do *nothin'*. You got it?" They nodded.

Goldman, clicking his carbine's safety off and on, grinned at Wilhelm. "Hey," he whispered, "soon's we hear 'em over there, I'll whip 'at big door open and you can ketch whoever's there from behind. Okay?"

"For God's sake, Goldman, you heard what Sarge said! We ain't s'posed to do *nothin'* till he gets back!"

Goldman, carbine in his right hand, stepped over to the big door and laid his left hand on the latch. "Ready?"

"No, dammit! I ain't...." A squeak, a shuffle from the other side and Goldman yanked the door wide open. Wilhelm stopped in mid-sentence and threw his carbine up to his shoulder.

Across the rump of an old sway-backed, slab-sided cow, Dolan's white-hot stare met his. "Jesus H. Christ, Wilhelm!" the sergeant shouted, "Didn't I tell you *not* to....?"

Goldman, snickering softly, slammed the door shut and slipped back across the room. Lips pursed, Wilhelm lowered his weapon and heaved a sigh. Oh, God, I'm in for it now.

Charko came through the outer door with Dolan right on his heels. "What in the billy-blue hell you think you're doin', Wilhelm?" Dolan's face glowed pink in the whitish light. "You coulda killed me over there, boy!" Tobacco juice squirted into the dirt at Wilhelm's feet. "You keep on, and you'll be haulin' an M-1 up at the front. I'll ship your ass out so quick it'll be draggin' crap!" He looked at the other two men, both grinning. "You think this is funny?"

"No, Sarge, we just…." Dolan's glare cut Charko short. Goldman turned away and pulled out a pack of Camels.

Dolan pointed a finger at Wilhelm's chest. "You pull that kinda shit up at the front, kid, and them dogfaces'll put you on 'fuck-up patrol' so the Krauts can get a shot at you."

Wilhelm squeezed his lips together, but the words tumbled out anyway. "Yeah, but, dammit, Sarge, Goldman pulled the door open and…." The look on the sergeant's face stopped him. His eyes dropped to the floor.

Dolan chewed and spat. "Charko, get upstairs and check it out, then get back down here. I'm gonna need you on the radio." He squinted at Wilhelm. "Awright, kid, if you're done fuckin' up for the day, get on in the front room and check it out. Goldman. Back him up."

Heart thumping, Wilhelm turned and forced his feet to carry him and the weight of his many crimes into the living quarters. Gray-gauzy light streamed through the big front window to his right; a large wooden table with slat-backed chairs all around sat before it. The edges of the table looked fuzzy, as in a dream. He thought to wipe his glasses but remembered he'd lost them on the ship coming over. The pot-bellied stove in the center of the room, its crinkled smoke pipe poking through the ceiling, softened his mood. He would sleep next to it, if Dolan said okay, warm and comfortable in his sleeping bag.

On the long wall across the room, a crippled couch slumped under a large, gold-framed picture. "My God!" he mumbled, "It's The Crucifixion! These Krauts are Christians! I didn't realize they were just like us, uhh…." the thought choked off when he remembered Goldman there behind him. "But they go right on killin' people, don't they? Killin', killin', and more killin'."

It struck him that he was a Christian, too, albeit not a very serious one, and had come here to kill people. The thought faded when his eyes fixed on an open doorway in the far corner of the room. The deep, menacing darkness inside made his belly contract. Check it out, he wondered, or wait for Dolan?

"Okay in here, Wilhelm?" The sergeant stood looking into the room.

"Yeah, looks okay, Sarge."

Dolan pushed past Goldman and looked around. He pointed at the open door in the corner and nodded at Wilhelm. The eternal question—Why me?—flipped across the corporal's mind. He stepped across the room and hesitated.

"Looks like a landing, Sarge. Maybe a stairway to the left goin' down to the...."

"Well, go on! Check it out!"

Wilhelm stepped into the gloom and squinted down the stairs into the darkness. Suddenly, a red-white muzzle-flash, a deafening roar, and flakes of plaster flew at him. He threw himself back into the room, the butt of his carbine slamming down as his head hit the floor. For a few seconds, he neither felt nor heard anything. Then the ceiling came into focus, his eyes burning, full of grit. He felt, smelled heat, something black, something burning. A tall black shape stood over him. This is it. I'm dead and gone to hell. His eyes followed the object all the way to the ceiling. From the floor, the stove looked a deep, ominous black.

"Get up, Wilhelm! You ain't hurt! C'mon! Get up! Get up!" Dolan, shouting, leaned against the wall next to the cellar doorway, a grenade in his hand. As Wilhelm sat up, the sergeant pulled the pin, allowed the safety handle to fly off, and tossed the grenade around the corner into the stairway. They heard it bounce twice, hit a wall at the bottom, and roll. The explosion, ear-shattering in the small room, brought The Crucifixion down behind the couch and a blizzard of plaster off the ceiling. Wilhelm thought of snow falling back home.

Dolan jumped into the stairwell, sprayed 45s down into the darkness, and swung back into the room, the muzzle of his gun smoking. Goldman, apparently enjoying himself, squinted down the barrel of his carbine at the doorway. He turned and grinned down at Wilhelm. Dolan was removing a second grenade from his ammo belt when a guttural shout came up the stairs. *"Kamarade! Kamarade! Bitte! Nicht Schiessen! Nicht Schiessen!"*

Wilhelm, on his feet now, retrieved his carbine and brought it to bear on the doorway. The slow thump of hob-nailed boots sounded on the stairs.

Dolan, still next to the doorway, waved Goldman left and Wilhelm right. "Careful! He's carryin' a burpgun! He moves, kill him!"

Charko, carbine at the hip, crept into the room from the foyer, his face pale.

A tall, square-bodied German, hands reaching for the ceiling, limped out of the darkness. *"Kamarade! Kamarade! Bitte! Bitte! Schiess nicht! Schiess nicht!"* The man's bloodshot eyes flashed around the room at the four muzzles pointing at him.

Goldman, a growl in his throat, stepped forward and shoved the muzzle of his weapon into the German's midsection, pushing him against the wall. *"Bitte,* my ass!" he shouted. "Hands up all the way! *Hände hoch! Hände hoch!"* Without warning, the small soldier slammed the butt of his carbine into the man's underbelly. The soldier doubled over, coughed, and spat at the feet of his attacker. "Why, goddam you! I'll...."

"Awright, that's enough, Goldman! Get away from him! Get away!" The sergeant stepped in and shoved Goldman back. He turned the German around, shoved him against the wall and proceeded to search him up and down, inside and out. The sergeant found the man's wallet and shoved it inside his field jacket, saying, "G-2'll wanta see this."

Finished, Dolan shouted, "Awright, you, down on the floor!"

Still facing the wall, the German didn't move.

Having heard Goldman speak some German a moment ago, Dolan turned to him. "Goldman, turn 'im around and get 'im on the floor. Keep his hands on his head."

Goldman, grinning, shoved the muzzle of his carbine into the prisoner's back. *"Umstehen!"* he growled. Slowly, the German turned, red-rimmed eyes glaring.

"C'mon, you bastid. *Hände am Kopf! Schnell! Schnell!*"

The man folded his hands atop his cap. Goldman's carbine moved as if to strike again. *"Sitzen! Godammit! Schnell! Schnell!"* The prisoner dropped to the floor.

Wilhelm stared at the German, his ruddy cheeks, sharp nose, and protruding ears. Like Dad's, he thought, and mine, too, I guess. He looks like cousin Carl—my uncle's big, stupid kid. Called him Junior instead of Carl. He rubbed the scar between his thumb and forefinger, a reminder of the lighted four-inch firecracker Junior had tossed at him one Fourth of July. Stupid, stupid, stupid.

"This bugger's the one what damn near blew your head off, Wilhelm." Goldman said, grinning. "You wanta have a little talk with 'im, or maybe I could do it for you."

"No, don't hit him anymore, Goldman. Don't hit 'im any...." Wilhelm stopped when he saw the sergeant staring at him.

"You almost fucked up again, kid. But this time it was *your* ass on the hook." He chuckled. "Next time you stick your nose around a blind corner like that, you're li'ble to pull back a bloody stump."

Remembering clearly that Dolan had *told* him to look around that corner, Wilhelm stared back. Next time, he told himself, I'll ignore you, you sonofa—a little voice in his head, his dad's, he was sure, immediately vetoed the thought.

Dolan's grin expanded into a full-fledged smile as he looked around the room. They'd got themselves a prisoner their first day at the front. Could get him an extra stripe. He walked over to the landing and looked down into the darkness.

"Awright, Goldman," the sergeant's finger stabbed toward Goldman, "you and Wilhelm stay with the prisoner. Keep him down, hands on his head. And, you—you keep your hands off 'im. He's gotta be healthy, so G-2 can grill 'im. You got it?"

"Don't worry, Sarge. I won't gut the sumbitch 'less he makes a move I don't like." Goldman's head canted sideways, a sly grin on his face.

"C'mon, Charko, fire up your flashlight. Let's go down and see what else is in the cellar. We gotta finish checkin' out this place toot sweet, so we can get on the air."

The two men disappeared down the stairs, Charko's yellow beam cutting the dusky darkness on the stairs. Wilhelm watched from the landing, while Goldman, that half-grin still on his face, stood staring down at the prisoner.

Half a minute passed. Suddenly, a yell, then carbine fire and the staccato roar of Dolan's gun. Goldman leapt around the corner into the narrow stairwell and stared over Wilhelm's shoulder into the darkness.

Suddenly, a black boot slammed into Goldman's back, catapulting him into the stairwell and knocking Wilhelm sideways against the wall. He hung there, watching Goldman crash down, until he realized what had happened. Tearing back up the stairs and across the empty parlor, he heard the squeal of rusty hinges and the slam of the front door. He pushed through the door and fell over the high stone threshold into the snow. "Dammit," he yelled, scrambling up.

He saw a black boot disappear around the back of the truck. "My goddamn cousin is gettin' away, and Dolan is gonna blame me for it!" He ran to the front of the truck, slammed his weapon across the hood and took aim. The German's dirty green coat, a bobbing target as the German high-stepped through the snow toward the woods, sat nicely atop the carbine's front sight.

"Halt!" Wilhelm shouted. "Halt, you bastard! Halt!" I can't shoot him in the back. You ain't *never* supposed to shoot a man in the *back*. The carbine fired. The runner swayed but kept going. The small rifle fired again, and this time the target went down, arms outstretched, into the snow.

Wilhelm felt numb, completely without feeling. He held up his hand and glared at his trigger finger. "You shot him. You shot him in the back, you dumb...." Inside the glove, his finger seemed without remorse. Crazy, he thought, I must be going crazy!

Goldman, carbine up, came running around the truck, cursing aloud. When he saw the German face-down in the snow, his jaw dropped. "Way to go, Wilhelm! Way to go, buddy!" He went to the fallen man, rolled him over with the barrel of his weapon. "Deader'n a fuckin' doornail! Good shot, Wilhelm! Damn good shot!"

Something deep inside Wilhelm snapped. "Dammit, get away from 'im, Goldman!" He rushed around the truck. "Get the hell away from 'im!"

Surprised, Goldman faced his buddy. "Who the hell you think you are, tellin' me what to do?"

Dolan ran up between the two men. "Okay, okay! Knock it off! Get back! Both of you! Get back!"

Wilhelm dropped to his knees beside the dead German. Up close, the big man's high cheekbones, eyebrows, and hairline seemed to confirm Wilhelm's surmise: he was family for sure. The rough, bloody edges of the wide hole in the man's chest, the exit wound of Wilhelm's bullets, had bled copiously. The dead man's wide, blue eyes stared into Wilhelm's. To him, they seemed to carry some kind of message.

"Goldman, you and Charko go on and unhook the radio, take it outta the truck and into the house. Set it on that table by the front window. I'll be there in a minute." Goldman, eyes still on Wilhelm, nodded and backed away slowly.

One hand on Wilhelm's shoulder, Dolan squatted down next to him and looked at the body in the dirty green coat. "It's okay, kid. I know how you feel. The first one's always the worst." He looked hard at Wilhelm. "You *had* to plug him, kid. You *had* to. He'd a told 'em about us soon's he got back, and they'd a come after us soon's the sun went down."

He pulled Wilhelm to his feet. "You did good. Now, let's get to work. The radio's gotta be on the air soon's we can get it heated up."

"Sergeant?" Wilhelm's half whisper was barely audible. "Could I see his wallet?"

"The Kraut's wallet? Sure. If you want."

The leather folder held several pictures: an old man and woman sitting stiff-backed in front of a younger couple with a big blond soldier between them, dated June, 1941, then a young woman with long blond hair, the name "Hildegaard" in German script at the bottom. The soldier's *Soldbuch,* his paybook, gave his full name: Klaus Hermann Langer, III.

"Thanks, Sarge." Wilhelm tried to smile. "I just wanted to know who it was I…."

Dolan nodded. "Yeah, okay. Okay. Let's get to work."

Dark clouds and the sounds of big guns rode in on the east wind. I want to be back in school, Wilhelm was thinking. What I wouldn't give to be there right now. This minute!

# CHAPTER 3

▼

# O TANNERBOM! O TANNERBOM!

With the radio ensconced on the table in front of the parlor window, an aerial strung, and their first transmission logged, the team started a fire in the little stove and brought in their duffle bags. Wilhelm's sleeping bag fit the lumpy couch perfectly. He and Dolan would use it between shifts on the radio. Hot chow was only a five-minute walk away, and things in the East lay cold, white and quiet.

Next day, as Wilhelm sat alone at the radio, the flash and roar of the German's burpgun, the bouncing green coat, the dark, bleeding holes in the dead man filled his mind. Thinking how easy it had been to take a life, he held up his hand and flexed his forefinger.

Just then, Goldman walked in. "Whatcha doin' there, Wilhelm? Givin' 'im a peptalk? Workin' him up for next time, huh?"

Wilhelm glared. The radio emitted its dying-dog whine, so he leaned in close and tweaked the fine-tuning knob. "Damn Krauts' jamming signal is really somethin'," he said, ignoring Goldman. "You tune out one signal and another one comes in right behind it."

Goldman smiled. He moved to the stove and held his hands up to it.

Wilhelm was wondering how Charko was able to get Division's signals to come in so clear and clean. Musta got some kinda special training in the Air Corps, he mused. Too bad we didn't get some of that.

Stomping the snow off his feet, Dolan came in and stopped next to Wilhelm. "Check in with Division, yet?"

"Yeah, Sarge." Wilhelm pointed at the log sheet. "A coupla minutes ago."

"Where's Charko?"

"Upstairs," Goldman said, grinning. "Found some Frenchie stuff up there. Second Division guys musta left it. Y'oughtta see it, Sarge. Some a' them French babes got tits the size of a...."

"He just got off the radio, Sarge," Wilhelm inserted. "Said he'd been on since oh-four-hundred and was gonna hit the sack a while."

"Yeah, okay. Goldman, go out and rev up the truck. Make sure the battery's okay." Dolan waited until the front door slammed, then swung one leg over the corner of the table. "You okay, kid? Get over shootin' that Kraut okay?"

Wilhelm looked up, surprised. "Oh, yeah, Sarge, I'm okay. I feel fine."

"I been wondering, why'd you wanta see his stuff, anyway?"

Wilhelm looked away, his mind racing: Should I tell him? Will he think I'm some kind of nut or what? "Well, to tell you the truth, Sarge, the man sorta looked like somebody I knew back home."

"Wilhelm's German, ain't it? Were you thinkin' he might be a relative, or somethin'—right?"

Wilhelm swallowed hard. "Well, yeah, Sarge. He looked a lot like one a my cousins." He waited for a reaction but got none.

"Awright. I don't give a damn if you got a German name, as long as it don't affect your job. Nobody in this team hangs back when the shootin' starts. You got that?"

"Yeah, Sarge, I got it. You don't have to worry about me." Feeling warm inside, Wilhelm smiled at the fine-tuning dial and made another infinitesimal adjustment. He was glad everything about his German descent was out in the open now. *Dolan is all right. Takes a real interest in his men. Bet my Dad did that, too.*

Things settled in. Hot chow at the cook shack next to Regimental HQ, quard duty around the house at night, two-hour shifts on the radio, and sleep when the work was done. *Not too bad for a combat radio team,* Wilhelm thought. *Not bad, at all.*

On the third day, the corporals got mail, Christmas and Hanukkah presents, cookies, cake, scarves, sweaters, socks, and underwear. Wilhelm had to wipe his eyes after reading the note his mother had placed in the soft wool scarf she sent him. He could see her in the living room sitting next to his dad, knitting and laughing at Bob Hope's jokes on the radio. Her favorite. He realized how little he had appreciated her, and he vowed to do more when he got home.

Dolan, who had received no mail, surprised his men when he volunteered to cover the radio while they went out and cut a "tannerbom" for Christmas. They picked up their carbines and trotted out the door before he could change his mind.

Wilhelm, struggling across the field in front of the house, turned and looked back. Dolan sat, feet up, next to the radio looking down at something. "Probably checkin' out Charko's Frenchie pictures," he mused. Snow squeaking beneath his boots reminded him of hunting with his dad and Uncle Ray in the cornfields back home, the time he missed with both barrels and his dad shot the rabbit in full stride with one shot. *Bet I could kill one now at a hundred yards,* he told himself.

"Awright, here's a good one."

Wilhelm, wondering why his Jewish comrade was so interested in a Christmas tree, shook his head. "It's too big, Goldman. We'll never get it in the house."

"Hey, I got the axe, so I pick the fuckin' tree. Okay?"

"Okay, okay. Anything you say—boss." Wilhelm turned away. "You and me better keep an eye peeled, Charko. We don't wanta get caught out here by some damn Kraut patrol, or somethin'."

Charko laughed. "You're a real pussycat, y'know that, Wilhelm?"

Wilhelm stopped under a big, black pine and faced east. Charko stood watching Goldman on his side under the little pine, cursing and hacking away at the trunk.

A Christmas tree, hot chow, and a warm bed—not too bad, Wilhelm thought. When spring comes, we'll beat it across Germany, meet the Rooskies in the middle. The war'll be over, and I'll be on my way back to school, maybe even in time for…no, dammit, we still got the Japs to fight! "The Golden Gate in Forty-Eight," the guys were singing coming over.

The wind had dropped, and the ebony pines, ice crystals glistening on every needle, no longer shed their covers. What a delicious silence! Wilhelm was reminded of Hattie May and Frank's old place outside Indianapolis—the "crick" fishing with Dad and Frank, then sitting around in the musty old parlor, with Frank twanging politics and Hattie Mae in her flowery smock serving fresh-baked muffins and comb-honey right from the hive. God! Those were the days!

A buzz in the tree above his head jarred Wilhelm from his reverie. Winter-time bees here in Belgium? A little twig, its layer of ice hanging tight, spiraled down and stood straight up in front of him. Another buzz, and another, and another. "Hey, Charko!" Wilhelm shouted, "Somebody's firing at us!" He threw himself down and brought his carbine to bear on the woods before him. "Charko! Where the hell are you? Charko! Charko!"

When he heard Wilhelm shout, Goldman grabbed his carbine and crawled behind the little pine, Charko behind him. Wilhelm got up, bent low, scooted across to his buddies. "What the hell's going on?" he asked. "We must be two, three miles from the front lines." No comment. They lay in the snow listening, waiting.

Goldman rolled out from under the tree. "Fuckin' tree's too big anyway," he said, weapon at his hip. Facing east, he shouted, "This'll teach yooz bastids to mess with us when we're tryin' to celebrate Christmas." He fired three times into the woods.

"For chrissake, what'd you do that for, Goldman?" Wilhelm's pale face went pink. "We don't want to get into some kinda firefight out here with nobody around to...."

"Ah, for chrissake, Wilhelm, there ain't nobody shootin' at us. Some dogface up there prob'bly dropped his M-1, or somethin'." Goldman wallked off toward the house, axe and carbine in hand, Charko followed him, his boots placed carefully in Goldman's tracks.

Wilhelm walked backward, keeping watch. "Three times? Some dogface dropped his M-1 three times?" Wilhelm hissed. "You're nuts, Goldman. Ain't no question about it, somebody fired at us!"

Goldman grinned. "Okay Wilhelm, if you say so. But I'm done choppin' for the day. Cut the next one yourself. Closer in so you won't get spooked so easy."

Wilhelm cut a small tree, and he and Charko carried it into the house and set it up. To Wilhelm's relief, nobody mentioned his "big scare" to Dolan. Somebody *was* firing, he told himself, and he would never believe otherwise.

After chow that evening, they decorated the tree with bits of toilet paper and spread their presents around it. Goldman taught them the

German words to *"O Tannenbaum" and "Stille Nacht"* and, with Dolan attempting harmony, they sang until fatigue and the radio's constant demands brought them to a stop.

Eventless days: snow falling, wind blowing, temperature dropping, the house warm, almost cozy. Wilhelm learned to pick Headquarters' dits, dahs and di-dah-di-dah-dits from between the jamming signals, and Dolan, because things were so quiet, decided to omit guard duty after midnight.

One evening, Wilhelm, feeling rested, dug out his chemistry book and, flashlight in hand, retired to the corner behind the stove. Dolan lay asleep on the couch, Charko slept upstairs, and Goldman manned the radio.

"Whatcha doin', buddy? Hey, you ain't readin' a *book,* are ya?" Goldman, smiling mischievously, whispered across the room.

"That's what they call 'em, Goldman. You oughtta try it sometime. You might like it." Wilhelm lowered the tome against his knees, hiding the title.

Goldman left his post, hunkered down in front of Wilhelm, and lifted the book. "Oh, my God! *Elements of Organic Chemistry!*" He blinked and stared at Wilhelm, as if he were a stranger. "Hot damn, buddy, that's the stuff my old man said kept him outta medical school." Goldman's hard, sallow face softened. "He's smart, too, my old man, real smart. You gonna be a doctor or somethin'?"

"Nah." Wilhelm didn't look up. "I'm gonna be a chemist. Like mixin' stuff together to see what happens." He saw himself being world famous, inventing medicines that cured all kinds of diseases, getting rich. One of his professors at I.U. had said, "MDs don't do science. They just feed the medicines chemists make to their patients. *We* do the *real* science." That had done it for him; he would study chemistry and do real science.

Goldman proceeded to tell a long story about how he'd worked at Wiley Tar & Chemical and how fat and sassy the redheaded technician was and how he took a dump in one of the samples one time and the "Dago" boss nearly went nuts trying to figure out what was wrong with it. He rocked back on his heels and laughed so loud that Dolan rolled over and cursed aloud. Said he'd saved the place from blowing up when the power went off one time and a big pot overheated. The place stunk so bad he didn't go back and get his last week's pay.

Goldman and I actually have something in common, Wilhelm thought. "I tried to get a job in a chem lab the summer before I joined up," he said. "Didn't have enough college, so I got a job in a drugstore instead." He wished they could talk chemistry, but if Goldman knew only "Wiley Tar," it wouldn't be very interesting.

Goldman went back to the radio and left him to his reading. The first chapter, *Structure and Bonding in Organic Molecules,* seemed interesting at first, but the distant sounds of war, the straight, hard wall against his back, and cold ache in his toes kept Wilhelm from concentrating. Every time he looked up, the small soldier was grinning at him. Maybe Goldman wasn't such a bad guy after all.

# CHAPTER 4

▼

# HERE THEY COME!

The sharp jangle of the telephone tore Wilhelm from a sound sleep.

"Yessir!" the sergeant shouted. "I heard 'em, Sir. Lock and load all weapons. Yessir!"

Wilhelm reared up, rubbed his eyes, and squinted through the icy darkness at Dolan.

"Yes, *Sir!*" Dolan repeated. "We'll keep a sharp lookout, Sir. Yessir!" Dropping the phone like a hot rock, Dolan threw back his head and yelled, "Awright, you guys! Goldman! Charko! Drop your cocks and grab your socks! The Krauts're comin'!"

Wilhelm, his brain slowly extracting meaning from the sergeant's words, sat staring. He heard and felt the roll and thunder of a massive barrage. Insides tightening, he dropped to his feet and pulled on his boots.

"Lieutenant says the Krauts jumped off about an hour ago, Wilhelm. They're attackin' all up and down the line. The phones'll be out, so we're gonna be busier'n a one-legged shit-kicker around here."

The radio chirped. Dolan picked up the headphones and shoved them at Wilhelm. "Get on the set, kid, and stay till Charko gets down here. Then get out and start the truck." He grinned. "Better jack a round in the chamber of your carbine before you go out. You might need it."

Sitting shivering in the truck, Wilhelm could hear the growl of tanks amid the roar of artillery, machine-gun, and rifle fire a couple of miles away. Heart thumping, he thought he could hear every bullet snap, every shell whine and whomp into the ground. *They're coming and we gotta stop them, oh, God, we gotta stop them.* The idea kept running through his mind.

When 88s and mortars slammed into the woods between the house and Regimental HQ, he left the engine running and ran into the house. The radio spewed dits and dahs furiously, as Charko's pencil poured five-letter groups of code into the logbook.

"Leave it, Charko! Ever'body in the cellar!" They followed Dolan down the stairs, waited a bit, and ran back upstairs. Again and again it happened. Between trips to the cellar, Wilhelm kept the truck running, delivered messages to HQ, and, alternating with Goldman, spelled Charko at the radio. Dolan, long-faced, stayed next to the radio, decoding and encoding messages to and from Regiment.

During a hiatus in the shelling, Wilhelm, starting Kratus, noticed holes in the hood and web-like cracks in the windshield. "You been indoctrinated, Kratus, old girl," he said affectionately. "Indoctrinated all to hell. Too bad we can't take you in the cellar with us."

About noon, Wilhelm, on his way to the truck, saw a long line of riflemen coming across the mile-deep snowfield before Regimental HQ. "Sarge! Sarge!" he shouted, running inside. "There's a whole buncha men comin' across the field out there! Looks like a whole company! Maybe a…."

Dolan brushed past Wilhelm into the yard. "Christ-a-mighty! Could be Krauts! We better…." He ran back in the house. "Goldman, get upstairs at the window and keep your eyes peeled. "Wilhelm, you and Charko pick a spot and take a bead on 'em. We gotta protect that radio or we'll be cut off completely!" He ran to the big front window to watch the advancing spots on the snowfield.

Wilhelm propped his carbine on the stone threshold at the front door and took a bead on the strangers. They were still too far away for his weapon to reach.

Charko lay down next to him. "Buncha Krauts out there, huh?"

"Can't tell for sure if they're Krauts or not. But there's a helluva lot of 'em, I can tell you that!" Wilhelm swallowed hard and tried to think. "Some'll prob'bly come around through the woods, Charko. Why don't you keep an eye over there and I'll cover the path to HQ." How the hell are we gonna stop all those guns, he asked himself. There's too damn many of 'em. Too damn many.

A tall figure suddenly filled Wilhelm's sights. "Don't shoot! Don't shoot!" the man shouted, throwing up his hands. "Lieutenant Clark here. Sergeant Dolan? You there?" Without waiting for an answer, the officer dropped his hands and came forward. Wilhelm's finger tightened on the trigger. "That's C Company out there in the field, Sergeant! C Company! They're pullin' back to new positions!"

Dolan stepped over Wilhelm into the yard. "Goddamn it, Sir! Why don't somebody tell us what the hell's goin' on around here! We damn near't opened up on 'em!"

"Well, you been told now, Sergeant. Just get back on that radio! Now!" The lieutenant turned and stomped off through the snow.

"Some shit!" Dolan snorted. "Awright. You heard the Lieutenant. Let's get back on the radio!" He looked up and waved at the upstairs window. "Goldman! Get your ass down here!"

"Whew! That was close!" Wilhelm got up off the dirt floor and wiped his knees. "Feel like I just been pardoned by the President."

Just before dark, they heard a deep guttural roar above the house. "Air power," Wilhelm shouted. "We'll show them bastards now!" He ran outside and looked up, ready to wave. His jaw dropped as his eyes focused on a big black bird coming east to west across the sky.

Charko ran up. "What the hell's that?" he yelled. "Looks like some kinda bird! I bet it's one a' them flyin' bombs the Krauts got. Read about 'em back in England."

Wilhelm's head shook. Charko went on: "Carry two-thousand-pounders and fly all by themselves. When they run outta juice, they fall down and go *boom!*" Dolan and Goldman joined them, watching in awe as the big short-winged machine farted away to the west.

"Why don't somebody shoot it down, Sarge?" Wilhelm asked.

The sergeant grinned. "And what do you think would happen to the dumbass that brought it down?"

Wilhelm's eyes went wide. "Oh, yeah. Be kinda dumb at that, wouldn't it? Kill everybody around there." Dolan nodded and walked off.

After dark, the sounds of battle receded to the west—St. Vith— where the General and the rest of the Signal Company hung out.

"Think they might call us back, Sarge? Get us outta here?"

"Nah. They need us up here. Besides, we couldn't get back there now if they called us." Dolan looked closely at Wilhelm. "We ain't goin' noplace, kid. Not till somebody comes after us."

Yeah, we're expendable, Wilhelm thought—four guys Division can replace any time they want.

That night, as Charko squeezed incoming messages from among the jamming signals, Wilhelm and Goldman walked guard around the house. They were amazed by how the radio's whine seemed to ricochet off the snow and frozen pines. Any passing patrol would hear it and come hunting. Little icy rocks of snow battered Wilhelm's pinched face, his watery eyes constantly scanning the black and white spaces around the house. To him, guard duty was a solemn duty. He'd walked guard many times in basic, in sunshine, sleet and rain back in the States. But *this* was the real thing and he knew it.

Coming around the back corner of the house for perhaps the twentieth time, he saw something move alongside the outhouse. "Hey! Did you see that? Over there." He grabbed Goldman's arm. "Is that a tree, or...." Before he could answer, Wilhelm fell prone in the snow, his carbine aimed at the slim, dark object some thirty feet away.

Goldman hit the ground next to Wilhelm. "What the hell you doin'? Ain't nothin' but bushes over there!"

"See it? It ain't movin' with the wind like the other stuff." He remembered being warned by the sergeant back at Benning to stand perfectly still if caught in the open at night. The Krauts will do the same, he said, so you gotta be really careful at night.

"I'm gonna find out who you are," Wilhelm muttered. He took aim and fired once, twice, three times. His target didn't move.

Eerily, a voice came to them out of the sky: "Who's firing? Who's firing?"

"Jesus Christ, Wilhelm! HQ's hollerin' at us! That whole fuckin' bunch's gonna be firin' at us!"

"Well, dammit, if that's a Kraut, you'll be damn glad I killed the bastard."

"What the hell's going on?" Dolan, grease gun in hand, ran up behind his guards and hunkered down.

Wilhelm twisted around. "I fired at that thing over there, Sarge. Couldn't tell if it was a man or...."

"It's a tree, Wilhelm! Been there ever' time I been out here!" Dolan frowned.

"Well, hell, Sarge, I didn't wanta take a chance, so I...."

"Yeah, yeah. Okay. Just be careful what you shoot at. The colonel gets one in the ass, we'll be in shit up to our necks." He turned and disappeared into the darkness.

"Yeah, if the Krauts don't get us first," Wilhelm mumbled.

They heard Dolan speaking to someone around front. Goldman snickered. "See there, Wilhelm, you woke up somebody over at head-fuckin'-quarters. They'll be after your ass tomorra for sure."

"Yeah, well." Wilhelm got up and walked over to the outhouse. "It's not a tree," he muttered. "It's a fuckin' bush! A Kraut bush, and I killed it deader'n a doornail!"

# CHAPTER 5

▼

# SURROUNDED

Pack up and pull *out!* That was the order. Pull *out,* not *back.* Pull *out.*

Wilhelm was, by now, totally disoriented, his mind numbed by gar-
bled code, his body exhausted from lack of sleep and slogging around
the house in total darkness listening for the approach of death from the
east. Gray-faced and narrow-eyed, his nerves strung tighter than the
E-string on his old guitar, he licked the rotten taste of chlorine-water
off his lips, shifted Kratus into low-low, four-wheel-drive, and pointed
her across the white, glistening field toward the Siegfried Line. Beside
him, face white-gray with fatigue, sat Sergeant Dolan. Goldman and
Charko lay on the wooden benches in the back, trying to get some
sleep.

During the previous night, Wilhelm had dreamed of German
potato-masher grenades bursting through the window, followed by
howling, bayonet-jabbing Krauts—a scenario he'd practiced many
times at Fort Benning. Mouth open in a silent scream, he squirmed up,
reached for his weapon and tried to get out of bed. Charko, at the
radio, got up and, chuckling, shoved him down. The dream came

again, this time with Sergeant Wilhelm's squad tossing grenades and doing the bayoneting. At 4 A.M., time to hit the radio, he was more exhausted than when he'd hit the sack.

"Where we goin', Sarge?" Wilhelm's voice barely cleared the whine of the gears.

Dolan tuned slowly to Wilhelm. "We're gonna join up with the 422$^{nd}$ and follow them outta here. Radio says the General's leavin' St. Vith and pullin' back. Bastards got us surrounded."

Unbelievable, Wilhelm thought. A goddamn radio operator one day and on the run the next. I'm not a dogface. I'm a *radio operator,* and I ain't *supposed* to do infantry shit. As the truck approached the edge of the snowfield, they came to a line of GI trucks alongside a thick pine woods. "That the Siegfried Line down there, Sarge?" He pointed at a concrete bunker deep among the trees.

"Yeah, I think so. Park at the end of the convoy and turn 'er off. Save gas. We're gonna need it." Dolan got out and waited for Charko and Goldman to come around. "You guys stay here," he said. "We'll be gettin' orders purty soon, so don't get yourselves lost." He went off up the convoy. Wilhelm got out and joined his buddies.

They stood looking at the row of black bunkers in the woods. "I hope we ain't movin' into one a' them fuckin' t'ings," Goldman muttered, kicking at the snow.

"Yeah. They don't look too damn comfy to me." Charko's dark, round face stood sharp against the snow's white glare.

"Sarge says we're goin' back with this bunch," Wilhelm said. "I'm bettin' we don't go anyplace till after dark, though." He slammed his cold feet together. "Think I'll take a look-see inside one a' them things. Wanta go?" Heads shook as Charko and Goldman turned and climbed back into the truck.

The bunker's doorway, black on black in the side wall, was almost invisible. Looking in cautiously, Wilhelm found the only light inside coming from a narrow aperture in the wall to his right. A figure, breathing deeply, sat high up on some kind of seat before a machinegun silhouetted against the odd snowlight. As Wilhelm's boot crunched loose dirt on the floor, the sleeper awoke, spun around, and dropped to the floor. The glint of a bayonet and rifle barrel sent Wilhelm's hands flying. "Hey! Buddy! Don't shoot! I'm from Signal Company!" The gunman stepped forward and stared. Wilhelm's eyes went wide. He recognized the soldier. "Well, I'll be damned! I know you. You're, uhhh…."

"Hey, for chrissake, you guys, we're tryin' to get some shuteye over here!" A white blob in the far corner of the bunker was shouting. "Keep it down, will ya! Keep it down!" A ghostly face floated there for a moment and faded out.

M-1 still in hand, the soldier whispered, "You're Signal Company! What the hell you…."

"Hey, you're Weehunt! It's me, Jimmy Wilhelm. From Second Platoon back at Benning. Remember?"

"Well, Jimmy Whoever, git over here where I can see you better." Hand still offered, Wilhelm advanced into the light from the machinegun slot. "You come up on me like that again, buddy, and I'm li'ble to blow your fuckin' head off."

Wilhelm stepped in closer. "Guess you don't remember me. Second platoon. Back at Benning?" Wilhelm remembered Weehunt very well. No more than five-one or two, the undisputed strong man of the platoon. Weehunt's short, powerful arms and stump-like legs set him apart from the rest. He could do fifty pushups on one arm, fifty on the other, and bet you a dollar he could do a hundred more on both.

"Heyyy, Wilhelm! Yeah, I remember you. Where'd you come from, buddy?" Weehunt took the offered hand, squeezed and shook it. "You got in the 106$^{th}$, too, huh? Lucky buggers, ain't we?" Weehunt's high pitched hee-hee bounced off the walls. The far corner, perhaps recognizing the source, lay silent.

"Yeah, we're lucky all right. Krauts got us hemmed in. Resta the Company's back at St. Vith takin' off with the General. Some shit, huh?"

The Great Cocksman, the "Cunt-huntin' Runt" they called him. Weehunt would sneak out of camp every weekend, come back and tell us stories about all the girls he'd screwed. Had the longest, thickest dick in the platoon. Guys came from all over the company to get a look at it. The sergeant came in to take a shower one time, and, after he stopped laughing, ordered Weehunt to take it off so he, the sergeant, could take it with him to town. The guys, kissing in with The Man, rolled on the shower-room floor laughing.

"Nice place you got here." Wilhelm said. "Just like home, huh?"

"Yeah, if you want to freeze your ass off." Weehunt sniffed. "Any shootin' up your way when the Krauts come through?" He grinned. "They went around us."

"We didn't see hardly any. Some 88s, that's all." Wilhelm shuffled his feet. At Benning, he'd considered Weehunt out of his class, physically. He felt uneasy around him—not scared, just uneasy. Wished he could go into town with him sometime, though, just to see how "it" was done. "Well, I'm drivin' the truck. Better get back. Sarge'll be lookin' for me."

"Had any since you got over?" Weehunt snickered, a hungry look on his face.

"Any?" Wilhelm's eyebrows rose. "Oh. No. Never got out of camp in England. Came over on an LST and drove straight across France. Hardly had time to take a leak."

"Me neither. I keep thinkin' about all that Jawja pussy goin' to waste back there. Good ole Phenix City. You remember?"

"Yeah. I tried 'em a coupla times," Wilhelm lied. "Pretty damn good, I thought." He ha-ha-ed.

"Hell, ones I had was a lot better'n that, buddy. Them Jawja gals got great pussy." Weehunt let out a little whoop.

"Yeah, well, I gotta get back. See you later, buddy."

The air outside felt almost warm after the clammy cold inside the bunker. Wilhelm swung his arms, banged his feet together, walked out onto the concrete tank traps east of the bunker, and looked around. Girls, he mused, that's all Weehunt ever thinks about. He grinned. Of course, there's Cindy back home, her long, dark hair and small, round breasts bobbing. Weehunt would be after her in a minute. "I would certainly never do anything like that," he said aloud. Then: "Ha!"

*     *     *     *

The cold and dark in the back of the truck was worse than Weehunt's bunker. "Kratus is *my* truck. *I* oughtta be drivin'. *I* oughtta be drivin' her, no matter what," Wilhelm mumbled. His steel helmet thumped across the bench as he rolled over. "Damn bench is hard as a rock." He kicked and squirmed like a spoiled brat. "Damn sweater and bunchy longjohns ain't worth a shit, neither. Just keep the cold in." Fingers tingling, he rubbed his gloved hands together. "I'd be warm if I was drivin', dammit!" Could be worse, though. Charko's out in the dark leading the truck with his flashlight. A pain in the ass but the best damn radio man we got. No question about it.

"Hey, Goldman. Cold over there?" Wilhelm shouted above the whine of the gearbox.

"Nah. 'Snice. Real nice." Goldman rolled over and stared. "You better get some shuteye, buddy. We're gonna give them Krauts some of their own shit tomorra. Li'ble to be a little rough on a softie like you."

Wilhelm put his hands between his thighs, pulled his knees up tight and closed his eyes. The gauge in his belly registered empty, the tumescence in his groin surprising him. Vibrations, he decided—the vibrations do it. He rubbed his crotch, and Cindy popped up. "Damn," he mumbled, "shame on me."

The crack of machinegun fire, barely audible, leaked through the plywood walls. A slow American 50, he thought, and a quick German 9 millimeter. Sounds like they're firing at each other. He reached under the bench and pulled his carbine out to where he could reach it. His fingers ran down his left legging to a thin shape above the ankle: the knife, his dad's, was still there. His dad's long, sad face rose up, refracted colors from the knife blade flickering across it. "Take this, Jimmy," he'd said, holding the knife by the blade. "Saved my life more'n once down in Haiti," he said. "You might need it over there." Wilhelm could tell the words hurt the old man. I don't need it, he'd thought, I'm a radio operator. I won't need it. Now, listening to the guns down the road, he wondered if his dad's words hadn't been prophetic after all.

A long burst from the German gun rattled the walls. Quickly, the American gun answered. The guns were closer now, much closer. On the blood-red screen behind his eyes, Wilhelm could see the gunners crouched behind their guns, ammo belts humping, brass jackets spinning away into the snow. He remembered the snap, the scary, gut-wrenching crack of machinegun bullets above his head on the infiltration course at Fort Benning. Dammit, he wanted to shout, I ain't supposed to be here! I ain't no goddamn dogface! I'm a fuckin' *radio operator!*

"You hear them guns, Goldman? Seems like we're heading right for 'em."

No answer.

"Sure as hell, we're gonna have to go out there and take care of them damn guns," he muttered. "Hey, Goldman!" The sounds of heavy breathing came from the other side. "I think maybe we oughtta haul ass outta here! These walls ain't gonna...hey! for crissake, don't you hear them guns? How can you sleep with 'em firin' right down the road from us?"

Wilhelm rolled over and stared at the wall, heart thumping, panic constricting in his throat. "C'mon, Dolan," he hissed, "you oughtta be able to see the muzzle flashes by now! You gonna drive right between 'em? You keep goin', I'm getting' outta here!

"Whyn't you just shut the hell up!" Goldman shouted. "Sarge knows what he's doin'."

Wilhelm imagined bullets spurting through the plywood walls, his body writhing, mouth open screaming in pain. Something inside shouted, 'Get out! Get out and run! Run! Run! Run!' He lunged to his feet, swayed across the steel floor to the top-hinged rear door and pushed it open. A cloud of exhaust engulfed him. Coughing, eyes burning, he threw one foot over the tailgate and hung there a moment, the voice in his head shouting, "Don't do it, Jimmy. Don't jump. It's wrong! It's *bad* wrong!" As his grip tightened, the truck suddenly swerved and braked. The sudden stop threw Wilhelm back inside, the overhead door banging shut behind him. He fell onto Goldman's legs.

Goldman reared up. "Godammit, Wilhelm! What the hell you doin' sittin' on my legs?" The 50, then the quick German gun fired off to one side, off to the left.

Wilhelm coughed, shook his head, and pushed to his feet. "Musta been walkin' in my sleep or somethin'," he croaked.

"Well, for chrissake, you wanta walk, get out and walk! But stay the hell offa me!" Goldman flopped down and turned toward the wall.

Back on his bench, one gloved hand under his cheek, the other between his thighs, Wilhelm breathed deeply and tried to relax. I'm a rotten soldier. Why, oh why, did I give up my deferment. I was born to be a doctor or a chemist, not a goddam soldier. He felt for the knife at his ankle. His dad's face glared, eyes Marine-hard.

The sudden silence woke Wilhelm. The truck had stopped. He heard Charko whine and Dolan's whispered reply. The word "dig" stood out. "Don't tell me we're gonna hafta dig foxholes in that frozen shit out there," he whispered. "Sarge must be off his rocker." The hard red clay and hot sun back in Georgia came to mind. Wouldn't mind a little sweat in my eyes right now, he mused. Wait a minute. That stupid flyboy out there *wants* to dig a hole! Probably never dug a hole in his life. "Hey, Sarge," he thought to shout, "make 'im dig a hole big enough for all of us!"

The back door swung open and Charko, his mouth a tight, pink line, crawled inside, dug his shovel from his duffle bag and dropped back outside. Wilhelm stretched his legs, rolled over and listened: digging sounds, the shovel grating, Charko grunting. Wilhelm smiled.

Suddenly, the digging stopped and a scratchy voice shouted, "Oh, God! Hey, Sarge! Help me! I need help!"

Dolan, still behind the steering wheel, turned to the wall behind him and whispered into the hole above Wilhelm's head, "Hey, Wilhelm! Goldman!"

"Yeah, Sarge. What?"

"Charko's got a problem. Get out there and shut him up! He's gonna bring the whole fuckin' German army down on us! On the double!"

"Okay, Sarge. Soon's I get my boots on." Wilhelm grinned into the darkness.

"Boots on! For chrissake, Wilhelm, this ain't no God damn trainin' exercise! Keep your boots on at all times! You got it?"

The boots he'd never had off clicked together in midair. Wilhelm lay back, grinning. Why don't *you* go shut him up yourself, *Mister* Dolan? Goddam sergeants never *do* anything. "Hey, Goldman! You hear the Sarge? He wants us to go out and...."

Goldman groaned and sat up. "I git a-holt of that fuckin' flyboy, I'm gonna cut his fuckin' balls off!" His feet hit the floor. "Talks like somebody already did it, anyway. Ain't worth a flying fuck, now the radio's down." Goldman turned to the wall, "Hey, Sarge, why don't we let 'im take care a his own shit? He ain't worth worryin' about!"

"Goldman! Get your ass out there! Now! And keep your voice down!" The sergeant's fist thumped the wall as he spoke.

A frigid wind met them as they dropped out into the snow. "I gotta piss before I do anything'," Goldman whispered. Both men stepped away and relieved themselves, steam rising from their yellowish streams. They scanned the wind-blown bushes for Germans, then, incidentally it seemed, looked for their bitchy compatriot.

Charco's cries came from between the truck and the woods, his voice rising and falling with the wind. They found him on the ground, one leg extended into a snowdrift, the other leg invisible, missing. Goldman, carbine at his hip, stood watch between the hole and the woods, while Wilhelm, grinning mirthlessly, squatted next to the fallen man. "For Chrissake, Charko, what the hell're you doin'? Sarge's madder'n a wet hen!"

Charko grabbed Wilhelm's arm. "C'mon, Wilhelm, cut the shit and get me outta here! Pull me up! Pull me up!"

"Up? Why? Can't you...."

"Just pull me up, goddamit!" Charko pulled at Wilhelm's arm. "My leg's down in some fuckin' hole or somethin'! C'mon, pull! My foot's freezin'!"

"Okay, okay! Keep it down!" Carbine slung on his shoulder, Wilhelm shoved his forearms into Charco's armpits and forklifted him up. A nasty sucking sound slipped from beneath Charko, the missing leg, wet, cold and dripping, appearing intact. Wilhelm stepped back. "Boy, you get into the god-damndest messes, don't ya?"

"Wait a minute! Wait a minute!" Charko let go of Wilhelm's arm and dropped to his chest in the snow. He shoved one arm, glove, field jacket, overcoat, and all down into the black, watery hole and came up with a water-spouting boot. Sitting now, he emptied the boot and with a loud grunt forced it on his foot. Up again, he limped around in a circle, sucking air between curses.

"C'mon, let's get back in the truck," Goldman hissed. "Yooz all done diggin' for now, Br'er Rabbit?"

"Yeah. Fuckin' foxhole's fulla water anyways."

"Dumbass! I coulda told you that!" Wilhelm shook his head. "You can't dig foxholes in frozen ground!" It sounded right anyway.

A barrage of burpgun fire! The three men hit the ground and crawled under the truck. "See what yooz did, you dumb bastid!" Goldman growled, "You're gonna get us all killed yet!"

"Well, hell, I can't help it if some damn farmer puts a hole right where I wanta dig my...."

"Shut up, back there, you guys!" Dolan's voice came from behind the left front wheel. American M-1s and 30 caliber machineguns began firing. As quickly as it had started, the firing stopped, and Dolan climbed back into the driver's seat. "Okay, you guys." Dolan looked around. "Go get some sleep. The Krauts're gone for now, but, now they know where we're at, they'll be back."

Inside the back, Wilhelm and Goldman grabbed the benches, and Charko flopped atop the duffle bags. Artillery and small arms thumped and crackled in the west, harbingers of the day to come. They slept anyway. Like rocks.

# CHAPTER 6

▼

# CAUGHT

One hand on the steering wheel, the other still on the gearshift, Wilhelm frowned across Kratus' hood into the ditch. A second convoy, going the other way, roared past on the road above.

"How the hell do they expect me to stay on the goddamn road with all those monster two-and-a-half-tons crowding past?" Wilhelm sighed. "And now he wants me to leave her! Abandon her in the ditch!" He stared up at the sergeant standing in the road. "Not on your life, *Mister* Dolan!" he muttered. "Nossir! Not on yo' life!" Drawing himself up, he met the sergeant's stare. "I'm gonna stay with her, Sergeant! I'm not gonna...."

"Wilhelm, goddammit, get your ass up here! On the double!" The sergeant, standing between Charko and Goldman, pumped his fist up and down, the doubletime signal.

Wilhelm shook his head. "No! I'm staying here with her!" Dropping his voice, he said, "Taking my stand with good old Kratus." He smiled around at the steering wheel, the gearshift, the empty seat beside him.

When he turned to look up the ditch again, the sergeant was breathing in his face. Dolan swung the grease gun off his shoulder. "Get outta the truck, Wilhelm, or I'm gonna shoot you where you sit."

"No, Sarge. I'm...." Disobeying a *direct order*! Dad would beat my butt good.

"What the hell's the matter with you! You scared? You want us to do your fightin' for you?" Dolan reached in and yanked the corporal out into the snow. "Get your ass up there in the road! *Now,* Wilhelm! That's an order!"

Mouth quivering, the boy plopped down in the snow at the sergeant's feet. Dolan pulled him up, spun him around and shoved him up the side of the ditch. Goldman and Charko, lying atop the idling two-and-a-half-ton in the road, grinned as Wilhelm came up toward them.

Dolan shoved Wilhelm against the tailgate of the big truck and leaned in close. "Listen to me, soldier! You pull any more shit like that, and, as God is my witness, I'll blow you away. Understand? You understand?"

Wilhelm stared, thinking: God? What's *God* got to do with this?

"Now, get up top and keep your eyes peeled!"

Wilhelm pulled himself onto the tailgate. Balanced there, he met the dirty, grinning faces of the men inside who had seen his stupidity and heard Dolan's shout. He hated them. All of them. Up on top, he crawled to the front and lay between Goldman and Charko. Rearing up, he reared up and looked back at Kratus, her exhaust flaring like a cat's tail in the wind. "Goodbye old girl," he muttered. "I'll be back." The Krauts'll get the scarf Mom knitted. Shoulda had it on, but it was too "good." Good for what? What kinda "good" could there be in this godforsaken place? There he is again—God. Sighing, he stared ahead, chin on his hands.

The big truck roared and jerked forward. Through the fog and blowing snow, Wilhelm could make out the captain's Jeep at the front of the convoy. The long string of trucks that had forced Kratus into the ditch had disappeared behind them. As they moved along, a copse of pines replaced the ditch on the right, a row of farm buildings appearing up ahead beyond the trees. On the rise to his left, he saw a monstrous tank with a black cross on its turret, white-sheeted men all around it. It ground steadily up the slope, exhaust blowing black smoke into the snow-laden wind. A Kraut tank. A whole company of infantry! They musta seen us by now. He watched, fascinated, as the tank stopped and began firing into a hotel-sized clapboard building at the top of the hill. The turret traversed back and forth methodically, gradually dismantling the building. Counting the seconds between muzzle flashes and the gun's roar, he tried to calculate the distance to the tank, but his muddled brain couldn't handle it. Six or eight rounds and the building collapsed, smoke and fire obscuring the men running from it. The German infantry fired furiously, the ripping, tearing sound of automatic weapons echoing across the field.

"My God! They all got burpguns, and all we got is these peashooter carbines!" Goldman snarled, staring over Wilhelm's shoulder at the hill.

As the convoy came to the row of barns, a terrific explosion came from up ahead. The three corporals rose on their knees as the truck jerked to a halt. The captain's Jeep lay on its side, burning, the muzzle of an 88 jutting from the fog into the road. The tank gradually appeared, a gray ghost that swiveled about, its gun pointing at the third and last barn in the row. Men were yelling, jumping from the trucks, some crawling beneath them.

"Ho-lee shit!" Goldman shouted. "We gonna get a chance to kill us some Krauts, now! C'mon, Wilhelm, let's go get 'em!"

"Oh, God, we're in for it now!" Charko mumbled, putting his head down.

Wilhelm lay quietly, wondering what to do.

"C'mon, you guys! Wilhelm, Charko, get down here!" Dolan, already in the road, pumped his arm and ran into the tall barn next to the truck. Wilhelm and Charko looked at each other, then followed Goldman off the truck into the barn.

The three men found their sergeant kneeling at an open window looking out on the snowfield behind the barns. "Looks like there's a couple hundred of 'em," Dolan said, watching the enemy form a line parallel to the row of barns some distance off. "They're getting' set to…oh, shit, there's another tank! They brought their heavy stuff, come lookin' for a fight, awright!" He sat back on his heels. "Fix your bayonets, and, Wilhelm, you get up in the loft and keep your eyes peeled. Kill anybody that tries to get in close."

Wilhelm nodded and went to the ladder he'd seen as he entered. "And Wilhelm!" Dolan shouted. "None of your shit up there! Just do your job! You got it?"

"He doesn't trust me," Wilhelm mumbled, climbing up. "Hell, I guess I wouldn't either." The words, "Kill anybody that…." kept running through his mind. His head began to throb.

"Charko, you and…Charko, get away from the door and get over here!" The corporal came over, dropped the butt of his carbine on the ground, and stared down at the sergeant. "Set up at that window over there," Dolan pointed right, "and keep a sharp lookout. They're li'ble to come at us from that side, too." Charko blinked, but he didn't move. "Charko! You hear me?" Dolan started to get up.

"Yeah, yeah, Sarge, I hear ya." Charko's face went sour. "I'm goin', I'm goin'." He sauntered to the far window and, standing well back from it, began to attach his bayonet.

"Goldman! Get over to that other window." Dolan pointed to his left. "Don't fire till you hear my gun. Ever'body! You hear? Don't fire till you hear my gun!"

Wilhelm, still on the ladder, had begun to feel sick to his stomach. How'm I gonna know *his* gun from all the other goddamn guns? I hafta shoot, I'll shoot! Light-headed now, he kept telling himself he would shoot Germans, cousins, first, second and/or third. Eyes just above floor level, he scanned the cracked, knot-hole-decorated walls of the loft. On his belly, he crawled to the only window in the side wall and looked across the ten or so feet to the neighboring building. "That space down there is mine," he mumbled. "Anybody comes in that space down there is dead meat." He felt tough, strong, his carbine loaded with German death.

To his left lay the American trucks in the road, the hill, the burning, collapsed house, and the German tank. Ragged flames from the captain's Jeep leapt high above the adjacent barn, black smoke decorating the gray sky overhead. Gone just like that, he thought. Wonder what it feels like to…he heard a snap overhead, sucked down against the floor and rolled away from the window. The "thwock" of that German round hitting the wall filled his mind. Little, piping voices sounded: "Bang, bang, bang," they yelled…kids, he imagined, playing war, pointing something, broomsticks or something, out the window. What the hell? Am I…am I going nuts? One round and I'm cracking up!

The roar of firing in the snowfield grabbed at Wilhelm. Real bullets now, real war. He crawled to the wall and squinted through a knothole. The wind made his eyes water. Feet pounded in the road, running into the barn below, men shouting. More running, more shouting. A tank heaved into the snowfield and came into view. Can't be the one that blew away the captain. Must be another one! The big, gray-brown machine, farting black, swung around and pointed its 88 at the barns, white-cloaked infantry around it. "Efficient bastards, these Krauts. I oughtta know, I was raised by 'em," he muttered. Lucky buggers downstairs got stone walls around them; all I got is these rotten boards full of holes around me.

One after the other the tanks fired, bits of wood and stone flying, the roar bouncing around the loft. Shouts, the crash of a building collapsing, more running, more yelling, chaos, pure chaos down in the road. Wilhelm crawled back to the side window. A big American, bareheaded and coatless, climbed into a Jeep, cocked the rear-mounted 30-caliber machinegun and began firing, his whole body quivering with the recoil. Guttural, ground-shaking sounds now—an engine roaring, treads clanking. Before the young soldier's ammo belt was empty; a gun, a big gun, fired at close range. The orange-yellow blast enveloped the man, the Jeep, and his gun. The flash warmed Wilhelm's cheeks, and blue-black spots bounced inside his eyes. When he opened them, the heroic soldier, the Jeep, and his gun were gone.

Wilhelm looked down toward the snowfield. He saw a white-cloaked figure at the corner of the adjacent barn, the muzzle of a burpgun dark against the snow. Almost invisibly white, the German studied the window below Wilhelm, the one next to Dolan. The man looked up, saw Wilhelm, and lifted his weapon. Wilhelm, a split second earlier, was already firing. Three times, three rounds, and the German went down, his gun spraying the stone wall next to the lower window. Wilhelm sucked air and told himself it was all right. He'd done his job, like the Sarge said to. Oh, hell—he had to grin—I fired before Dolan did. Saved his ass, though, didn't I?

The end barn in the row gone, both tanks went to work on the second, the one next to Wilhelm's. He watched the wall across from him sag, ready to go down, the men inside now in the road, running, crawling under the trucks. Now Dolan began to fire. About time, Wilhelm wanted to shout, but didn't. All three guns down below were firing. He rolled to a crack in the wall and rapid-fired the rest of his clip at the line of white coats across the field. He saw a German drop. Did I do that? He loaded another clip and crawled back to the window.

They're gonna hit us next, he thought, as a rash of bullets slammed through the loft. Nose on the floor, he lay stretched out behind his steel helmet. When the German fire slowed, he crawled to a knothole and emptied another clip into the German line. Nine lousy rounds, he thought, and their burpguns throwing hundreds at us. Back at the window, he could see the tank that had demolished the building on top of the hill rumbling down toward the road, its band of ghostly killers close around it. Two tanks here and one on the way! We gotta haul ass outta here! Now!

Bullets cracked through the walls in earnest now, ricocheting off the rafters, splinters flying. The Sarge and the men downstairs were firing, the tanks in the field growling toward the last barn. Theirs. Wilhelm crawled over to the ladder and looked down. Men crowded into the little room, faces pale, eyes wide. Some lay in the straw; others sat fingering weapons, listening to the battle. Goddamn Headquarters warriors, typewriter jockeys, and coffee hounds! Why don't they get to the windows and kill some Krauts? He reloaded and crawled back to the wall. I can't go down yet. Sarge needs me up here. He's depending on me. I got the best shot up here.

He found a knot-hole close to the floorboards and fired until the breech of his carbine stood open, his last clip empty. He lay listening to the thump of his heart, to the guns, waiting for the chirp and roar of an 88. He felt a warm wetness in his underwear. It moved down his leg into his boot. He pushed up and looked down. Damn! I pissed in my pants! Dad's knife is down there. Wait'll I tell him, he'll.... An ear-shredding explosion shook the barn. The far corner of the loft was gone, wood and stone flying in all directions. A four-by-four beam fell across Wilhelm's legs. Another slammed across his helmet and rolled off. A crescendo of large and small guns, loud, continuous. He rolled over, shoved the four-by-fours aside and, on belly, toes, and fingernails he snaked along the floor to the hole. Grabbing the top rung, he pulled himself down chin-first, hand-over-hand. At the ground, he tucked, rolled, and sat up. His carbine, released at the top, stood butt-up on its bayonet nearby. "A rifle standing on its bayonet means a dead soldier," the big, gruff sergeant in his favorite Saturday matinee always said. "I ain't dead," he mumbled. "Not yet, anyway."

Dolan, Charko, and Goldman ran past. "Wilhelm! C'mon! Let's go! Let's go!"

Wilhelm jumped up, yanked his carbine free and, behind Charko, ran for the door. A shell hit, and a piece of rock slammed into his back. He knocked Charko aside and fell into the road, his back throbbing. He squatted against the wall next to Goldman, the cold stone welcome against his burning clavicle.

Goldman stared at the dark streak on Wilhelm's leg. "Tough up there was it, buddy?" he asked, grinning.

Wilhelm turned to the sergeant. "Hey, Sarge," he pointed down the road. "Whyn't we go down to the end of the convoy and…."

Dolan's head shook. "See them white sheets scootin' by down there? For damn sure, we can't go that way." He spat. "Sittin' here ain't a helluva lot better, though, is it?"

As if to emphasize the thought, two shells hit the barn behind them almost simultaneously. The roof fell in, bits of rock and wood whizzing, bouncing off the trucks sitting in front of them. Men ran out, yelling, diving under the trucks. The wall behind the ex-radio team swayed but stood its ground.

"What're we gonna do, Sarge?" Goldman shouted above the roar.

Three white-cloaks suddenly appeared between the trucks and, burp-guns pointing, stepped before the four Americans. The muzzle of one tall young German's gun motioned upward, as his sharp eyes stabbed into Wilhelm's. The American slid up the wall, back aching, eyes fixed on the muzzle of a Schmeisser. His fingers opened, and his carbine fell into the muddy snow. Back stiff against the stone wall, Wilhelm knew the next few seconds might be his last.

# CHAPTER 7

▼

# THE ACCIDENT

The dirty face of his captor—a soldier not much older than Wilhelm—broke into a wry smile when he saw the wet streak on his captive's leg. He mumbled something to the *Feldwebel,* and both men grinned. Wilhelm, hands in the air, had surrendered, his weapon on the ground. What would his dad think? Would he ever see Mom again, Fritzie, his room, his home? Suddenly, he was turning, his nose and mouth slamming into cold stone, the salt taste of blood on his tongue. A hand probed his pockets, his crotch, and down his legs, stopping above the dark, wet place. A bang and his helmet bounced away in the snowy wind pouring through the broad-meshed wool cap on his head. A strange, liberated feeling.

The four Americans were marched around the fallen barn into the snowfield behind. Already gathered there, a crowd of pale-faced, snuffling Americans stood slamming their feet together in the snow. Wilhelm rubbed his nose and licked his swollen lip. He felt strangely naked, his carbine, helmet, even his web belt and canteen gone. Money, wallet, and watch gone, too—hardly worth thinking about. The feel of the German's fingers on his privates lingered. At least the knife was safe. Wet or dry, it was still available. Good old Dad.

Wilhelm pulled the wool cap off his head and ran gloved fingers through his filthy hair. Goosebumps covered his neck and arms. Captured! Still alive! Still alive! The goosebumps confirmed it. He put the hat back on and pulled the flaps down tight against his ears. He looked around at the Germans. Keep us or kill us? Mow us down like rats and be rid of us? Germans are efficient, frugal. I know, I was raised by them. The guard with the upside-down stripes looks okay. Got a big voice, like Dad, like Grandpaw. The *Feldwebel*—Wilhelm knew a sergeant when he saw one—spoke rapidly to a two-striper—a *Gefreiter* or *Obergefreiter,* he didn't know which. He tried to hear, to read their lips, but they spoke too fast. If they start shooting, I'll hit the ground, crawl under somebody, play dead. Do these guys know about the Geneva Convention? Hell, combat soldiers, real killers, wouldn't give a damn even if they did know about it.

Wilhelm looked around at his buddies. Dolan's chaw was probably his last; Charko and Goldman sucked cigarettes and counted those left. Drag-beggars and butt-snatchers stood around, sniffing their smoke.

A long nerve-jangling burst of burpgun fire roared, reverberating through the woods at the edge of the field. The prisoners stirred as if a giant eggbeater had swung into action. The renegade gun fired again, the *Feldwebel* shouting, a detail of guards joining him as he took off toward the woods. Silence now, blessed silence. Maybe that's it. "All they wanta do is scare the shit outta us," somebody said.

Acid gurgled up, reminding Wilhelm that he hadn't eaten for two, three, maybe four days. What day was it anyway? Time was slippery. He dipped up some snow and let it melt on his tongue. Flat-tasting, like the distilled water in the lab at school. What I wouldn't give for some of that hot coffee and gooey sugar rolls we used to have between classes.

Wait a minute! He turned away from his buddies and shoved his hand down through his overcoat, field jacket, and wool sweater, all the way to his shirt pocket. Yes! It's still there! How could I forget half a D-bar? He pulled the lump of chocolate out and held it in close, broke off a piece and slipped it into his mouth. Wonderful! He just let it melt on his tongue. Jaw motionless, he looked around at his friends. I'll share the rest with them later. But it depends on what they share with me.

The wind whipped across the field, sharp ice crystals biting Wilhelm's cheeks. He looked across the field. Black spots in the snow, the dead, the wounded. Some sat up, holding an arm or leg, moaning, crying. The Kraut I killed at the barn is probably buried under it, he thought. Am I sorry I killed him? No. It was him or me. If I hadn't, I'd be the one buried over there. The game's called "The Quick and the Dead." I'm quick, he's dead—this time. This time, anyway.

"Looks like they're lining 'em up," Dolan croaked, his voice gone hoarse. "Stay close. Last thing we wanta do is get separated." Strange, Wilhelm thought, the Sarge looks smaller, shrunk up. No longer in charge, I guess.

They formed a rank: Dolan on the right flank, then Wilhelm, Goldman, Charko, and a corporal they didn't know. Twenty ranks, five men to a rank. A German unit. A "Los! Los!" from the guards, and off they went toward the woods. Good, Wilhelm thought, let's get the hell away from here. Get out of the wind and get some chow. A mound of meatloaf, steaming mashed potatoes covered with brown gravy rose in his mind. He licked his lips and swallowed hard.

As the column strung out across the snowfield, Wilhelm turned and looked back: the tail end of the column lay out of sight in the blowing snow. So many men, so easily captured and so quickly! We fought like babies, like the fucking greenhorns we are. We stink to high heaven!

In the woods, the column slowed and stopped. Wilhelm could see a *Feldwebel's* head up front, his hand in the air. When the hand dropped, a shout and the column moved up. What's going on? When they reached the *Feldwebel,* Dolan's rank stood on the brink of a snowy cut down through the pines, guards posted along both sides. When the *Feldwebel* dropped his arm and shouted "*Los!*" they took off down the hill at a trot. But Wilhelm's stride widened and, arms pumping, he fought to keep his flying boots under control. A giggle rose in his throat. He'd felt like this running down the hills in Garfield Park back home.

Looking down, he saw the toe of his boot catch a thin, black wire. It rose up in front of Goldman, then Charko, a small, metal cylinder jumping up between Charko and the strange corporal at the far end. A burst of flame and it exploded. The blast blew Charko off his feet; his body, like a broken mannequin, slid away down the hill. Goldman, Wilhelm, and Dolan went down like a row of dominoes, slipping and sliding. Lying on his back, dazed, Wilhelm looked straight up through the pines, the mysterious black wire rising again in his mind. Blinking, he sat up and hugged his knees.

Back up the hill, the next rank of POWs stared down at them, heads shaking. Down the hill, motionless in the snow, lay Charko, with his head twisted unnaturally to one side. Wilhelm half crawled, half slid down to him and leaned in close. Sucking sounds came from a hole in Charko's throat, blood spurting, making a pink mush out of snow. Looks like a snow-cone, Wilhelm thought. Charko's face, a mangled mass of blood and bone, made him cringe. He pressed three fingers against the spurting artery, his glove warmed by Charko's blood. The sucking sound became a gurgle, and stopped.

A gloved hand, big and wide, slid across Wilhelm's shoulder, grasped his wrist, and pulled his hand off Charko's neck. Wilhelm looked up into the squinting blue eyes of a red-bearded American giant. "What the hell you doin'? Let go!" he shouted.

"Might's well let 'im go, buddy. He ain't gonna make it no way." The big man leaned down and examined the dead man's wound. "Bleedin's stopped. He's dead. We gotta move on 'fore these Krauts git to shootin'."

Wilhelm yanked his arm away and jammed his fingers back into Charko's wound. "Get away! I gotta stay with 'im and…."

"C'mon, you cain't he'p 'im no more. He's gone." The voice was soft, calm. "Jus' leave 'im. God'll see to him." The redhead pulled Wilhelm to his feet. "C'mon, let's git on down the hill."

Wilhelm allowed the stranger to lead him along the side of the path, Americans now running past. Looking back, he saw the Germans drag Charko off the hill. "The bastards just dropped him in the woods," he muttered. His new friend seemed not to hear.

They met Dolan and Goldman at the bottom of the hill. Wilhelm, eyes on his feet, felt guilty. "God-a-mighty, what a helluva way to die," he said. Covering his eyes with his right hand, he realized the glove was gone, his hand cold, clotted blood between his fingers, the palm sticky, the nails black underneath. He scrubbed it down the front of his overcoat and kept his eyes on it. "Never liked ole Blackie much. But, damn, I never…." Tears ran down his cheeks and dripped off his chin. "I didn't see that damn wire! It just jumped up outta the snow and…." He looked at Dolan. "It was too late by then and—hell, I liked ole Blackie a lot." A small voice inside asked, "Did you kill anybody in the war, Daddy?" and a man's voice replied, "Sure did, son! Shot me a buncha them Germans over there." Hands clapped amid peals of laughter.

Dolan pulled Wilhelm's hand away and looked hard at him. "Don't sweat it, kid. Any of us coulda tripped that mine. Just happened to be you. Don't sweat it. Ain't nothin' you can do about it now."

The column of prisoners re-formed at the bottom of the slope and moved off toward a little town barely visible in the distance. Head down, Wilhelm watched his left foot—the killer foot—swing through the snow like it always did. Got me a killer finger and a killer foot, too, he thought. That same little voice inside now said, "Ain't nothin' you can do about it now, Jimmy. Ain't nothin' you can do about it now." He looked up at the dark, rolling clouds and sighed. Forget it, he told himself. Forget it. Forget it. Forget it. He knew he'd never forget it.

The stranger walking next to Wilhelm smiled and said softly, "Sorry about yo' buddy, fella. Lost one m'self, back there at the barns."

For the first time, Wilhelm saw the man's wide blue eyes, broad mouth, and scruffy red beard. His calm, quiet voice sounded to Wilhelm like that of Captain Blanchard, a preacher back at Benning. The stranger took off his glove and offered his hand. "Name's Lumley, Bott Lumley. Medic, 104$^{th}$ Recon. M'friends call me Lum."

Wilhelm scrubbed his bare hand on his coat again and took the medic's hand. A medic? Why the hell didn't you do something for Charko back there? I hope he moves on.

"Mah whole outfit's gone. All 'cept me." Lumley blinked, turned away, and cleared his throat.

Wilhelm forced a smile, still wanting to ask why Lumley didn't do something. "Name's Jimmy Wilhelm. That's Sergeant Dolan and Izzy Goldman there. Hundred and Sixth Signal."

Lumley grinned. "Ahhh, code squeezers." The others grinned.

"Appreciate you stoppin' back there, Lumley." Dolan's eyes flashed at Wilhelm. "This kid breaks up sometimes. *Somebody* needs to take charge of 'im."

"Fuckin' Kraut tanks did a job on us, didn't they?" Goldman, face twitching, sounded friendly. Wilhelm, incredulous, swung around and stared.

"Yeah. We was in the first barn the tanks hit. Mah buddy Dink run out and got a Jeep 30 going purty good, but...." Lumley looked down at his feet.

"I saw that. Took real guts." Wilhelm squinted at Goldman, the "gutsy" one.

"Me and ole Dink played football together back home. Played jus' like he soldiered, ole Dink did. Like a wild dawg." Wilhelm nodded, picturing a dog in a football helmet behind a machinegun. "Not but twenty years old, ole Dink was. Same as me."

The column tramped into the little village, people along the street shouting what sounded to the Americans like obscenities. Outside the town they stopped in a broad snow-drifted meadow, with fences all around. As the column broke up, the Germans posted guards all around. The ex-radio team, minus one plus a medic, banged their feet together and stood in close, shielding each other from the wind as best they could. Goldman bent low in the middle and lit one of his last cigarettes. Drag-beggars charged in from all directions. Charko's broken face, and spurting blood hung in Wilhelm's thoughts. I couldn't help it! I couldn't help it! filled his mind.

"Where d'ya s'pose we are, Sarge? From the front lines, I mean." Goldman's pale dirty face twitched in the freezing wind.

"Can't be too far. Night comes, maybe we can find us a way outta here." Dolan looked around at the fences, the guards. "Some a' our boys might be comin' this way purty soon. You never know."

"Yeah, sure," Wilhelm mumbled. "Shoulda showed up three hours ago." He looked at Lumley, who nodded and smiled.

The wind scoured the field, snow swirling into the prisoners' faces, the sky darkening. The cold clawed into their coats, up sleeves and down necks. Wilhelm, shivering, wondered how it felt to freeze to death. Chin jammed into his collar, he thumped his feet together. Snow piled up against his leggings, his knees and calves going numb.

"We gotta get down. Over there against that post." Dolan slogged over to the corner and pointed. "Set down there, Wilhelm. The rest a' us around you." They arranged themselves with Wilhelm in the middle, Dolan in front leaning against him. "We'll change off later on." The sergeant closed his eyes and leaned back.

Goldman leaned forward and whispered into the sergeant's ear. "Guess 'at means we ain't goin' no place tonight, huh, Sarge?"

A guttural shout cut the darkness. Everybody stiffened. A *Feldwebel*, almost invisible in the blowing snow, stood on a pile of wood just outside the fence. "*Steh'n Sie* off fence! Off fence! *Schiessen!*—uhh." Someone next to him muttered something: "Schot, Schoot! Ve schoot! Vill shoot!" Goldman giggled. The noncom conferred again with his translator. "Lorries *am morgen kommt. Zum Zug,* umm, *zum train geh'n.*" He stood, apparently waiting for a response from his audience. A guard moved up the fence and stopped at the corner post behind Wilhelm and prodded him.

"Musta been a teacher," Wilhelm murmured, getting up and away from the post. "Waitin' for questions from his students. Wish to hell he'd a stayed a teacher. I coulda stayed in school, maybe."

Getting down off his perch, the *Feldwebel* smiled. "*Gute Nacht!*" he shouted. "*Gute Nacht!*" They heard his translator snicker.

"*Gute Nacht* to you, too, you sumbitch," Goldman shouted, loud enough for the Americans to hear.

"You get alla that, Goldman?"

"Yeah, Sarge. Said we're ridin' trucks to the train in the mornin'." Goldman shook his head. "Waddaya wanta bet there ain't no fuckin' trucks?'" He doused his half-smoked cigarette in the snow and shoved the butt inside his field jacket. "I think we oughtta get outta here while we still can, Sarge. These old fuckers guardin' us ain't gonna to shoot nobody."

"Them 'old fuckers' are *Volkssturm,* Goldman, and they'll shoot your ass just like any other Kraut. Get that through your thick skull, you'll live to see tomorra." Dolan's pale blue eyes met the bright, black ones under Goldman's wool cap. "Our lines 're at least twenty miles westa here. Other side of the Kraut offensive. You wanta wade through all that, you go ahead. I'll see you in heaven, if you make it." He sighed. "Keep your drawers on, Goldman. Our boys could be comin' along any time now."

The little man leaned away, lips pursed, cheek twitching. "Yeah, Sarge. If you say so."

The four men had moved away from the fence and arranged themselves in a rough square with their backs leaning in, faces outward. In the windy, black-and-white night, the ex-radio team, minus one plus a medic, each man's back balanced against the others, hunkered low into the belly-deep snow. When one had to get up to relieve himself, they shifted, cursed, and re-established themselves. Snow fell during the night, the prisoners and guards alike disappearing into the frozen whiteness. "I'm Dreaming of a White Christmas" bounced across Wilhelm's mind. They're singing it back home right now, he thought. I can't hear it, but they're singing it. They're singing and dammit I'm not there!

# CHAPTER 8

▼

# BOXCARS AND BOMBS

Dawn finally broke, a gray-white wind cutting the prisoners' pale, drawn faces. Hungry and miserable, they moved about, slamming feet together. The voice of the *Feldwebel* faded in and out as he stood above the crowd shouting, *"Kein lorry! Spazieren! Vawk! Ve Vawk!"*

Goldman rolled his eyes, his grin saying: I told you there'd be no trucks. Ve valk! Ve valk!

"Ain't gonna git us nothin' to eat, Ah guess," Lumley said, passing through the gate into the road.

Goldman, automatically disliking the stranger, looked up into the tall southerner's face. "Don't see nobody eatin', d'you?"

Lumley smiled and turned away.

The truck and tank tracks frozen into the dirt road made walking difficult. The guards ignored the Americans' complaints unless they stepped off the road, then they shouted, waved rifles, and threatened to shoot. Small units of German soldiers marched past, forcing the POWs off the road into the ditch. Sometime around noon, the column wound past a tank idling in the middle of the road. As Wilhelm came abreast of it, the monster, like a massive iron stallion, reared up and leaped forward, crashing down beside him before grinding away. Wilhelm, looking straight up, found himself on his back in the ditch.

"Most got ya, did he?" Lumley, smiling, offered a hand.

"Sonofabitch tried to run over me!" Ignoring Lumley's hand, Wilhelm just lay there. It felt so good to stretch out, he'd stay down and maybe the guards wouldn't see him.

"C'mon! Get up outta there!" the sergeant yelled. "These guards ain't blind, y'know! C'mon! Get up!"

"Did you see that bugger, Sarge? He almost…." Wilhelm allowed the redhead to pull him up and onto the road.

Dolan grinned. "Hell, that driver couldn't see you from where he's sittin'. He was just drivin' like he always does."

*     *     *     *

After a long, cold, and windy day, with no food, and snow for water, they slogged into the little town of Gerostein, a railhead. Alongside a crushed tank and a wheeless truck, they slept, leaning against each other as before, in the middle of the muddy road.

Shouted to their feet before sunrise, they marched through the village to the railyard, to rows of boxcars they were to inhabit. The guards cut the column into units of sixty men—twelve ranks, five men to a rank. Back to the wind, feet slamming together in the gritty, black snow, Wilhelm watched German soldiers march past, packs bouncing, weapons stiffly upright, jackboots synchronized. Without knowing the words, he understood the *Feldwebel's* commands. Short-order drill, the same in all armies, all done "by the numbers."

"Look at them bastids," a prisoner down the column said. "You'd think they was winnin' the fuckin' war."

"They was where I was," another man said, chuckling. Nobody laughed.

A platoon of young Germans, their slim, white necks straining under heavy steel helmets, stopped across from the POW column. Narrow bodies under heavy packs, rifles twisted on their shoulders, they looked a pitiful sight.

"Look at that." Goldman grinned. "Them young Krauts won't last a minute at the front." He pulled himself up and, like the combat veteran he considered himself to be, reviewed the troops. "Ain't got no idea what they're in for."

"Well, it ain't their fault, y' know." Lumley looked into Goldman's narrow eyes. "It's the bugger that sent 'em here that's doin' wrong. Ah hate to see young 'uns like them sent off to die like that. Makes me mad."

"Makes you mad, huh? If one of 'em was to draw a bead on you, you'd kill him, though, wouldn't ya?"

"That ain't a fair question, Goldman, and you know it," said Lumley softly. "Ah wouldn't want him dead just 'cause he's young, neither."

Goldman snorted. "'At's bullshit, Lumley, and *you* know it." They turned away from each other.

At the far end of the train, a column of tanks—elephantine machines with trunks of steel—roared across the tracks, scree spraying, black smoke fouling the air behind them. Next, a small German, old and bent, puttees wrapping his skinny legs, came along leading a horse that pulled a wooden cart, a large pot of something steaming in its belly.

"Well, I be dog, look at that," a wag said. "Got the biggest fuckin' tanks in the world, but their chow comes in a horsebucket." This time several men laughed. "I had me a gun," another man said, "I'd kill that sumbitch and grab his soup." More chuckles.

Guards came trotting down the column shouting, "*Los! Los!*" Sounds like "Lost! Lost!" Wilhelm thought, lost somewhere in fucking Germany. His feet hurt, his back ached, and his eyeballs felt like they'd been rolled in sand. The past week rolled across his mind: "Cousin" Junior, with holes in his back, Kratus idling in the ditch, the Kraut going down with burpgun spraying, the young one feeling his crotch. Chaos, that's what it was, total fuckin' chaos. And then there was Blackie, poor Blackie. It wasn't my fault, but, like Sarge said, anybody could've kicked up that mine. Fuckin' war is driving me crazy! I *hate* this, *hate* it, *hate* it! A wisp of dirty, gray smoke smeared back along the train and swirled past his head. "God, if I could do that," he mumbled, "rise up and fade away like that, I'd...." Tears welled up. He swiped them away with his bare hand.

Lumley, poking frozen mud off the bottom of his boot, saw Wilhelm's tears and quivering lip. "You okay, Will," he said softly.

"Yeah, I'm okay." *Will?* Nobody's ever called me *Will.*

"It wasn't your fault, y'know. About yo' buddy, Ah mean. So don't be unhappy with yo'se'f. I mean you...."

Wilhelm looked away. "Yeah, I know. Dolan already told me all that. Just leave me alone. I don't want to talk about it." Especially to you, he thought, a lousy medic like you.

Goldman pushed his wire-rimmed glasses up his humpbacked nose and said to no one in particular: "I just wish to hell we'd a tried to take off yestidy. We get on this fuckin' train, we ain't *never* gonna get back to our lines." His eyes flashed at the sergeant. "We coulda made it if we'd a gone that first night."

The sergeant stared, his lips locked in a straight line.

"Maybe." Wilhelm squinted at the small soldier. "You felt so damn strong about it, whyn't you go on and take off? At least we wouldn't have to listen to you bitchin' about it alla time." Immediately he wished he could take it back, at the same time meaning every word of it. A feeling of ah-what-the-hell washed over him: I'm still alive, and I ain't hurt. He pulled out the remains of his D-bar and held it up. "Hey, you guys! Look what I got!" Holding it close to his belly out of sight of the men all around, he broke it into four roughly equal pieces and held them out in his palm. "C'mon, let's finish it off. I'm tired a carryin' it around." A weak grin.

Surprised looks and smiles all around. "Hey, thanks, Will," Lumley said. Dolan rolled his bit in the foil from his last piece of tobacco, but Goldman tossed his in his mouth and, making soft, happy sounds, chewed, and swallowed it. Wilhelm found the largest piece still in his palm. Smiling, he allowed his bit to melt on his tongue. An only child like me, he was thinking, *never* gives away anything, especially candy, under these conditions! He felt warm down deep inside. But these guys are my friends, my *only* friends, and I *need* them. Another wisp of that gray smoke swooped past him and faded away. Somehow, to him it seemed just greasy, gray smoke now, nothing more. He couldn't stop smiling.

Dolan kicked at the steel axle sticking out in front of him. "Damn it to hell! We don't get in one these fuckin' cars pretty soon, my feet're gonna freeze up hard as a rock."

"Mine too, Sarge," Lumley said, slamming his feet together hard. "Ah gotta get these shoes off and rub mine, else Ah'll be standin' here on stumps." The big redhead looked over the heads nearby down the column. "Wonder when these buggers is gonna get us somethin' to eat. Mah belly thinks mah throat's done been cut." He pulled a small, red, gilt-edged book from his overcoat pocket and flopped it open. Mouth working, he began to read. The others looked at each other.

"Awright, here we go," Dolan said, pointing at an approaching German guard. "*Los! Los!*" the German shouted, waving the unit along the train. They stopped at an empty boxcar, and, one by one, hoisted themselves up into it.

"God damn! Smells like horseshit in here!" Goldman stomped his feet. "We gonna live in this crap the resta the way?"

"Shut up and c'mon!" Dolan yelled. Light from a brakeman's tower, a cupola in the corner, illuminated a hole in the far left corner. "Looks like the shithole over there! Let's grab the other corner!"

Wilhelm dropped in between Goldman and Lumley, left arm pulling up his knees, bare right hand between his thighs. Dolan, on the floor in front of Wilhelm, took off his shoes and began to rub his feet. Lumley did the same. The soft odor of dirty socks, attenuated by the cold, brought locker rooms, naked bodies, and snapping towels to Wilhelm's mind. Hated that class, he remembered. Give my right arm to be back there now, though. The boxcar door slammed shut, and a steel bar scraped into place. Except for the light from the cupola and the cracks in the walls, all was dark. The wind found its way through the walls and up between the floorboards. Wilhelm, shivering and belly growling, felt something sink inside him. He wanted to cry, but wouldn't allow it.

Hours passed before the train rumbled and began to roll, stopping and starting, grinding and squealing its way into Germany. Fingers numb, feet burning cold, Wilhelm could not shake the feeling of being lost, lost forever in some strange, distant place he'd never been before. Where are we going? When will we get there? Reminds me of those long, boring Sunday afternoon rides with Mom and Dad. But this ain't Sunday afternoon. And I really am lost.

It was dark when the train slowed and a rumble, like a shiver, rolled down the train and through the car. Shouts and curses bounced around as several men got up and struggled through the crowded men to the walls. A foot or a finger, an arm or a leg stepped on, even brushed against, brought curses, sometimes fists.

These guys are hungry and mean. Maybe they'll let us out to get some chow. I need a place to stretch out and lie down and a blanket to get warm. He tried to stretch his legs and got kicked. Just when he thought he couldn't sit another minute, he began to breathe deeply.

Is Goldman, here against my left arm, thinking the same things I am? Nah. He's tough. A New Jersey street-tough. And Lum—big, strong Lum on my right—he's got his little red book, his God, and all that to keep him going. Wonder if all that praying and Bible reading and stuff actually *does* anything. Maybe I'll borrow his book sometime and check it out. The Sarge, of course, is really tough. Like my dad. Made outta concrete.

"Hey, Lum," he heard himself say. "Whyn't you stop all that prayin' and mumblin' for a while, huh? You're driving me nuts!"

The white blob that was Lumley's face swelled as it turned toward Wilhelm. "C'mon, Will, it's Christmastime, boy. You oughta be doin' some prayin' your ownse'f."

"Yeah, well, maybe sometime. But not now. Not right now." It's Christmas? My God! I forgot all about it! They're eating Christmas dinner back home, I bet, and listenin' to Christmas music on the radio. Mashed potatoes, brown gravy, and big white slabs of turkey—I can smell 'em and taste 'em! And here I am growlin' my guts out in a goddam boxcar on my way into *Deutschland,* Krautland, *der* fucking *Vaterland.* He closed his eyes and tried to stamp Christmas dinner on his mind.

Suddenly, a plane came in low and fast across the rail yard, and a reddish light flickered into the car. A voice came down the brakeman's tower over the shithole: "It's a flare! That plane dropped a flare over there!" Men jumped up and crowded against the walls to look through the cracks.

"It's the Red Cross, I bet," somebody shouted. "Lettin' ever' body know this here's a POW train."

A tall soldier, the six stripes on his sleeve flashing pink in the thin light. grinned. "Shit, boy, there ain't no Red Cross 'round here. That's a target flare. Night-bombers comin' to blow the town and this fuckin' train all to hell." Men at the big sliding door began to push and shove at it.

Bombs thumped in the distance, the car vibrating, shivering. "Them's the giants' feet." Dolan's voice came from the darkness in front of Wilhelm. "I heard 'em before back in France. They step on you, you're *kaput*. C'mon, let's see if we can haul ass outta here." Sirens and the snap of anti-aircraft guns cut the air. The men, cursing and shouting, lifted and pushed, at the door.

The man in the brakeman's tower dropped to the floor and shoved into the middle of the melee. "Is there a little guy in here?" he shouted, "one what could get through that bobwire up there? He could git out and open the door!" He looked all around. "C'mon, somebody! Anybody! Anybody!"

"Here! I'll do it! Put me up there and I'll do it!" Goldman's voice faded into the growing roar of engines in the sky. He rose into the tower on a square of hands, his feet disappearing into the darkness.

"I'm out! I'm out!" Feet thumped across the roof, then nothing.

"Damn, he's done broke a leg," Lumley breathed into Wilhelm's ear.

Slowly the steel bar rattled across the door. Before it was half open, prisoners were pushing out into the thundering night, yelling, falling, and running. A wall of sound, along with the wind and flying snow, filled the night. The giants' feet thumped into the railyard, and the whole world shook.

Wilhelm bounced off his buttocks onto his feet and ran, knees high, head back, arms flailing. Shouts of "Bombshelter! Over here! Over here!" rose out of the darkness. The stream of men turned toward a building across the yard, as bombs high-pitched whine changed to a low hum before each explosion. "*Diiive, diiive! diiive!*" they seemed to scream. And Wilhelm did. Again and again, down into the snow, his nose meeting cinders, chest and knees burning at impact. The earth tossed him up, but gravity slammed him back down again. A sharp pain in his chest. A broken rib? A heart attack? In the middle of the field, he ran into a barbwire fence, men hanging on it, climbing, yelling. Avoiding the barbs, he eased up and over, but, on the other side, found himself caught, an arm and a leg hooked. The arm free, the lower barb held fast. Bent, pulling at it, he sees a hand, square-cut nails clean enough to pass inspection, reaching in, pulling the twisted hook away. Dolan's hand. It's Dolan's hand! Wilhelm threw a quick smile at his savior and turned to run. A bomb screamed in close. He barely beat it to the ground.

Suddenly, no more bombs. Only the drone of engines and the wail of sirens filled the night. But he ran on, a long snow-covered building looming up. The bomb shelter? He ran into a black wall, bounced back and almost fell. Turning, puffing, he leaned against it and slid down. Prisoners, the lucky ones, hit the wall around him.

Wilhelm looks around for the Sarge. Dolan? Where is he?

Flames flashed behind the building, the town burning, the clouds above now blood red. Wilhelm squinted along the wall. "No shelter for POWs," he murmured. "Shoulda known." Thinking more clearly now, he looked himself up and down: no pains, no wet, bloody holes. Not a scratch! You're a lucky bugger, Jimmy, he told himself. Somebody upstairs likes you.

But what about the Sarge? Wilhelm looked out across the field at the fuming craters and the dark lumps in the snow. Is he out there? With those dead guys? The thought hit him hard: "Somebody up there," his eyes flashed up at the clouds, "really *does* like me." The train, he saw, stood untouched, all its doors gaping open. "Shoulda stayed in that boxcar, insteada running out there. How stupid can you get?" He looked for his path among the craters and along the fence. Minutes ago, Dolan was with me. Helped me get loose. I gotta go out and look for…no, I can't, I can't go out there again. Not now.

He looked down the wall again. Where's Goldman? He had a head-start. Oughtta be around here somewhere. And Charco and, no, wait, not Charco, dammit, not Charko, he's dead. Wilhelm's bare right hand, the palm webbed with fine, black lines, the long, ragged nails tar-black underneath, floated up before his eyes. "Charco's blood. I gotta forget him! Sarge said to forget him. Oh, no, not another one! The Sarge too? But I didn't make him stop and help me. He did it himself. It ain't my fault if…. you can't blame me…. who the hell am I talking to, anyway?

The scream of the sirens atop the warehouse dropped to a growl and groaned away into the wind. Wilhelm's chest, the bone right in front, began to throb. Feeling around, he felt a lump there and reached inside, deep. My God! A piece of German bread, rock-hard and dark, the crust crumbling in his fingers. "Well, I'll be damned!" he muttered aloud, "It's the piece I saved from the hike!" He broke off a corner and shoved it in his mouth. Dry and hard, smelling of pine-tree sawdust, he wanted to spit it out but swallowed it instead. After all, it was edible once upon a time.

Looking up at the wall, he saw a sign painted on it. *Wertheimer Gesellschaft, Limburg.* So that's where we are, *Limburg.* Hey, that's where that stink-cheese Dad likes comes from! Has to keep it in the garage, it stinks so bad! He grinned and sniffed. Only the sharp stench of high explosive filled his nose.

Suddenly, planes and ack-ack and wailing sirens on the far side of the town filled the air. The ground thumped and rolled, the clouds roiling blood-red. He had a sudden urge to run, but his feet refused. No bomb shelter, no stupid running, he thought. Back against the warehouse wall, he pulled his knees up, covered his ears, and tried to think about—about what? The Sarge? Goldman? Lumley? The new guy. "Please, God," he whispered, "let them be okay. I need 'em bad, God. I need 'em awful bad." Eyes dry and hot, he stared up at the clouds, waiting for…for what? An answer? A voice from heaven? Even if He *is* up there, He ain't gonna listen to me; I never went to church; he doesn't even know me. Forget it. Fuck it.

The second raid over, his fear subsiding, Wilhelm got up and moved among the prisoners crowded into little groups, voices muted, feet bouncing together. They're awful quiet, he thought. Expecting the guards to forget them? Ha! But why ain't they takin' off? Escaping, like they're supposed to? Yes, Jimmy, and why ain't I takin' off? Hell, it never crossed my mind. Supposed to, at least that's what they said back at Benning. Sarge was here, he'd know what to do.

A familiar stocky shape appeared down the wall moving his way. Wilhelm, eyes big, lurched forward and waved his arms. "Hey! Hey, Sarge! Sergeant Dolan! Boy, am I glad to see…." The soldier stared, frowned, and swung by, two stripes on his sleeve pink in the flashing light. Wilhelm turned and watched the man disappear into the crowd.

"Hey, is that you, Will?" Lumley, smiling, hopping on one foot, came out of the crowd toward him. He dropped a heavy hand on Wilhelm's shoulder and eased himself down into the snow, the injured leg held straight out.

"Lum! Where you been, boy? You okay?" Wilhelm stared down at the redhead's gimpy leg.

"Yeah, 'cept for this here leg. Piece of one a' them bombs got me, Ah guess. Ah was jus' fixin' to open up my pants and take a look at it when Ah heard your voice." He winced. "Gimme a hand here, will ya? Ah gotta see where this blood is comin' from." He unhooked the cord and pulled his legging off.

Wilhelm squatted down next to the big fellow and helped him peel away the bloody pantsleg. Seeing Lumley's wound, he felt guilty about being so healthy.

Lumley pressed on the artery up near his groin and the flow of blood slowed. "Put your finger on right here, Will, and press down good'n hard. Gotta make me a tourniquet." He twisted the bloody stocking into a cord, pulled it around his thigh above Wilhelm's finger, his squinting blue eyes brimming. "Oh, God! It hurts like the billy-blue hell!"

"You seen the Sarge anywhere?" Wilhelm asked, ignoring Lumley's pain.

"Seen 'im runnin' out there. Ain't seen hide nor hair of 'im since, though. You ain't neither, huh?"

Wilhelm shook his head and looked away. "No, I ain't," he said. Would I ask if I had? This guy's just plain stupid. A stupid damn Southerner medic and a lousy one that. Coulda helped Charko and didn't do a thing. Helps himself, though.

The wind had picked up, and the congealed sweat in Wilhelm's crotch and armpits had gone cold. He dropped into the snow next to Lumley, pulled his knees in tight and wriggled his fingers and toes. His wounded leg dressed again, Lumley dropped back on his elbows and stared up at the clouds. The sirens had gone silent, leaving only a cold, windy silence. Now the flare on the factory sputtered and went out.

Through the pall of acrid smoke in the railyard, a line of guards appeared coming toward the POWs.

"Here they come, Will. What're we gonna do?"

"Huh? Oh, uhhh, yeah." Wilhelm, his mind back on the hill, Charco's blood pulsing through his fingers, the sucking sound from the dying man's throat slowly fading, roused himself. "I don't know, Lum. I ain't thought about it."

"It's gonna be mighty hard to find the Sarge and Goldman in this crowd. Course, they could be out there somewhere." Lumley's eyes flashed at the railyard. "I'm guessing', well, we oughtta jus' go on back to the train and…."

"Yeah, that's what I was thinkin', Lum." Wilhelm sighed. "I hate like hell to go back in that fuckin' boxcar, don't you?"

"Yeah, Ah do, Will, Ah sure do. But Ah don't know what else we can do."

"S'posed to take off, y'know." Wilhelm mimicked Dolan's hard look. "That's what they told us at Benning. Remember?" Head canted, he stuck out his chin and squinted at Lumley. "Tell you the truth, though, Lum, we ain't got a chance in hell of gettin' back to our lines from here." Dolan wouldn't have said that.

Lumley nodded. "Yeah. And if the Krauts was to ketch us wandering' around in there," his eyes flashed toward the woods at the end of the warehouse, "reckon they'd just shoot us down and be done with it."

Lips pursed, Wilhelm stared at the oncoming guards.

"Ah'm fixin' to say a little prayer, Will, before the guards git here." Lumley had his palms together. "Whyn't you c'mon and join in?" He closed his eyes and began: "Our Father who art in Heaven, hallowed be thy name…."

About halfway through, Wilhelm began to mumble the words. He knew them, all right, he'd heard them often enough in the boxcar. After the "Amen," he grinned and stared at his feet.

Lumley chuckled. "You done good, Will. Real good." He slapped his buddy on the back, leaned in hard and heaved himself up. "Come on, let's get on back. Goldman and the Sarge're probably over there, wonderin' where we're at."

The two men began to pick their way across the yard, Lumley leaning, Wilhelm straining to support him. A soft warmth had replaced the ache in his chest, and, in spite of Lumley's weight, he felt strangely light on his feet. Did the prayer do that? No! Hell no, he told himself. They passed craters and dead men, the wind clearing the smoke in little patches. Light from the burning town beyond the warehouse bounced off the clouds, lighting the field. At the barbwire fence, now bent and twisted into the snow, Wilhelm stopped and checked the approaching guards. "The Sarge was right here helpin' me get off the fence, Lum. Right here. Let's take a quick look around." They searched along the wire in both directions until the guards pointed back and *Los-Los*-ed them toward the train.

The mixed stink of horse and human feces greeted them at the boxcar door. "Home-sweet-home," Wilhelm sang, sniffing. "Good ole home-sweet-home."

"Well, well, lookey who's here! The heroes're back!" Goldman, a bloody gash on his cheek, left arm cradled in his overcoat, appeared from the dark inside the car. He squatted in the doorway and spat into the snow. "Thought yooz guys'd be back at the Company by now, drinkin' hot coffee and loadin' up on them powdered fuckin' eggs." He dropped over the edge of the car and dangled his legs.

The returnees hoisted themselves up on either side of Goldman and looked him over. "Looks like you got mashed up some, there, buddy,"

Wilhelm ventured. "We looked all over for you on the other side. You just get back?"

Goldman, left eye squeezed shut, lips pressed together, rocked back and forth on the edge of the boxcar. "Me? Back? I ain't been no place. Opened the fuckin' door and the whole fuckin' crowd a yooz run right over me!" He spat and wiped his mouth on his sleeve. "All I gotta say is, to *hell* wit' alla yooz! To *hell* wit' the whole fuckin' buncha yooz!"

"Well, at least you got all your fingers and toes, buddy." Lumley, loosening the cords on his legging, held his leg out straight. "Some of them guys that run over you are still layin' out there, y'know."

"Yeah, yeah, I know. I seen 'em. You ain't tellin' me nuttin'." Goldman pulled off his wool cap and ran his gloved fingers through the greasy black hair. "Tough shit is all I got for 'em." He shook his fist at the field. "That's all I got for alla yooz sumbitches! Tough shit!" He sighed, closed his eyes and rocked back and forth. Wilhelm thought he looked like a small abandoned child. "When you and them bastids got through runnin' me down," Goldman mumbled, "I couldn't do nuttin' but roll back under the car. I got behind one a' them wheels and shook and cried like a fuckin' baby. Shit in my pants, too, I think. Smell it?" Covering his eyes with his good hand, he began to rock again, faster now.

Lumley put his arm around the little man and held him. Wilhelm turned away. The idea of one man hugging another one repelled him. His dad had never hugged him; the Wilhelms never did anything like that. No kissing, either. He swung his legs and watched the guards herd the rest of the prisoners back to the train. Looks like everybody decided to come back to the train like we did. I just hope we did right.

Goldman wiped his tear-streaked face on his sleeve and took a deep breath. "So yooz guys went right up the middle like a couple a fullbacks, huh? Lucky bastids, ain't ya?" His face cracked into a smile, the first since they'd seen. His sore arm appeared from inside his coat and, fell across Wilhelm's shoulders, while the other flung itself around Lumley's neck. "Hell, I guess I was lucky, too," he whispered. "What about the Sarge? Yooz see him anywhere? Is he—gone?"

Lumley opened his mouth, but Wilhelm spoke. "I ain't seen 'im, Goldman, not since I hung up on that fence out there. Looks like them giants he was talkin' about got him." Wilhelm blinked and looked up at the scudding clouds. "We're on our own now, buddy. On our own from now on."

Even though the wind was picking up, Lumley pulled out his little red Bible and opened it. "Y'all've heard of the twenty-third Psalm, ain't you?" Neither Wilhelm nor Goldman nodded, but he reached across and held the book in front of Goldman. Wilhelm grabbed and helped hold it there.

"Ah think now'd be good time for us to, uhhh, read it out, so: The Lord is my shepherd, I shall not want...." A few stanzas later, Wilhelm, then Goldman, joined in. "He maketh me to lie down in green pastures...." Some of the men entering the boxcar stopped, hunkered down behind them and joined in. With many voices speaking, Lumley began again at the beginning, their white exhalations rising into the wind like smoke from a signal fire.

Later, Wilhelm sat in the cold, dark corner of the car, his eyes closed, a strange feeling warming his chest. A strange, new feeling, one he'd never had before. Later, in his dream, he ran into "the valley of the shadow of death," hard, cinder-black snow rising up again and again, howling, whistling bombs falling, and the pain in his chest filling the night. He ran, looking for a nonexistent bombshelter, got caught on a roll of barbwire when Dolan appeared, freed him and walked off into the darkness. He awoke in the dark, breathing hard, the shithole calling.

# CHAPTER 9

▼

# HOME SWEET HOME

Shouts of "*Los! Los!*" and the rush of frigid air—colder but cleaner than the fetid air inside the car—woke Wilhelm. When he finally got his sticky eyes open, they met the filthy overcoat of a prisoner stretched against the wall above him. The man, now moving away toward the door, had apparently spent most of the night leaning there on one arm or the other.

Wilhelm slid up the wall and looked through the crowd into the railyard. "Christ," he muttered, "we're still in Limburg—craters, dead men, and all. Ain't they never gonna move us anywhere?" He closed his eyes and slid back to the floor.

A strange sound—an American voice, soft and urgent—cut through the din of snuffling, groaning men. "I'm Chaplain Hendersen, men. I'm bringin' you all Christmas cheer from home."

Christmas cheer? Wilhelm wanted Christmas dinner, not Christmas cheer. Fuck the cheer. Bring on the turkey! He wanted to, but he didn't shout it.

"Come on out and join in," the minister intoned. "Jews, Catholics, Protestants! Everybody's welcome! Come on out! Come on out!" Wilhelm reared up and looked. Half a dozen guards, their dirty faces drawn with fatigue, formed a semicircle around a tall, thin American whose pale lips protruded from a streaky, gray beard. A secret sun seemed to glow in his eyes.

Most of the prisoners, stretching and yawning, dropped out of the car into the snow. Their scruffy faces showed little interest in the chaplain's words as they turned to relieve themselves in the snow. Lumley, however, jumped out of the car, shook the chaplain's hand, and told him of his Baptist background. His presumed congregation assembled, the minister lifted his Bible and began to read—yes, it was the story of Christ's birth.

Wilhelm walked over and leaned against the boxcar door, fascinated by the chaplain's gray-pink lips in the surrounding hair, the beard jumping back and forth in the wind. What a helluva strain it must be, he thought, to go down the train reading that same crap over and over to a bunch of brainless, starved-out POWs. He's either off his rocker or a Section Eight, ready for medical discharge.

"What the fuck's he think he's doin', yammerin' on like that?" Goldman plopped down in the doorway, and Wilhelm joined him.

"What's it look like he's doin', Goldman? He's bringin' *The Message* to the sinners." Wilhelm stared at the small soldier. "Christmas Cheer. Ever hear of it? You people ever do any celebratin'?"

Goldman grinned, hawked, and spat.

Wilhelm took off his glove and turned both hands palm up, his right palm still webbed with Charko's blood, the frayed nails still black-edged. Behind his eyes, he saw the mine jump and explode, Charko's broken body sliding down the hill, blood spurting. He shook the picture away and put his left—and only—glove back on.

Snow-laden wind swept over the car, across the railyard, and rose, like a woven sheet, up and over the warehouse. Just like back home, he thought, the snow blowing up and over the Sturms' house next door. He saw the kitchen table now, holding steaming bowls of mashed potatoes and brown gravy, slabs of meatloaf, bread and butter and, oh, God, if I could only be *there! Home!* Christmas or no Christmas, just *home, eat* and *eat* and *eat,* until....

A moving black spot, fading in and out through the snow-curtain, caught Wilhelm's eye. Slowly, the spot became a man, old and bent—a man leading a horse pulling a wagon. He wore a peaked hat from another time, a greenish-gray coat roped and tied around his narrow middle. Struggling through knee-deep drifts toward the train, the old man's black, knee-high boots rose and fell like the pistons of an archaic engine. The little caravan stopped not far from the chaplain's Christmas service; the bent German, staring at the spectacle, leaned against the horse's flank, white balloons puffing from both their mouths. Rested now, he moved to a nearby crater; he stooped and pulled a lifeless leg up out of the snow. He dragged the body to the wagon, wrapped his arms around it, and gently, almost lovingly, hoisted it onto the wagonbed.

Leaning again on the horse, the man studied the train, the boxcars, and the prisoners. His jet-black eyes met Wilhelm's, and he frowned quizzically. The boy, puzzled, stared back. Was there a kind of recognition in that look? Did Wilhelm resemble someone the man knew? A cousin maybe? The German went back to his task, their eyes not meeting again.

The service over, Wilhelm watched a few prisoners crowd around the chaplain, smiling, nodding, shaking his hand. He wished he could join in, but he just couldn't, or wouldn't. Most of the "congregation" took the opportunity to stretch their legs, pee, or defecate in the snow. They had a little freedom and enjoyed every minute of it. Now, the guards *Los-Los*-ed them back into the boxcar, the chaplain and his entourage of guards moving along to the next car.

Goldman grinned. "Damn if I ain't glad that's over. I had to go through that fuckin' valley of death again, I'd shit."

Wilhelm felt like slapping the small man's face. "You're somethin', you know that, Goldman? I was just thinkin' how tough it must be for that preacher to…aw, hell, you don't give a shit about nothin', do you?"

"Oh, c'mon now, buddy. I give a shit, course I do! But that's about it." Goldman nodded toward the railyard. "See that little Kraut out there pickin' up them bodies? Now *he's* really doin' somethin' *for* us. Somethin' *real*. Somethin' you can see."

A loud fart came from the car behind them, the sound magnified by the big, hollow space. "Ha! Ha! Ya hear that, Wilhelm? That's what I think about all that crap. The opiate of the people, somebody said once. And I believe it! I really believe it!" The tic had twisted his face until his left eye was almost shut. "That fuckin' chaplain wants to do somethin' *for* us, why don't he get us some *Christmas chow?* Get 'em to let us out of the car once in a while so we can take a decent crap. That Bible reading's the best he can do, he can go to hell as far's I'm concerned." He got up and went back into the car.

Wilhelm kept his eyes on the little German in the railyard. His wagon full now, the man struggled across the field toward the warehouse, the wind shoving him this way and that. Wilhelm, suddenly aware of the erstwhile congregation scrambling for space behind him, slid quickly along the wall and squeezed in, albeit reluctantly, next to Goldman.

Lumley, humming softly, a smile middling his scraggly beard, dropped into the space next to Wilhelm. The boxcar door slammed shut. Darkness and the familiar stench of horse and human offal filled the car. "What'd you think of it, Will?" Lumley whispered.

"What? The service? It was okay, I guess. Nice of the chaplain to come and...." Wilhelm smiled mirthlessly at Lumley's big shadow. "But it's too bad he didn't bring us some chow, a little turkey and dressing, though, ain't it?" Wincing, he realized he was repeating after Goldman.

"Yeah, I guess." Lumley hesitated, "But did you hear what he said— what he had to *tell* us?"

"Yeah, I heard 'im, Lum. I heard 'im." Wilhelm frowned. "Mostly, I was watchin' that little Kraut out in the field. Wonderin' what he was gonna do with them bodies he was pickin' up. Pile 'em somewhere, I bet, and let 'em rot." Wilhelm sighed. "Y'know somethin', Lum? That man looked at me like, like he knew me. One a my Kraut cousins, I guess." Oh, hell, Lum wasn't with us back at the house. He doesn't know what I'm talking about.

"He looked at you, huh? Well ain't that *inter-restin'?*"

Wilhelm, a little surprised at Lumley's tone, said, "I heard most of what your preacher said. I didn't mean I...."

"He warn't *mah* preacher, Will!" Lumley's head shook. "Y'know, they's times Ah don't even *know* you." The big man loosened the legging on his bad leg, leaned back, and closed his eyes. "Just 'cause Hitler's a rotten bastard don't mean the rest of 'em are." He pulled the twisted sock out of his pocket and tied it tightly around his thigh.

"Well, I hope so, Lum. I sure hope so." If I'd've got killed by those bombs last night, Wilhelm wondered, would anybody back home ever know what happened to me?

"That's crap, Lumley, and you know it." Goldman's sharp voice cut the darkness, his breath bathing Wilhelm's cheek. "A man's life ain't worth shit around here, and froze-up dead bodies ain't even worth that.

The Krauts'll toss them bodies in a hole somewheres, throw gas on 'em, and burn 'em." He smiled into the darkness. "But don't worry about it, guys, it ain't got nuttin to do wit' yooz." Goldman, chuckling, shoved his feet out into the darkness. "Hey, look at this!" he shouted. "I got me a whole damn yard for my feet!"

The boxcar jerked, squealed, groaned, rolled forward, and stopped. Nowhere, Wilhelm told himself, we're going nowhere.

# CHAPTER 10

▼

# OUR NEW HOME

Next day about noon, a grinding jerk came down the train.

"Hey, they're hookin' up an engine," a voice shouted. "We gonna move ass outta here!"

"My God, I hope so." Wilhelm shifted, twisted around, and stretched his arms over his head.

"Ah, 'at don't mean nuttin'. We seen it before, ain't we?" Goldman's voice faded into the swelling screech of steel against steel.

Wilhelm breathed a sigh. "Hot chow and a warm bed. C'mon, you bastards, let's go! Let's go!" The car jerked, rocked, and ground to a halt. A moan ran through the crowd. Wilhelm, an ex-fighting man, used to standing in line, waiting hours for orders—for chow, for come-what-may—groaned in disappointment. With the bombing, the death, the everlasting hunger and cold, he had hit bottom, his patience gone. Real men, his training had taught him, do not scream. But that's what he wanted to do—scream.

"Come on! Come on!" Wilhelm bounced hard against the wall, remembering Dolan's rocking in his seat on the Schnee Eifel. "Let's go!

Let's go! Move! Move!" he cried. "Get us some chow, build us a fire, find us a fucking bed!" He looked around at Lumley. "I know, let's set this car on fire and get some heat in here!" Somebody across the way chuckled. Wilhelm slumped against the wall and closed his eyes, desperate, thinking to die would be to get free.

Other prisoners sat silent and motionless in the hazy light, their mouths shut, eyes half open. An hour, maybe two, passed. Suddenly, a gust and a train roared past, the car rocking, shuddering in the vacuum it brought; then a rumble and the car jerked forward. Hope, like water in a big, dark, open pot, sloshed around the car.

"Go! Go! Go!" Wilhelm reared up and shouted. Suddenly the whole car was shouting, "Go! Go! Go!" As the train picked up speed, the wind whistled through the walls, burst up between the floorboards, and whirled down the cupola. Smiling, Wilhelm shivered, pulled his knees against his chest, and rested his head on them. Cold snowlight splashed through the cracks in the walls, the faces across the way strobing off and on. It reminded him of those flickering Saturday afternoon movies at Fountain Square: "Tom Mix," "Flash Gordon," "The Lone Ranger." Now he was following that cute girl with the beautiful smooth round butt swinging around the Square. How beautiful she was! He was in love, again. What *was* her name?

The train's rolling motion felt good, but only in daytime. He felt bad at night—the total absence of light, those bulky bodies leaning into him, stepping over and around him. He hated them all. Dangerous, too, was the chore of getting to the shithole and back. A finger or toe stepped on, a bumped shoulder could bring curses and a fist from the darkness.

The car began to slant, the train rising, the temperature falling, inhaled air freezing in Wilhelm's nose. Below 5 degrees now, he decided.

Around midday, their fourth in the boxcar, the train halted again. Doors all along the train ground open, the POWs dropping out into the blinding sunlight, blinking, looking around. Wilhelm squinted up at the pale blue heavens and filled his lungs with deliciously clean mountain air. He smiled, stretched, and swung his arms, the snow underfoot, crisp and crunchy, reached almost to his knees.

"Smell that, Lum? Good clean air? Damn near't forgot what it smells like!" He smiled—another thing he'd almost forgotten—at Lumley. "Cold, though, ain't it? Damn cold."

"Yeah, shore is, Will. It shore is. Purty place, too, ain't it? Sorta like the Jawja mountains, 'cept we don't never have snow this deep and this kinda cold." He rubbed his beard and stared at the hills beyond the train. "Ever been to the Jawja mountains, Will?"

"No." Wilhelm said, chuckling. "On'y thang Ah ever saw was reyud-mud in them reyud-wawtuh swamps at Fo't Bennin'." He congratulated himself on his Jawja accent. "Never knowed they *was* any mountains down theyuh." The super-flat Indiana cornfields near his home came to mind. "Nothin' but a few li'l heels in Indiana whur Ahm from, y'know." He smiled, expecting some comment from his Southern buddy. Nothing.

"Yooz guys ain't never been to the Catskills, have ya? They're a helluva lot prettier'n this. This is crap. Germany is crap." Goldman opened his overcoat, unbuttoned his fly, and proceeded to pee a yellow hole in the snow.

Wilhelm followed suit, thinking of Dolan and the tobacco-brown holes he used to make. "Gone but not forgotten," as Dad always says. He's right here in my head. Wonder if that's what preachers mean by The Resurrection?

A group of pale-faced women in heavy coats with dark cloths covering their heads came out of the little station next to the tracks, a detail of soldiers carrying a big, steaming pot behind them. POWs from up and down the train came running.

"Hey, look at that! *Hausfraus!*" Wilhelm grinned. "That's what my grandpaw used to call my mom when he came to dinner: a *hausfrau.*"

"Yeah, well, don't go all gooey on us, Wilhelm. Not till you see what kinda shit they got for us, anyway."

"Oh, shut up, Goldman! Just shut up!"

They shoved into the melee rushing toward the big pot. Guards "*Los-Los*-ed" the men into line. Given a large spoon, a single dipper of soup in a metal bowl plus a chunk of brown bread topped by a dollop of ersatz butter, Wilhelm and his buddies sat against a boxcar's wheel and ate like starving dogs, smacking lips and sucking fingers.

"Y'know, it's hard to believe those Kraut women went to all this trouble just for us." Wilhelm squirmed against a cold, hard steel axle. "Bet the German army didn't have nothin' to do with it."

"Yeah, Krauts're wonderful people all right. Your grandpaw would be proud," Goldman sneered. "But why ain't these wonderful people feedin' us ever'day? And why're they takin' so fuckin' long to get us to camp? Hell, Germany ain't even as big as Texas. We aughtta be half way to China by now."

"Maybe we could stay here and let these ladies take care of us." Wilhelm returned. "Whadaya think, Lum?"

"Oh, yeah. That'd be real nice." Lumley grinned. "Ah'd love thet."

*     *     *     *

Two days and many stops and starts later, the train rolled into a station and stopped. Wilhelm and his buddies got up and looked through the cracks. Guards and guard towers and barbed-wire-topped fences met their eyes. "Looks like we're here, boys," Wilhelm announced.

After several hours passed: "Shit. The bastids're jus' gonna let us sit here and starve to deat'. That way they can jus' haul us off and dump our bodies somewheres." Goldman spat on the floor.

When the boxcar door finally slid back, the men crowded through and dropped into the gritty, black snow along the tracks. Lined up and counted, their group of sixty moved out. They shuffled through the muck and mud, cowed and broken like a crowd of old men.

"Stahl-a-mer IIIB. Ar-bite makt fry? What's that mean, Goldman?" Lumley stared at the sign arching above the gate to the camp.

"*Stalag IIIB*, Lumley. It says, 'Work makes you free.' They want you to work your ass off for 'em. But we don't have ta work. Geneva Convention says corporals don't hafta work."

Wilhelm chuckled, lifted his arm, and kissed the two stripes on his sleeve. No more boxcar, no more bombs—maybe—heat and a bed and regular chow—maybe. Would they be mistreated? Beaten, or worse? He'd heard rumors. We'll see, he thought. We'll see.

*          *          *          *

"Hey, look, they're breakin' us up into small groups. Let's drop back to the end of the line so we can stay together." Dolan would've said that. He really is still here, Wilhelm told himself.

They spent the next two days in a barn, waiting, sleeping on straw, a do-it-yourself "latrine" in the corner. They welcomed a dipper of hot tea and a piece of sawdust-laden bread each morning, and a beet-top or, with luck, a thin barley gruel in the evening.

On the third morning, the crowd at the registration tables had thinned, so Wilhelm, Lumley, and Goldman joined the line. Wilhelm and Lumley removed their wool caps, brushed their hands through their hair, and stood up straight for the photograph to come. Goldman did nothing, wild and greasy hair protruding from under his cap show-ing his disdain for the coming confrontation with the enemy.

The registrar, a *Feldwebel,* his high, broad forehead and hatchet-sharp nose shining in the yellow light, the pale blue eyes nar-rowing as Goldman stepped before him. "Your unit?" The registrar's words came hard and sharp.

Goldman's face darkened, tic buckling his left cheek. "Isadore Gold-man, Tech Corporal. Serial Number 356 498 61."

Isadore, so that's his name, Wilhelm thought. Went to school with an Isadore, yeah, Isadore Feldman, ugly kid, real ugly.

"*Und your unit?*" The German shouted, bunker-slit eyes boring into Goldman's.

"Isadore Goldman, T/5, 356 494 61," Goldman reiterated, looking down his nose at the seated German.

The rows of medals on the *Feldwebel's* chest fluttered as he slid his hands flat across the table. Goldman's chin rose. "*Goltmann, eh? Isadore Goldtmann. Jaaa? Du bist Jüdisch, ja?*"

The German's familiar *Du* instead *Sie* lowered automatically Gold-man's standing in the world. Goldman mumbled, "One more time, you dumb fuckin' Kraut." He kept his voice low. "Isadore Goldman, T/5, 356 494 61."

Eyes bulging, the *Feldwebel* looked as if he might explode. A *Haupt-mannn,* empty right sleeve dangling, rose from a desk in the corner and limped up behind the registrar. When the captain whispered into his subordinate's ear, heels clicked and the *Feldwebel's* head bobbed. As the officer stumped back to his corner, the *Feldwebel* wrote something on the form before him and waved Goldman away.

"*Nächst!*" he shouted. "Your unit?"

Wilhelm's lips quivered. "James Wilhelm, T-5, 352 494 77."

"*Your unit?*"

Having heard it many times at home, Wilhelm recognized the accent, the tone. "James Wil...."

"*Ja, Ja, Ja!*" The German scowled. "*Vilhelm. Eine deutsches Name, ja? Sie sind* Cherman, *ja?*" Wilhelm recognized the polite *Sie*.

"American, yes. *Mein Grossvater ist von Deutschland gekommen.*" Pride shone from Wilhelm's face.

"*Ahh, gut. Sie sprechen deutsch, ja?*"

"*Nein.* I mean, no. Well, just a little. *Nur ein wenig.*" Wilhelm wasn't sure it was a good idea to let the Krauts know he understood their language, however small his understanding was.

"*Nächst!*" The German looked past Wilhelm at Lumley, the last American in the barn.

Lumley, having registered without difficulty, joined Wilhelm and Goldman at the end of the long line outside. From the tall red smokestack on a low, flat building at the head of the line, the wind smeared black smoke in their faces. "Ah thought the Krauts was s'posed to be smarter'n that." Lumley slammed his feet together in the snow. "Looks like they'd a knowed better'n to ask about our units and all. Wudn't no sense to it."

Goldman clapped Wilhelm on the back. "Vell, vell, Vilhelm, you fuckin' Kraut, you. You shoulda told him you could talk Cherman like a native. Mighta got you a nice goldbrickin' job in the camp here."

"Yeah, well." Wilhelm smiled. "I notice you didn't say nothin' about it, and you know a helluva lot more Kraut lingo than I do."

"That sumbitch tagged me for a Jew right away, so I figgered to play dumb." Goldman watched his feet bump together. "*Mein Grossvater* left this fuckin' hole a long time ago. Just like yours did. But I bet yours didn't hafta leave to save his ass like mine did." He sighed. "I don't want nuttin to do wit' dese bastids, 'cept maybe on the end of bayonet."

"Wonder what the Sarge'd say about tellin' the Krauts you know German." Wilhelm squinted and pursed his lips. "I wish he was here. If we coulda only a found him out there, maybe we coulda saved him, or somethin'."

"How 'bout these here new dogtags we got?" Lumley dangled his in the wind. "What did that Kraut call 'em, kreeg-somethin'?"

"*Kriegsgefangener* tags. *POW* tags." Goldman turned back to Wilhelm. "Yeah, sure, buddy, we all wish the Sarge was here. But you said you looked and you didn't find 'im. Sooo?" The small soldier's eyes narrowed. "Yooz guys didn't know where I was neither, did ya? Didn't go lookin' for me, though, did ya? Huh? Huh?"

"Awright, Goldman, don't get your balls in an uproar," Wilhelm said, smiling broadly. "You were outta the car first, so we thought you'd made it okay." He looked at Lumley for confirmation. "It's just I keep thinkin' how the Sarge always knew what to do and…."

"Yeah, well, he ain't wit' us no more, so just *forget* about 'im. Okay?" The cut on Goldman's cheek went bright red.

Wilhelm stared down the line at the red brick building. "That smoke feels kinda warm don't it." He rubbed his cheeks.

"Everwhat they's doin', must be some kinda fahr in there. Shore like to stick my feet in it."

Goldman chuckled. "I heard some guy up ahead say it's a dee-louser. Ever had yer big ass dee-loused, Lumley?"

"No, Ah ain't. Don't even know what a…louse is."

Eyes flashing around, Goldman leaned in close. "They're little bugs, Mr. Lum, and they crawl around your balls and you're a-hole and chew on 'em. And them bites can make you sick." He tipped back and laughed. "Even first graders back in Jersey know 'bout 'em. Scratch your crotch in school and the teachers'd send you home. I used to scratch up a storm, let 'em ketch me, then take off down to Moe's and shoot pool. More damn fun."

"Never heard of louses, Goldman. A course, we ain't 'vanced like y'all up North." He gave Goldman a friendly push. Goldman quickly shoved him back.

By the time Wilhelm stumbled into the building, his toes were numb and his teeth chattered. A blast of deliciously hot air poured over him from the darkness. "Christ! What're they doin' in here?" he shouted. A bolt of fear ran down his spine—they're *burning* something! What? Relief came when he saw women behind a counter and other men disrobing rapidly. Smiling, he unbuttoned his overcoat and began to work his way through his clothes.

Staring at the women as he took off his pants, Lumley whispered, "How's come we gotta git nekkid in fronta all them girls?"

"Don't worry, big man. They ain't gonna faint when they see that monster cock a yours." Goldman stared at Lumley's emerging privates. "Ain't big as it used to be, though, is it?"

Wilhelm stowed his dad's knife inside the lining of his overcoat, tied his shoelaces together, and hung everything on a wire hanger he found on the wall. He approached an especially buxom girl at the counter. From the expressionless look on her face, he realized his embarrassment was silly, that his privates were nothing special, to her or to anybody else. She's seen so many peckers by now, he thought, she's not even looking at mine. A little grin and she accepted the hanger holding his clothes, his life, his total possessions and disappeared into the darkness behind her.

Nude now, but warm, very warm, the three buddies followed a line of men through a second door into the snow and wind outside.

"Ah cain't believe they took our clothes and put us back *outside* agin! Ain't never seen *nothin'* like this!" Lumley folded his arms against his chest and worked his knees up and down, the gash in his calf blue with cold.

"The dirty bastards!" Wilhelm cried, swinging his arms and stomping his feet. He hugged himself and joined his buddies in a tight little circle. It was getting dark and a night wind had risen.

"Shit, Lumley, ain't you figgered it out yet? These bastids want us to ketch somethin' and die, so they won't hafta feed us anymore." Goldman's teeth chattered as he turned on Wilhelm. "What ever happened to that fuckin' Geneva Convention you keep talkin' about? I git back, I'm goin' right to the top, to the fuckin' *President* 'bout this!"

A shout went up as a big door up front slid open, and the guards began to hustle the prisoners inside. The floor lay wet and slick, the room thick with the stench of dirty feet, filthy armpits, and assholes; light bled into the darkness through slits near the ceiling. A ripple of fear ran down Wilhelm's spine as the door slammed shut behind him.

"What the hell we doin' in here?" Wilhelm said, his voice thin, weak.

"Yeah, that's what I'd like to know. What the hell's goin' on, anyway?" Goldman yelled, his voice harsh, wild.

"Yeah, that's whut Ah'm wonderin', too," Lumley added. "That's whut Ah'm wonderin'." He reached up and tapped a pipe near the ceiling. "They's a showerhead up there. Maybe we gonna get a wash-up."

Suddenly the pipes rattled and a flood of Baltic-cold water rained down on the crowd. Amid much dancing about, shouts for washcloths and soap filled the room. The men rubbed and scrubbed at themselves with their bare hands, stomping and yelling. "Hey! There's some soap over here! On the wall over here!" a voice yelled. The men, their eyes becoming accustomed to the darkness, grabbed little gray bars off a narrow shelf and rubbed it on themselves.

"Soap, shit," Goldman muttered. "More like a mix a sand and gravel."

But the water stopped almost as quickly as it had started, men with soapy hair, armpits, and faces cursing and frantically wiping themselves. A door on the far side of the room slid open, and the prisoners, still squee-geeing themselves, stepped through it expecting...what?

As Wilhelm came into the big lighted space, large, strong hands yanked him sideways. A white-clad female simultaneously inserted a long, glistening needle into his right pectoral muscle, injecting something unknown into his shivering chest. Shoved on into the room, he was blown almost off his feet by a blast of frigid air from a monstrous fan in the far wall. Goosebumps blossomed, and every muscle in his body contracted. He went into a chaotic dance—a mixture of twisting and twitching over which he had no control. Coming slowly to his senses, he stretched and rolled his right arm, the time-honored movements of a freshly inoculated soldier. Lumley and Goldman, arms folded across their chests, stood frozen in the corner next to the fan, grinning at him. "Did you guys get stuck like I did?" They nodded. "Wonder what that stuff was, anyway."

"Don't worry, buddy, you ain't gonna die 'cause of it," Lumley responded. "Prob'bly just a tetanus shot."

The three buddies cowered together out of the fan's draft, shivering and rubbing themselves, watching the faces of the other men as they were injected and slowly moved into the room, struck by the fan's blast. A weird and silly spectacle. Fully aware, himself, of the surprise, the sudden fear those men felt, Wilhelm chuckled. Goldman laughed. Lumley smiled, too.

Now a door next to the fan opened, and the guards shooed the mass of naked men back outside, pointing them toward the delouser building. Inside the warm building, they ran to the pile of hot clothing on the counter awaiting them. The women brought more clothes from the ovens in back, even as the men clawed through the pile for their own.

Lumley pulled on his shorts and yelled, "Boy, oh boy, mah sciv-vies're really hot. Wish they'd jus' stay that way!"

Almost dressed, Wilhelm rescued his dad's knife from the overcoat lining and replaced it in his left legging. "Yeah. Ain't it wonderful? This warm stuff is great!"

"Oh, my, yes!" Goldman's voice dripped sarcasm. "The bastids screwed up and let us have a little heat for a change."

Back outside, they lined up five to a rank, as always, and marched into the camp proper. The three buddies and several other men were assigned to one of the long brick buildings on a street dark with boot tracks in the dirty snow. The little band of newcomers pushed aside a heavy cloth just inside the door and found themselves in a large room filled with men and multi-decker beds. It smelled of coal smoke, dirty socks, and the bad breath of the great unwashed. Across the front, tall windows looked out on the street, cold air falling off the glass and slid-ing along the concrete floor. Long wooden tables sat along the win-dows; a couple of sheet-metal-topped stoves, a red brick chimney rising between them, lay before the forest of beds.

Each newcomer was issued a pair of blankets, thin, blue and ragged; they got a large spoon—a "Hoosier tablespoon" Wilhelm decided—and an all-purpose metal pot called a "dixie" like the one they'd been loaned for soup in the mountains. Besides these treasures, each man received from the sergeant of the barracks three 1" x 5" x 30" pieces of wood.

"What the hell are these for, Sarge?" Goldman asked, tossing the boards back and forth, hand to hand. "We gonna paddle each other when we're bad, or somethin'?"

"Bed slats, Corporal. Bed slats. You stick 'em across the space inside the bed frame and lay on 'em." The round-faced Master Sergeant, Matt Sharkey, his voice deep and authoritative, looked down his nose at the little man. "Take good care of 'em, pal, 'cause you ain't gonna git any-more." A big, gaunt, rawboned soldier, his face lined and shriveled due to lack of nourishment, Sharkey carried what might be called an "aca-demic" stoop. An ex-teacher, Wilhelm guessed.

"I'm supposed to *sleep* on these *three* little, bitty, fuckin' pieces a wood? 'At's bullshit, Sarge! I can't...." Goldman saw the sergeant's face go pink.

"Find yourself a buddy, soldier, and you'll have *six* little, bitty, fuckin' slats to park yer little, bitty fuckin' ass on." The sergeant, head of Barracks #7A, glared and moved to leave.

"Yeah, okay, Sarge. Okay. But how about we get some chow? We ain't had nuttin since the fuckin' cows come home."

"Awright, Corporal, git this straight! And the rest a you, too," the sergeant scanned the new arrivals. "We eat when the Krauts say we eat. Usually after *Appell*. That's when they count us. Rutabaga soup tonight, maybe, a potato, if we're lucky." He looked at each man, made a quick about-face, and was gone.

# CHAPTER 11

▼

# A COLD DAY IN HELL

The available beds stood in the back row, behind which tall windows shed light and let cold air into the room. Lumley sighed, walked over to one of the windows, and looked out. Without a sleeping buddy, he would have to sleep without the heat of a second body next to him. The big redhead walked off in search of a buddy among the new arrivals.

"Heat rises, so I think we oughtta set up in the top bunk." Assuming he and Goldman would share a bed, Wilhelm stood looking around inside an empty three-decker bedframe.

"Hell, ain't 'nough heat back here to worry about." Goldman stepped inside the frame next to Wilhelm and placed one slat in the center of the sleeping space and two together at one end.

Wilhelm centered one slat next to Goldman's and placed his other two at the far end. He slammed his hands together as if completing a terrible chore. "I'm slippin' through this damn thing in the middle a the night," he mumbled, "I'm gonna wake you up and take you down with me."

Grinning, they covered the slats with three of their four blankets and folded one at the foot. "We can cover up with that one and put both overcoats on top," Wilhelm said. "With our field jackets for pillows, it could be worse." He remembered sitting in the snow, sitting in the road, and that whole week sitting on that hard-bottomed boxcar.

Someone shouted, "Wilhelm? Is there a James Wilhelm back here?" A tall, blond soldier with the broad shoulders and narrow hips of an athlete stood in the aisle looking around.

"Yeah, I'm Jimmy Wilhelm. Over here." The tall stranger looked directly at him atop the bunk. Wilhelm wished he hadn't answered so quickly—a reflex the army had taught him.

"Jimbo! You from Indianapolis like the Sarge says?" The big blond put out his hand and smiled.

"Yeah." Wilhelm looked into the soldier's clear blue eyes and took his hand.

"Name's Bernie Danzig, Jimbo," the bright, smooth voice said. "But ever'body calls me Danny. I'm from good ole Naptown, too." Danzig's pearly-whites, dimpled cheeks, and cleft chin reminded Wilhelm of the rootin'-tootin' cowboys in his favorite Saturday afternoon movies. "Saw your name on the newcomers' list and thought I'd look you up."

"Good to meet you, uh, Danny." Wilhelm smiled. "A newcomer's list? Damn Krauts're organized, ain't they?" He introduced Goldman, who shook Danzig's hand, dropped off the bed and joined Lumley down the way.

"I'm from the south Naptown, down around Fountain Square. Y'know where that is?"

"Fountain Square? Sure! I used to go up there ever' Saturday to the movies. When I was a kid, that is." Wilhelm grinned. "Hey, Danny," he leaned in close, "you got any pull around here? We only got three bed slats apiece and…."

"Yeah, Jimbo, that's all anybody gits when they come in. There's a lotta tradin' goes on, though, and you can...."

"Trade? Trade what? I ain't got nothin' to trade. The shirt on my back, maybe." Wilhelm looked his new friend in the eye. "How long you been in here, Danny?"

Danzig beckoned and moved away toward the stoves. "C'mon, let's go up to my bunk. It's a lot warmer up there, and we can git us a cuppa coffee." His long white teeth flashed.

"Coffee? Boy, I ain't had coffee for a helluva long time." Wilhelm jumped down off his bed, and, licking his lips, tried to remember what coffee tasted like. It needs cream and sugar, but I better not mention that. Another thought: this guy's making coffee for me, a complete stranger from back home—would I do that?

The air felt warm up near the stoves. Wilhelm sat on Danzig's bed a few feet from the redbrick flue and waited while Danzig heated water, then poured it onto what Danzig said was powdered coffee in a couple of metal cups.

Wilhelm sipped and smiled, the heat bringing tears to his eyes. "This's *good*, Danny! *Real* good!" He swallowed a sob and squinted at his new friend. Thinking to hide that weak feeling, he said, "One thing I'd like to know, Danny, is where we are. The camp, I mean. Where 'bouts in Germany is it?" He wondered also where the coffee and the cups had come from, but didn't want to ask.

"We're over east, Jimbo. By the Polish border."

"The Polish border! Jeez! No wonder it took so damn long to get here." His tongue felt fried, but he tried to ignore it. "A long way from the front, then, ain't we? Not much chance our boys'll be comin' through here any time soon."

"No, but the Rooskies ain't far off. Radio says they 'bout got Poland wrapped up. You guys're lucky. You got here just in time to get liberated. Ain't heard their guns yet, but we're bettin' it won't be long 'fore we do."

"Radio? You got a radio in here?" Wilhelm's eyes flashed around. "The Krauts let you have a...."

Danzig laughed. "Hey, Jimbo! They don't *let* us have nothin'! There's a radio in *ever'* POW camp I been in, and I been in quite a few. A guy comes in and reads the BBC news to us ever' mornin'. Somebody keep's watch, o' course. The Krauts know we got a radio, and they bust in ever' once in a while lookin' for it."

Wilhelm, not wanting to ask too many questions all at once, took a long drink and changed the subject. "Where'd you get the coffee, Danny? The Krauts?" There it was, another question, anyway.

"Got a box from home last month marked CHRISTMAS." He chuckled. "M'folks're smart. They know not to write HANUKKAH on it."

Wilhelm's jaw dropped and clicked shut immediately. My God, Danzig is Jewish! Blue-eyed, blond and Jewish! Hard to believe. Generous, too, for a...oh, wait, what am I thinking? Got the idea that Jews are stingy and wouldn't give anybody anything from Grandpaw. He hates Jews, Polocks, Honkeys, Frogs, and just about everybody else over here. No wonder Goldman hates the Krauts.

"You know how these stalags work, Jimbo? What they're really like?"

"No, I sure don't. Nobody ever told us anything about bein' captured, so...."

"Well, come on over here and I'll show you around." They went to one of the front windows. "See that wire there, 'bout knee high? That's the *warning* wire. You don't cross it, or even touch it. The Krauts say they'll shoot you. But some guys can step right over it and nothin' happens. That's for tradin' purposes only, and you gotta check with the tower guard first. See, he gets a cut of ever'thing that goes past his line a sight." Danzig led Wilhelm around the beds to a back window. "That building's the latrine," he said, pointing. "Got about a hundred sittin' holes and stinks like hell. Not too bad in this weather, but it's really bad in summer. Maybe the Rooskies'll get us outta here before that." Grinning, he studied Wilhelm's reaction. "You have to go at night, make sure the guards see you're headin' for the shithouse. They don't like anybody walkin' 'round out there at night."

Back at Danzig's bunk, they sat down and finished their coffee. "Let's see, the washroom's over there between us and section 7B—cold water and soap made outta concrete, mostly. Don't drink the water unless you want the GIs—the trots, you know, the runnin' shits. Git clean snow out back where it don't git stomped on much and melt it on the stove for drinkin'." He thought a minute. "It's a great life, if...oh, I forgot about *Appell*. That's when the Krauts count us, mornin' and night. Tea before we fall out in the mornin' and soup in the evenin' after *Appell*." Danzig grinned. "That's about it, Jimbo. It ain't too bad, if you can stand it."

"Jeez, so we only get chow twice a day, huh? I was hopin' we'd at least...."

"That's it, buddy. Sometimes Red Cross parcels come in, but we ain't seen any for quite a while. Bastards're prob'ly eatin' 'em themselves. Krauts're gettin' pretty hard up, with all the bombin' goin' on. No mail or stuff from home anymore, either; trains're are out, I 'spect."

Suddenly, a group of POWs burst through the heavy cloth in the entranceway; a man, surrounded by four others, slumped inside, his head hanging, one eye black, the cheek purple-red. As the group passed slowly across the front of the room, hisses and boos came from POWs all around. A sign on the injured man's back proclaimed: "I AM A THIEF."

"My God!" Wilhelm whispered. "What'd he do?"

"That's what happens if you get caught stealin' around here," Danzig explained. "There's a group a guys that takes care a crooks like him. They beat the shit out of 'em and then parade 'em through all the barracks." He grinned. "Not much stealin' goes on in these camps, I can tell you that."

"My God," Wilhelm said again.

"I dunno what else they do to 'em, but I don't wanta find out, neither."

Wilhelm's stomach gurgled loud enough for both men to hear. Danzig smiled. "We'll be eatin' purty soon, Jimbo. Tell your guts to shut up and git used to waitin'."

Wilhelm smiled. "Yeah, well, they're already pretty well trained. We didn't git much comin' over here."

They sat a moment and watched the vigilante group pass through the door into 7B, the other side of the barracks. "By the way, Jimbo, you need any more slats? I got some extras I been savin', but I'm thinkin' the Rooskies'll be here pretty soon, and I prob'ly won't be needin' 'em." Danzig pulled a box from under his bunk and opened it. "How many'd they give you guys?"

"Three each. Me and Goldman been wonderin' how we're gonna sleep on six little boards, but, after that damn boxcar, I guess we can...."

Danzig dropped six slats into Wilhelm's lap. "There you go buddy. That oughtta help."

"Hey, Danny! Thanks a lot!" Wilhelm laughed and slapped the big kid on the shoulder. This Jew boy is something else, he thought. Nothin' like Goldman. In fact, I doubt the two of them would get along.

*    *    *    *

Three days later, the newcomers had pretty well adjusted to "*Krieg*-ee" life. Wilhelm had heard about a library, such as it was, near the far end of the camp. So he walked down that way, wondering what they would do if he didn't return a book. He was surprised to find so many books in English, from, he surmised, POWs who got them from home in the days when boxes had come through. The books were mostly old and moldy, but, to his joy, he found an elementary organic chemistry book a little older and moldier than the one he'd left in Kratus. He lay on his bunk, paging through it when Danzig came up and looked over his shoulder.

"Whatcha readin', there, buddy? God, didn't they have nothin' better'n an old chemistry book down there?"

Wilhelm grinned. "This is my kinda stuff, Danny. I've 'bout decided to be a chemist when I get back."

Danzig squinted up and down the aisle. "Hey, Jimbo," he whispered, "didn't you say you was a radioman or somethin' when you got caught?"

"Yeah. With the 106th Signal." Wilhelm tried to sit up, but Danzig held him down. "We were up on the line and…."

"Yeah, yeah, okay. I thought so." The big blond walked to the end of the aisle, looked around, and came back. "Look, Jimbo, ole buddy, I need your help. See, word just came down the Krauts're gonna hit our barracks this afternoon." His bright smile met Wilhelm's wide stare. "They're lookin' for the radio. It's no big deal, but, like I said, they do it ever' once in a while. Just to keep us on our toes."

Wilhelm pushed Danzig's hand away and swung his legs over the side of the bed. "Sooo?" he said, softly. "What's that got to do with…."

"Well, it so happens, Jimbo, that, believe it or not, *I* got the radio! It's up under my bunk." His pearly-whites flared in the weak gray light.

"Jesus! Really? *You* got the radio?" Wilhelm started to slide off his bunk, but Danzig grabbed him and held him up.

"Now listen, Jimbo, ole buddy, I gotta hide it somewhere before the Krauts get here." He pursed his lips and looked around. "See, they caught me with it once before, and I spent some time in solitary. So they're gonna be checkin' me out real good. Prob'ly why they're coming to 7A, thinkin' I'm the man. They're li'ble to hang me up by the you-know-whats if they ketch me with it again."

Danzig's heart-warming smile lit up his face, as his fingers began to massage Wilhelm's shoulders. "I hate to ask, but hows 'bout you taking it off my hands for a little while? Just till they get done searchin' my stuff."

The frown on Wilhelm's face stopped him. Thinking the free coffee and bed slats had come home to roost, Wilhelm stared. "And what if they come back here and search *my* stuff? They can find it back here just as quick as they can up front."

"Sure, but see, they won't do that." Danzig's tone was sharp now. "They won't come back here, 'cause they know you new guys wouldn't have it. They'll just hit the longtimers like me and the other guys up front." The big blond's eyes narrowed. "Besides, we know for a fact, they ain't got enough men to search ever'body. You guys back here ain't gonna have no problem."

"Jeez, Danny, I don't know. What if they *do* come back and they find it in my sack? You gonna tell 'em *you* gave it to me? Or am I just S-O-L?"

Chuckling, Danzig was massaging Wilhelm's biceps now. "Hey, c'mon, Jimbo, there ain't *nothin'* to worry about. I know these fuckin' Krauts like the back a my hand, and I'm tellin' you they ain't gonna bug nobody back here." He leaned back and squinted down his nose. "'Sides, would I get my li'l ole Naptown buddy in trouble over a lousy li'l ole radio?"

Like a bulletin in the Movietone News at the Fountain Square movie, his mother's words bounced across Wilhelm's mind: *"Never, ever do a favor for a stranger, Jimmy, until you get to know him."* His head rocked side to side, up and down, then side to side again.

"Oh, all right, Danny," he mumbled, knowing full well it was not smart. "Bring the damn thing back here and I'll hide it for you, but if...." No guts, he told himself. I got no guts at all.

"Good boy, Jimbo!" Danzig shouted, trotting back toward his bunk. "Good boy! Good boy!"

*    *    *    *

Midafternoon brought heavy clouds, low and dark, a blizzard on the way. Wilhelm lay on his bunk trying to read, while the radio, under the blanket next to him, kept distracting him. What'll they do if they come back here and find it? I ought to tell 'em Danzig gave it to me, but, no, I'll just have to spend time in solitary like he did. Yeah, but what if they're really mad and stand me up against the wall and...Jesus!

The sounds of hobnail boots, many pairs of hobnail boots, maybe a whole platoon of hobnail boots scraped into the barracks up front. The tables along the front wall crashed down; the metal plates atop the stoves banged into the floor and *"Raus! Raus! Raus!"* echoed off the walls. Wilhelm could see hands held up before the front windows as the guards moved along, searching the POWs. Some of the beds up front tilted and fell.

Bent low, Danzig came running down the side wall. "Jimbo! Jimbo! there's a whole buncha Krauts up there. Lot more'n I...they're gonna search the whole damn...you better take the radio outta here and maybe drop it outta the window, or somethin'." He spun around and duck-walked back toward his bunk. Wilhelm would've laughed aloud at the sight if he weren't so nervous.

"I shoulda shoved this damn thing down his fuckin' throat," Wilhelm murmured, tucking the precious electronic wonder inside his field jacket. Goldman, his bunkmate, grinned, turned away, and lay down.

Low to the floor like Danzig, Wilhelm headed for the back windows. "*Think* before you *act*, Jimmy." His dad's words flashed across his mind. "*Always* think before you act!" He looked along the wall under the back windows to a stack of toilet paper, sitting where it always did, roll upon roll upon roll. I'll put the radio in under there, and…no they'll kick that pile to pieces sure as hell. Toilet paper, ah, I'll take some and go outside and they'll think…. He grabbed a roll and, without a sound, opened one of the windows about a foot. Belly-down, he squirmed across the sill, the radio in its rag-sack, and fell headfirst into a four-foot-deep snowdrift. Blind and standing on his head against the wall, he listened for footsteps, then managed to roll over and sit up. He half-expected the muzzle of a burpgun in his face, but there was nobody there. Only the wind's mournful howl, the bump and crash of chaos inside the barracks came to him. He got up and pulled the window shut, shoved the radio inside his field jacket, and, as best he could, smoothed the snow beneath the window. Holding the roll of "necessary" paper where a tower guard could see it, he hurried, as expected of a man on his way to answer a "call of nature," into the latrine.

In the stinking darkness, he felt around for a couple of holes, sat down between them, took the radio out, and held it up. "What the hell do I do now?" tumbled from his throat. An idea bloomed. He opened his field jacket, pulled off his belt, and lashed it tightly around the radio. Pants, longjohns, and scivvies down below his knees, he scooted over and allowed the radio to drop between his legs into the hole. A swirling wind from below brought goosebumps to his whole body.

For the first time in weeks he saw his emaciated thighs and slab-sided calves. "My God, look at me," he whispered. "Nothin' but skin and bone!" He reared back and shouted, "God *damn* you fuckin' Krauts to hell! Alla you! Damn alla you to hell!" The words bounced off the invisible walls and came back at him. The first time I ever cursed the Germans, he thought. I ought to be ashamed of myself, but I'm not.

He sighed and peered down into the hole between his legs. Eyes now adjusted to the darkness, he could see a field of dark frozen lumps a couple of yards below. He slipped the metal end of the belt under his right buttock and looked down at the radio. It was safe for now. Underwear and pants pulled up as far as possible and elbows on knees, he covered his freezing ears with his hands. Not bad, he thought, prepared for a long wait, not bad for a punk corporal condemned to the shit house for the rest of the day. Solved the "Case of The Wandering Radio" and saved Danzig's ass at the same time.

A deep breath brought ice to his nostrils. Five above zero. An icy breeze circulated across his *glutei maximi* and dangling pudenda, his testes retracting into their ancestral home. He wondered if there might be long-term effects if he sat there too long and wished for some of Danzig's hot coffee. He wished, too, for a shaft of the broiling Fort Benning sun or, even better, a warm, tempting hug from Cindy. "Hell, if she was on my lap right now, I wouldn't be able to do a damn thing," he mumbled. "There'd just be *two* of us freezin' to death."

Girls. Sperm. The biology lab—the sweet, round face of his lab partner, Rosie, came to mind. "My gosh, Jimmy," she whispered, looking up from the microscope, "where'd you get all them cute squirmy little critters?" Before he could answer, she had clapped a hand over her mouth and run out of the lab. "I bet she knows by now where they come from," he said, laughing aloud.

Leaning to one side, he could see most of one barracks window through the latrine door. The commotion, shouts, and thumps could still be heard, but the noise seemed to be decreasing. "What if they do a count and find out somebody's missing? They'll come looking and...." As he spoke, three guards came along the barracks wall, kicking through snowdrifts. Two of them turned and peered into the latrine; they saw Wilhelm and came in. They seemed about to speak to him when he screwed up his face and emitted a massive fart. The Germans chuckled, shook their heads, and left him to his work.

The sun gone and the wind beginning to howl, Wilhelm sat on his cone-shaped bottom, going numb all over. He had shifted the belt to his other cheek, swung his arms and legs, rubbed his shriveled penis and the little empty sack below it. "What am I now? Man or woman?" he asked the darkness. "What is it with these people, anyway? Why are they always killin' each other over here? And why did we have to butt in?" They? How about me? "Why did I come over here? Why didn't I just refuse to join up? But no, I *had* to come help stop the Krauts! And another thing: people over here—Jews and Protestants and Catholics— all hate each other! What the hell's the difference? They all believe in the same God! Why can't they leave each other alone?" He slumped into the shithole. It was all too much for a nineteen-year-old boy to fig- ure out.

The darkness in the big room hung thick and heavy around him. Suddenly, he remembered: they're at *Appell* now, and I'm not there! The Krauts'll keep them out there all night. And they'll be mad as hell! They'll kill me in cold blood when they find out I...*cold blood!* Ha! What other kind is there?

He began to breathe deeply, began to feel a little warm inside, almost comfortable—Christmas—ham. Suddenly, strange hands pulled on his arms, trying to yank him to his feet. "No! No! No! Leggo! Leggo!" He managed to pull one arm loose and sit back hard on his belt.

"Shhhhh," a dark shape whispered. "Will! It's me, Lum! We're gonna get you outta here! Keep still, buddy. Keep still."

"Lum! God! It's Lum! Boy, am I glad to see you! I'm so damn cold I don't know what…."

"It's okay. It's okay." Lumley pulled harder.

"No wait! The radio! It's under me! Here! Wait!" Wilhelm, eyes blinking to stay open, grabbed the belt down under and pulled. The radio slid from between his legs, dangling before Lumley.

"Peee-yew! What a stink!" Lumley chuckled. The redhead took the smelly prize and handed it to somebody behind him. "Okay, now, Will, let's go!" Several sets of hands lifted Wilhelm off the seat, while others pulled up his underwear and pants. A blanket fell over his shoulders, as he rose up on a four-legged chariot and floated out the door. That ever-loving German wind struck the little convoy. "Oooh, it smells good! So clean and…." A shrill child-on-a-rollercoaster laugh poured out of him, his nasal membranes crystallizing immediately.

His tenders put Wilhelm in a reconstituted middle bunk up near the stoves, wrapped blankets around him, and poured hot, sweet tea into him. "He'll be all right," the big shape that was Lumley said. "He'll be fine once he gits warmed up."

Good old Lum, Wilhelm thought. "I'm all right," he mumbled. "I'm okay." Lum's a medic. He knows all that stuff. Smiling up at the hovering faces, he couldn't think why they were smiling at him. He rolled over, pulled his icy heels against his buttocks, and, chin tight against his chest, closed his eyes.

# CHAPTER 12

▼

# ON THE ROAD AGAIN

Wilhelm, known by now as the Shithouse Kid, got up the next day and grabbed a broom to help in the barracks cleanup. Danzig stopped him before he got started. "I'm sorry, Will," he said, "but I guess the Krauts dug up a lot more men than...." Wilhelm turned and began to sweep away from the big man. "I tried to warn you in time, but...."

"Yeah, sure, you warned me, awright. Two seconds before they started to trash the place." Wilhelm dropped the broom and joined a group of men on the other side who were lifting and reassembling beds. When he looked around, Danzig was on his way outside. That bugger's no friend of mine, Indianapolis or no Indianapolis, Wilhelm told himself. I'm never going to speak to him again.

After tea and *Appell* a few days later, Sergeant Sharkey, his florid face alight with pleasure, appeared among the bunks near the rear windows. "Lumley, Wilhelm, Goldman," he shouted, his thumb pointing back over his shoulder. "You guys're on potato-pickin' detail. Get your stuff on toot sweet and report to the Kraut sergeant outside."

Lumley chuckled. "Hey, Sarge, you don't *pick* potatoes, you *dig* 'em."

"No shit! Is that a fact?" The sergeant glared. "That Kraut'll tell you how ta git 'em. Do what he says, and you'll be okay." Turning to leave, he added, "Oh, yeah. Remember, this is not a *work* detail. As you know, noncoms don't work. You wanta complain, see President Roosevelt."

"Shit, Sarge, why you pickin' us?" Goldman, tic twisting his cheek, asked in his inimitable whine. "How 'bout them new guys what just come in? Whyn't you send *them* out to…."

Sharkey's squint changed to a sneer. "Get off your ass and move out, Corporal! That's an order!" He did a quick about-face and stalked off between the beds.

Overcoats, field jackets, wool hats and gloves in place, the newly appointed potato detail found a *Feldwebel* with a short column of prisoners waiting outside. "Oh, shit!" Goldman held a hand across his mouth. "Look who's our leader! It's that fuckin' Kraut what give me a hard time when we checked in. Remember? Name's Kruger, I think."

"Ahh, he won't bother you now we're in camp." Wilhelm shook his head. "Looks nicer'n Sharkey, anyway."

"Sure, Wilhelm, you ain't gotta worry about it." Goldman, head down, moved back toward rear of the column.

Picks and shovels loaded, the POWs pushed a two-wheeled wooden cart through the camp and out the front gate. The little heat stored in their clothing quickly blew away in a boreal wind that threw crystals of snow sharp as sand into their eyes. A quarter mile out, they turned into a windswept snowfield, rows of small mounds stretching off into the haze.

They worked in pairs, shovels scraping, picks bouncing off on the iron-hard earth. Great white clouds rose from the men's mouths. If a prisoner stopped for a moment, a guard moved in shouting, "*Los! Los!*" *Feldwebel* Kruger, short but broad in the shoulder, swaggered about, hovering, smiling, enjoying himself. He apparently liked watching Goldman, whose pick mostly bounced, barely cracking the frozen soil.

"Hey, Lum," Wilhelm hissed, "you see what I see? We gotta…."

"Yeah, let's git the Kraut's 'ttention and keep 'im from beatin' on the little guy."

"Okay. Let's stop and get 'im to come after us."

The next time Kruger stopped behind Goldman, both men, whispering and smiling, dropped their tools and hunkered down in the snow. They went back to work as soon as Kruger or one of the guards shouted. Finally, Kruger assigned a guard to monitor Goldman's miniscule progress and stood, cigarette in hand, behind Goldman's friends. Kruger's gonna catch on, Wilhelm thought, and have us all shot.

At last, Goldman threw down his pick and looked across the mound at the *Feldwebel*. "Go to hell, Kruger! I ain't diggin' no more. The Geneva Convention says I don't hafta…."

Kruger laughed, a gold incisor flashing in the gray light. He waved to the guards, and Goldman's buddies watched him be dragged away, his heels leaving deep streaks in the snow.

"Don't s'pose they'll shoot 'im, do you?"

"Nah," Wilhelm mumbled. "I don't think Kruger'd wanta lose his favorite Jew boy so quick. He's havin' too much fun needlin' him." He superimposed Kruger's face on the hard brown earth and swung his pick. When the first potato appeared, he forgot Goldman and began to plan how to steal it and the others he might find, too.

In spite of the almost impenetrable soil, hard brown vegetables did appear, were collected and thrown into the cart. As the heavy vehicle was pushed and pulled by the exhausted prisoners back to the camp, Wilhelm kept hearing the words "*Yid*" and "*Jud*" in the guard's rapid

German. Had Kruger dreamed up the potato detail just to *get* Gold-man? No, Kruger wouldn't go to that much trouble to…or would he?

A week passed before Goldman, face pale, with deep, dark lines wor-rying his forehead, stumbled into barrack 7A and went to Wilhelm's bed.

"Hey, buddy! Where you been all this time?" Wilhelm looked into the dark eyes staring over the edge of the bed. "You okay?"

With some difficulty, Goldman climbed up and sat next to Wilhelm. "Where the hell you think? Been in fuckin' solitary. Ceilin' so fuckin' low, I couldn't even stan' up. Slep' on a board so fuckin' narrow my ass hung off." Still in his overcoat, he lay back and pulled a blanket over himself. "Bread and water, 'at's all. Bread and water ever' day." Cracked lips pursed, Goldman's tic worked his cheek. "Nuttin but the best for the little 'Yid', y'know. Nuttin but the fuckin' best."

\*        \*        \*        \*

A week later, things had changed. "Them wheel-to-wheel Rooskie guns," as the long-timers called them, were shaking the windows, the walls, the men's insides. Questions: When will they get here? Do they know this is a POW camp? Will the Krauts run? Will they take us along, or leave us behind if they do? Should we be digging in?

Wilhelm stood at one of the big front windows, his "things," such as they were, in his blanket roll at his feet. He felt a little giddy watching the snow flash past, like the time on the way to Fort Benning he'd stood on a train and watched another one roar past. Those questions flying about the room made him giddy, too. Everybody, it seemed, had some kind of answer—everybody but him. His empty belly had taken a back seat to the big guns firing death in his direction. We're here, Wilhelm was thinking, three weeks and the war's already caught up with us. Fucking Rooskies'll put us in another camp back in Rooskieland somewhere and, who knows, we may never be heard of again. Old lady Holcomb, the history teacher back at school, used to say, "You're always making history, folks. Glory in it!" Well, c'mon over, Mrs. Holcomb, I wish you were here.

It's not been too bad, though, this camp, probably better'n where we'll go, *if* we go. The first night here was really something: that awful rutabaga soup, dirt in the bottom and black stuff floating on top, and then my race to the latrine around midnight, pants at my knees, the guard's searchlight on my bare bottom, his laugh echoing across the compound. Got to send a letter anyway:

> Dear Mom and Dad, I hope by now you heard that I got captured. I'm okay, not hurt or anything. I'm fine and hope you are, too. We get chow every day and I have a good bed and a roof over my head. Not as good as home, but I'm OK. I sure hope you are feeling okay, not sick or anything. See you when the war's over. Pet Fritzie for me. Love, Jimmy

Didn't say a damn thing. Danzig said the Krauts would tear it up if I told them how it really is in here. Wonder what the old Marine Sergeant will think when he finds out I surrendered. But they didn't have Tiger tanks and 88s and burpguns when he was in Haiti. Things are a helluva lot tougher now, Dad. That's what I'll tell him when…*if* I get home.

Wilhelm stepped closer to the window so he could see the *Volkssturm*, the old men of the camp guard, standing out in the *Appell* field, their rifles inverted on their backs. Damn Krauts love this military crap. Bunch of dumb sticks marching around like idiots in the middle of a blizzard, all ready to die for *der Führer, der Vaterland.* It's going dark. If we leave now, we'll be walking all night long.

Suddenly, half a dozen guards burst into the barracks. "*Raus! Raus!*", they shouted, then "*Schnell! Schnell!*" There was a hierarchy there, he decided: *Schnell* was worse than *Raus*, which was worse than *Los*. Yeah, *Schnell* was the worst word he'd ever heard in his whole life.

*       *       *       *

Lined up outside the front gate, five abreast as usual, the prisoners waited for the order to move out. The night threw hard, sharp pellets of ice in their faces, the cold making their ears burn. Feet bumping together, toes going numb, Wilhelm squinted into the wind, his stomach growling, the chaos of the day threatening to empty its small contents in the road. The chemistry book in his left hand, the gloved one, felt heavier than the blanket roll on his back. His left anklebone, no longer accustomed to the knife's scabbard, had begun to complain. He could still hear his dad's words: "It's longer than a dagger and sharper than a bayonet, Jimmy. Keep it close, boy, you might need it some time." Tears had glistened in the old man's eyes. "Don't worry, Dad," Wilhelm muttered into the wind, "I still got it, and I'm keepin' it real close."

"Got your little red book, there, buddy?" Wilhelm recalled his vow to read Lumley's Bible sometime.

"Yessir, Will. She's right here." Lumley patted his overcoat pocket. "I see you got your Good Book, too." Lumley's red beard was going white. "You're fixing to pay a mighty big fine, if'n you don't take it back on time, y'know that?"

"Yeah, well, I'm hopin' the Rooskies blow up the library and get me off the hook." Wilhelm hoisted the big textbook to eye level. "It's so damn heavy, I'll prob'ly hafta toss it before we get very far. Shoulda left it, I guess."

Lumley turned to Goldman. "Got everythin' you need, there, li'l buddy? Toothbrush, toothpaste, shavin' cream and all?"

Goldman was looking around at the guards. "These ole farts couldn't find their ass in a toilet bowl if they was sittin' on it." His cheek twitched. "It's gonna be one helluva night on the road, and this blizzard's gonna make 'em even blinder'n they are. Perfect for us to take off. How's about it?" He peered into the woods next to the road. "When we get out a-ways, we can make a loop in the woods, come back to camp, and wait for the Rooskies."

Wilhelm's head shook the whole time Goldman was speaking. "Not me," he said. "I'm staying with the crowd. I figger the bigger the crowd, the safer I am." He stared at Goldman, then Lumley. "Hell, the Krauts're li'ble to throw 'em back then we'd freeze our butts off out here waitin' for the Rooskies to find us."

"Ahhh, you're just chickenshit, Wilhelm. You got no damn guts at all."

Lumley, lips pursed, stood on tiptoes and looked down the column. He said nothing.

"Okay, do what yooz want. First chance I get, I'm goin'."

"Fine, Goldman. Go right ahead. I'm stayin'."

The *Volksturm* came down the column yelling and the column began to shuffle away from the *Stalag*. As they came over the railroad tracks, Wilhelm saw a row of boxcars on the siding, behind. Ridiculous as it seemed, he couldn't help but wish he were in one of them.

Down the icy road, broken by frozen tank and truck tracks, the men stumbled, slipped and slid, their heads down, eyes narrow against the wind. Remembering the sore groin he'd had after the long hike to the railhead at Gerostein weeks ago, Wilhelm took short steps, finding when possible the footprints made by men just ahead of him. The column, what he could see of it, had quickly deconstructed, each man, deep in his own private misery, beating a winding path among the others. The *Volksturm*, their little black Hitler mustaches going solid white, quickly lost themselves among the prisoners.

Every few minutes, the *Felwebel*s in charge shouted, "*Nach links!*" or "*Nach rechts!,*" herding the prisoners into a left- or right-hand ditch. Tanks, command cars, sometimes trucks with tall black columns behind the driver's cab rumbled past. Wilhelm was told they were "wood-burning trucks." Of course, he didn't believe a word of it.

As he slogged along in the darkness, snow packed the right side of his cap, his right sleeve, and the whole right side of his overcoat. Wind's from the right, he mused. That's probably north, meaning we're headed west—west toward the American lines and France and the Atlantic. In a burst of joy he turned to tell his buddies they were headed home. He found their heads bent, and looking down at their boots, walking like dead men. Their sadness hit him hard. He went back to watching his boots.

They walked, stumbled, and skated on for what seemed an eternity. Men stopped to relieve themselves, some even sat down in the ditch until *Los-Los*-ed back onto the road. "Hey, Lum," Wilhelm said softly, "where's Goldman? Is he…gone?"

"Ah don't know, Will. Ain't seen 'im in a while. Didn't say nothin' to me 'bout leavin'."

"Well, you know ol' heart-a-gold Goldman, he wouldn't say nothin' to nobody." Wilhelm smiled down at his feet. "Well, I hope he makes it."

"Yeah, so do Ah. We can take a look around next time we stop."

"*Next time?*" Wilhelm's head rose up. "Shit, Lum, we ain't stopped that first time yet! Or did I sleepwalk through it?"

An hour later, Goldman's hard, narrow face, pinched bone-white against the wind, appeared behind his two buddies, eyes on his feet. He ignored their questioning looks and knowing glances.

After what seemed an eternity, the blinding-white sheet covering the column, the woods, and the fields faded into a murky gray. The desire to sit down, lie back, and close his eyes tore at Wilhelm's innards. The guards be damned, he thought. I don't care what happens. I gotta get off my feet and...suddenly a round, dull-white, almost warm light, broke through the overcast above the trees. His spirits rose. He yearned to see and feel again the hot, bright orb that had made him sweat and curse back at Bennin'. Even his fingers, especially those on his bare right hand, seemed to come alive. He saw the Hoosier sun over the swimming pool in Garfield Park and the ball field where his dad had taught him to hit a high, inside fastball. Somebody—some *thing*—up there had saved him again.

They walked on all day. Early January, the day short, darkness already approaching; the wind picked up, and a thin snow began to fall. Hours of crunching through icy ruts and black ice, then diving into a ditch away from roaring vehicles, came and went. Snow allowed to melt on Wilhelm's tongue slaked his thirst but did little for the burning ache in his empty belly. The sounds of slogging feet seemed to slow, the column drifting to the side of the road. When it finally stopped, he stepped into the ditch, his knees buckled, and he fell back in the snow. Prisoners, half asleep on their feet, cursed as they slammed into those stopping in front of them.

Across the broad, white field next to the road, Wilhelm made out a dark, fuzzy rectangle only slightly darker than the sky. Was it a barn? A barn with straw to lie on, to sleep on, to die on? Oh, God, let it be a barn! The guards were waving, shouting, pointing. The prisoners began to run, stumbling and cursing, across the field toward the black phantom in the distance. Wilhelm, with Lumley and Goldman at his side, ran, too, desperate for a space under a roof. They jammed themselves into the melee at what was apparently the entrance and squeezed through.

Inside, Wilhelm stopped and extended his arms into a total absence of light unlike any he'd ever before experienced. His boots, replacing his eyes, kicked out, poking into the seamless carpet of bodies already spread before him. Among the sounds of men pushing and shoving around him, threats of eternal damnation rose from below. His boots found fingers, toes, bellies, and shins as he move forward. Suddenly, his boot found a flat place, a crack in the human carpet. He fell forward onto his knees, twisted out of his blanket roll and inserted it, pushed it, down between invisible arms and legs on both sides. The blanket roll beneath his head, he rolled on his side, inserted his hands between his thighs, and closed his eyes. What happened to Lum and Goldman, he wondered, as he began to snore.

*       *       *       *

The cold, gray light of day found a leg across Wilhelm's chest, another from the opposite side atop his ankles. Sitting up, he pushed them aside, hips, legs, and shoulders complaining bitterly. Remembering the men he'd seen in ditches along the road, he was glad to feel anything at all. Guards shouting, he got up, swung his blanket roll on his back, and picked his way through the crowd of groaning, cursing men. A cold wind met him at the door, the snowy gray sky low and threatening.

\*     \*     \*     \*

*Breakfast time:* eggs, sunny side up, stiff, hot bacon, crisp, buttered toast and jelly, please. The glowering sky answered, "You already got the *fast,* my boy, but you can't be *breaking* it for some time to come."

Shit, he thought, some shit. The so-called liver patty—a soft meat he wouldn't touch at home—and sugar cubes and leftovers from his one-and-only Red Cross parcel lay safe in his blanket roll. His belly shouted, "Eat 'em now!" but his head vetoed the request. No use using up reserves. Pulling his clenched fists up inside his sleeves, he found his left hand empty. Damn! The book! My chemistry book is…! He turned around and met the mob of sleepy-eyed, mean-with-hunger prisoners slogging toward him. To hell with it. It was too heavy anyway, a waste of energy. A familiar fear replaced the bacon and eggs: he wanted his buddies. Lumley's head stood above the crowd a few steps away.

"Looks like these buggers ain't got nothin' for us to eat this mornin', Will." The red-bearded one smiled down at him. "M'belly thinks mah throat's done been cut."

"Yeah, mine, too. Where's Goldman? Don't tell me he took off last night."

"Wouldn't s'prise me. Woulda been a good time."

The crowd began to move into the road, no *Appell,* no tea, not even a *Los!-Los!* Wilhelm took one step, winced, and grabbed Lumley's arm for support. "Damn groin's sore as hell! All that slippin' and slidin' tore me up again." Wilhelm hobbled along until the muscles warmed and began to move again. There they were again: the boots and the ruts and the sheeted black ice. He only hoped this might be their last day on the road. Ha!

At midmorning a crowd of refugees, in carts and on foot, split the herd of prisoners down the middle. If they're going away from the

Rooskies, Wilhelm reasoned, *we're* going *toward* them! That can't be right! Not even the stupid *Volksturm* would take us back that way! So which way *are* we going? South? North?

The long, sorry stream of human misery kept coming, children crying, horses neighing, slipping on the ice. A ragged young man leading a donkey and cart came along; a bearded, gray-faced old man, one hand holding onto the sideboard, the other swinging a cane, struggled along beside it. Inside the creaking box-on-wheels, an old woman, fever-bright eyes peering from under a black cloth, sat humming almost inaudibly to a tightly wrapped baby in her arms. Across from the crone sat a pale-faced young woman, blonde hair wrapped in a ragged red cloth. One arm enfolded a tiny girl, wriggling and babbling on her lap; the other attempted to confine a bright-faced boy who, reaching for his sister, tried to pull her hair. The pale cheeks, bluish lips, and solemn eyes of the cart's occupants projected their pain, their misery into the crowd of POWs.

Lumley suddenly halted, bent over, and covered his face. "Ah cain't *stand* this!" he cried. "This damn war and all this crazy sufferin'. It's too much! Ah jus' cain't stand it no more!" A prisoner, shuffling along behind him, ran headlong into the big redhead, almost knocking him off his feet.

Wilhelm pulled Lumley to the side of the road. "Hey, Lum, what's the matter, boy?" He bent and looked up into Lumley's face. "C'mon, Lum, don't worry about them. They're gonna be okay. They're doin' what they gotta do, what that sonofabitch Hitler is makin' 'em do. It ain't your fault, Lum, it's that fuckin' Hitler's fault."

Lumley straightened himself and wiped his eyes. "Yeah, Will, Ah know. Ah know. It's just gittin' to me, that's all." He sat down on the edge of the ditch and stared off into the woods. "Ah jus' need to set a bit and git me somethin' to eat."

Smiling down at Lumley, Wilhelm felt that familiar warmth in his chest. Sorry to see his best friend, such a big strong Bible-reading soldier, fold like that. But he couldn't help feeling proud of himself. It hadn't been *him,* the little guy who's always afraid, always scared, that had caved in. Just shows we're *all* alike. We're all made of the same stuff down deep *inside.*

Just then, Goldman, their missing comrade, came along the ditch. He looked closely at his two friends, and following their eyes, turned and stared into the woods. "I got some stuff. C'mon, let's eat. I'm starvin'," he said, opening his blanket roll. "These bastids ain't gonna give us nuttin'."

Acknowledging Goldman with a perfunctory nod, Wilhelm found the can of "liver patty" he'd dreamed about at the barn, spooned its contents onto a bit of black bread, and wolfed it down. Lumley finished half a can of Spam, fingering out the last bits, then licking the can clean. Goldman, sardine can upended over his mouth, snarfed the last of the little fish and joined Lumley in a lip-smacking contest. The three men, smiling inside if not out, lay back in the snow, and, eyes closed, savored the myriad tastes on their tongues and the rare esophageal sensations down below. A bit of warm heaven in the midst of a frozen hell.

CHAPTER 13

▼

# THE KNIFE COMES IN HANDY

That afternoon three horsemen, high-brimmed black hats hiding their eyes, galloped up the middle of the column, turned, and watched the prisoners slog pass. "SS Sonsabitches! Look out for 'em!" came down the column man to man to man. The riders sat on their horses a while, then rode back along the column, berating prisoners who, in the ditches, were relieving themselves or gathering snow for a drink. The guards finally called a halt, and, groaning with relief, the prisoners stepped off the road, dropped down and lay back in the snow. Stronger men gathered wood, built small fires, and heated water to mix with the brown dust labeled "powdered tea" by the Red Cross.

One SS horseman, burly and aggressive, stopped next to a burgeoning fire and gestured at the men huddled around it. He yelled and pointed toward the road. POWs up and down the column heard his guttural voice and craned their necks to see. The men at the fire stared up at the German, who now spurred his horse and, obviously enjoying himself, shouted again and waved his arms. The prisoners turned around, following him and his prancing horse. The rider, now having the attention of prisoners up and down the column, drew his *Luger*, fired it once in the air, and pointed it down at the tallest American in the group.

"What's he shootin' for? They ain't doin' nothin'." Wilhelm, standing on tiptoe, muttered.

"Sumbitch's shootin' 'cause he wants to shoot, that's what," Goldman sneered. "Rotten bastid's afraid to go after the Rooskies 'cause they might shoot back, so he...." The gun fired once more, and the tall POW disappeared into a cloud of smoke and sparks. His buddies, yelling, bent into the fire and pulled him away.

"That fella's shot," Lumley said, grabbing his blanket roll. "Ah better git down there and see whut Ah can do. Y'all go on. Ah'll ketch ya down the road a piece."

The SS trooper, shouting and firing like some kind of wild Indian, galloped into the road and joined his cohort already moving back the way they had come.

"Dirty rotten bastids!" Goldman screamed. "I had my rifle, I'd show 'em some shootin'!"

"Hey, Goldman! Sit down and shut up!" Wilhelm shouted. When he lay back in the snow and closed his eyes, the horse reared, the pistol fired, and the tall POW disappeared again, a scene he would see again and again before the march was over.

Lumley caught up with them on the road half an hour later. "'At boy took a bullet awright. Right between the eyes." His tone somber, he looked down as he spoke. "One a his buddies got his tags, and Ah said a couple a words over 'im. 'Bout all we could do. Hope somebody finds him and buries him."

That night, they got a dipper of barley soup and a loaf of black bread for each five-man rank. After bread crusts and forefingers had swiped every last spot of soup from their dixies, they lay down and smiled, enjoying once more the warmth and taste of food.

"Bastids could get us chow like that ever' day, if they wanted to."

"Ah doubt it. Ah ain't seen the guards eatin' much neither, have you? Ah don't think…."

"Goddammit, Lumley, I'm beginnin' to think you're part Kraut," Goldman snarled. "Forever takin' up for 'em like you wuz family, or somethin'."

"Hey. I'm the only part-Kraut around here. Lum's just tryin' to be fair like always." Wilhelm grinned.

"Shit, Wilhelm! These fuckin' Krauts don't know nuttin' 'bout fair! Dis here redhead *is* part Kraut! I know it!" Goldman's attempt to be funny fell flat. At least they spent the night in luxury: a barn with intact roof and plenty of straw, with stray potatoes here and there.

By noon the following day, an icy wind swept across the column, the sun a fuzzy yellow bulb ducking in and out among dark, hurrying clouds. Wilhelm's complaints of chilblains and numb toes fell amid those of frozen fingers, burning ears, and aching backs. In spite of all this he often heard a snicker, a laugh, and saw a smile here and there. The food effect, he decided. A shot of hot chow will do it every time. Tank and truck traffic dropped off, too, assuaging fears of death or injury by intent or accident. As he swung along, the swish and smack of his boots seemed a bit more rhythmic than before; his boots seemed to avoid the frozen ruts more easily than before. Germany can't be much wider than this, he thought. This has got to be our last day on the road! Warm beds and hot chow, boys, right up ahead!

It was, however, not to be. Even so, he and his buddies spent the night in relative comfort, almost warm and quite dry. Wilhelm smiled at the stink as he entered the little schoolhouse: just like American kids, he mused. German children stink, too. Since the floor was already occupied, he pushed the books off a shelf behind the teacher's desk and slid his weary body onto it. The redhead lay draped across the teacher's desk. Head on a stack of paper and feet on Lumley's back, he slept soundly. Who could ask for more?

Next day, their fifth on the road, during a rare midmorning break, Lumley went off to a barn and came out yelling, "Taters, ever'body! Over here! Over here! Taters all over the place!" The prisoners jumped up and took off toward the barn. Warily, the guards watched in apparent indecision, then, hungry too, followed the prisoners inside the barn. Some half hour later, prisoners and guards alike came back to the road, their pockets bulging.

Wilhelm dropped on the edge of the road, his hands full. "Anybody got any salt?" Nobody answered. He rubbed the hard, brown dirt off a potato and, squinting, bit into it. "Hard as a friggin' rock! Not much taste, either. Like eatin' a piece a concrete!"

"You don't want yours, pal, I'll eat 'em for ya," Goldman mumbled. "My belly don't give a damn what my tongue thinks."

Lumley spat on a clod of dirt on a big vegetable and rubbed it away. "Back home," he said, munching, "we usta sneak into ole man Lumpkin's garden on the way home from school and kick us up some taters. Some a the kids even carried salt with 'em. But Ah never did. Ah like 'em natchrul, like this." He looked at Wilhelm. "You eat 'em for real like this just once, Will, and you ain't never gonna eat 'em no other way."

Wilhelm grinned. "If you say so, buddy. It's all between the ears, I guess."

That night, they ate potatoes and slept on the black, oil-and-grease floor of a garage. A sign on the wall above their heads shouted

*RAUCHEN VERBOTEN;* the smokers among the POWs pointed and laughed. Those who had 'em, smoked 'em anyway. During the night, sirens wailed and the sounds of feet—many, many feet—came from the street outside. Bombs whined, whistled, and slammed down. The garage shook, windows shattered, and debris rattled heavy on the metal roof overhead. If you don't know where the bomb shelter is, Wilhelm remembered, stay where you are. The lesson of Limburg taught him to snuggle deeper into his blanket and hope for the best.

Next day, the POW column moved down the main street of a small village and halted before a church. Bells rang in the tall steeple that glistened in winter sun, as people poured through the wide front doors down the steps into the street. Most stopped and spoke with fellow parishioners. Sunday, Wilhelm thought, wishing he were standing there with family and friends, a hot, savory Sunday dinner only hours away.

Lumley squinted down at Goldman. "See there, Buddy, these German people are jus' reg'lar people, goin' to church of a Sunday. Jus' like us, the mommas talk 'bout their younguns and the men talk politics. Jus' like back home."

"How the hell do you know what they're talkin' 'bout? You don't know no German." Goldman, cheek twitching, glared at the redhead. "And they *ain't* like the folks back home, neither. Far's you know, they might be talkin' 'bout linin' us up and shootin' us down. You don't know nuttin!"

"There ain't a smooth bone in your whole *fuckin' body,* is there, Goldman?" Lumley snarled, his shoulder jumping as he blurted the four-letter word. "Ah don't *hafta* know what their sayin' to know what they're talkin' 'bout. And 'sfar's them shootin' us down, well…."

"They're all Krauts, Lumley, fuckin' goddam Krauts!" Goldman had begun to shout, "and 'at's all you gotta know 'bout 'em! They're the bastids 'at started this goddam war, and church or no goddam church, they can all rot in hell far's I'm concerned!"

"Awright! Awright! Knock it off!" Wilhelm jammed his good bare hand between the two men and stepped in between them. "You're gettin' some a the guys around here keyed up," he hissed. "So knock it off before somebody starts somethin'!"

"'At's a crock, Wilhelm! Ain't nobody gonna 'start nuttin! Not weak and hungry as we are."

"Awright, just drop it, will ya?" Internecine fights like when his parents yelled at each other always made Wilhelm nervous. "We got enough problems without you guys bitchin' at each other alla time." Dolan! Where are you, Sarge?

Most of the *Volkssturm* mingled with the crowd of churchgoers, smiling and shaking hands. A man in preacher's robes spoke with the boss *Feldwebel* and went back into the church. A few minutes later, several ladies, their Sunday-go-to-meeting dresses fluttering in the icy wind, came out with sandwiches and cups of a steaming liquid—*ersatz* coffee, Wilhelm guessed. The *Volkssturm*, backs to the prisoners, bowed deeply before accepting the ladies' offerings.

The prisoners muttered, licked their lips, and kicked at the ruts in the road. "Look at that! Sonsabitches're living off the land," one man said. "No wonder we don't get nothin'."

"That's what they call *Gemütlichkeit*," Goldman whispered. The dirty groove between his eyes squeezed deep and dark. "And one a these days they're gonna get it shoved straight up their ass, and, ohh, how I'd love to be there when it happens."

When they finished eating, the guards carefully aligned the column of prisoners (for the benefit of the onlooking church-goers, Wilhelm surmised) and marched them away. At a bend in the road just outside the village, a horse-drawn wagon came into view, a wisp of what looked like steam rising behind the uniformed driver. The word "Soup!" rolled down the column like a ball of fire.

Lumley stood on tiptoe. "Yeah. There's somethin' hot in that wagon, awright," he said. "Steamin' up real good."

Shouting, "Soup! Soup! We want soup!" the POWs broke ranks and rushed down the road toward the wagon, the guards shouting. Wilhelm and his buddies, among the first to arrive, were pressed in against the side of the wagon as the pimply-faced *Gefreiter* in the driver's seat fought to control the horse. An American sergeant stepped in, grabbed its bridle, and spoke softly to it. The horse allowed him to lead it and the wagon off the road, where the *Volkssturm*, rifles up, surrounded the cart.

"Hey, there's bread in there, too!" someone shouted. The word "bread" surged through the crowd, causing more shouting, more pushing. A rifle fired, then a second. The prisoners, quieted for a moment, then began to cry "Soup and bread! Soup and bread!" The *Volkssturm* had bayonets fixed when a *Feldwebel* jumped into the wagonbed and waved his arms. "*Ya! Ya!*" he shouted. "Zoop, *Ya! Brot, Ya!* Zoop *und Brot! Yaaaa!*" He flashed a broad smile and jumped down. The prisoners, knowing the drill, began to line up, five to a rank, dixies in hand.

Somehow, Wilhelm found himself standing among four men he'd never seen before. He knew better than to step away to look for his buddies. He'd lose his place for sure. "Zoop *und Brot*" first. Good ole Lum will find me, he told himself, that familiar lump of panic rising in his throat. He collected his soup and waited while the tall, dark prisoner the others called Volitch accepted the rank's loaf of bread. These guys're a "click," Wilhelm was thinking. I gotta stay close, or I won't get a crumb out of them.

He was right. Ignoring Wilhelm, the four men, moved quickly through the crowd and down the road. Wilhelm trotted along behind, his soup sloshing, eyes searching the crowd for his buddies. Volitch stepped off into a ditch and sat down on the far side; the other three men stopped and, backs to the road, began to spoon up their soup. Smiling, Volitch pulled a rusty kitchen knife from his coat pocket and nicked the bread in three places. When he saw Wilhelm coming along the ditch toward him, he hesitated but began to saw the hard, black loaf.

Wilhelm, stomach acid burning his throat, stopped at the edge of the group and spoke quietly. "You ain't cuttin' it right, there, buddy. There's *five* of us and you're only cuttin' *four* pieces."

Grinning, Volitch turned his strange slant eyes on Wilhelm and pointed the bent knife at the front of Wilhelm's overcoat. The other three men guffawed.

Wilhelm looked down. "Dammit! God damn it!" Holding his nearly empty dixie beneath the smear of soup, he used his bare right forefinger to squeegee what he could back into it. Volitch put his knife back into the bread and began again to saw.

Taking a step forward, Wilhelm shouted, "Hold it! *I* got a piece a that comin'. You gotta cut *five* pieces, not four!" Six eyebrows across the ditch went up, the eyes beneath them swinging from Wilhelm to Volitch.

The big man's lips pursed as he looked down his nose at Wilhelm. "Don't get your balls all het up there, buddy. You'll get yours, soon's I git it cut." He sawed again at the same place.

Wilhelm, his face hard, began to wonder if this was worth one lousy piece of bread. His father's face flashed across his mind, and he knew the answer. Bending as if to wipe the front of his coat further, he slipped his hand into his legging and came up with the knife. The six eyes at the edge of the road widened. "I got a knife, too, *buddy.* Sharper'n yours, I bet." He met Volitch's hard stare. "Gimme that bread and I'll cut it up for you." Wilhelm slowly rolled the knife in his fingers, its narrow, curved blade flashing in the cold, gray light.

"Awright, awright, put that fuckin' knife away, *buddy*. We ain't out to cheat nobody." Volitch looked across at his friends. "Are we, boys?" A weak, almost inaudible assent came back to him. He slid his knife to the butt end of the loaf and sawed a piece loose. "Awright, there's your fuckin' bread. Grab it and git the fuck outta here before I take your blade away from ya and cut your fuckin' t'roat wid it."

Wilhelm speared the dangling slice with his knife and, walking backward down the ditch, shouted, "Thanks a lot, guys. You're a buncha real fuckin' heroes!" He jumped into the road and walked quickly away.

Picking a spot at some distance, he sat down and sighing, held the bread on the knifepoint at eye level. "Thanks, Dad," he muttered. "I wouldn't a got it if it wasn't for you." He stuck the bread in his mouth and, munching on it, pulled the blade across the thumbnail of his bare right hand. It resisted the pull nicely. "Still sharp as the day you gave it to me, Dad. Coulda cut that sonofabitch's gizzard out if he hadn't come across, couldn't I?" He wiped the blade on his knee and shoved it back into its scabbard. His old vow never to use the knife as a weapon came to mind. "Naïve as hell, wasn't I, Dad? Didn't know nothin' about nothin' in those days." He found Lumley and Goldman staring down at him.

"Where you been, Will? We been lookin' all over for ya." Lumley sat down next to Wilhelm. "D'ya git your rations okay?" Wilhelm nodded. The redhead bent and stared at him. "You okay, Will? You're lookin' kinda puny."

"I'm okay, Lum. I got my chow, okay." Wilhelm's tone was sharper than he intended. "But it wasn't easy." The words just slipped out.

"Whaddaya mean, it wasn't *easy?*" Goldman, frowning, dropped onto his haunches in front of Wilhelm.

"Wellll, I had a little trouble gettin' my bread from some guys. But it worked out okay. I ain't worried 'bout it."

Goldman stood and looked around. "Point 'em out, and me and Lumley'll have a little talk wit' 'em."

Lumley shook his head. "No, weak as we are, we ain't goin' 'round lookin' for no trouble, Goldman. Will says he's okay, he's okay."

Silently, Goldman hunkered down again, tic twisting his cheek.

Lumley held out a piece of bread half again the size Wilhelm had eaten. "Here, Will, Ah had a piece left."

"No, dammit, Lum, I got all I want! Just forget it, will ya? Forget it!" The frown on Wilhelm's face faded. He felt sheepish. "Thanks anyway, buddy."

That night they were to be billeted in an abandoned village, its houses without roofs or windows. The homes, perhaps, of the refugees they'd passed sometime back. Lumley wandered about and discovered a cellar beneath one, so they burrowed in and slept like rocks down in the dirt.

Next morning, they had the usual snow for a drink, and again hit the road. The same dark shapes slipped and slid around them, but Wilhelm thought the men were more energetic than usual, talking, some even laughing. Was it the Zoop *und Brot* from yesterday? He shouted, "Hey, guys, let's see if we can find us another wagon full of chow, huh? Whaddaya say?"

A prisoner in front of him turned around. "One a the guards says we're stoppin' purty soon."

"I'll believe it when I see it," Goldman muttered.

"Yeah, me too." Wilhelm looked at Lumley.

The big redhead just smiled.

That yellow smear in the sky hung near its high point when the column passed a sign that said: *Lukenwalde. 3 Km.*

"Luckin Wald. S'pose it's the town of our dreams, Will?"

"God, I hope so. Anything's better'n walkin' this fuckin' road."

The POWs almost cheered when the column turned off the road into the little town. The street, covered by snow-whipped black ice and lined with empty houses, took the column past a half-burned school, its windows gone, walls broken and crumbling. Near the town square, they passed a bombed-out church, its twisted, bullet-scarred steeple threatening to fall on them. *Luckenwalde*—Hitler's legacy—drab and empty. I gotta remember this, Wilhelm told himself.

A barbed-wire fence loomed in the distance. The wooden arch over the gate carried a familiar sign: *ARBEIT MACHT FREI*. The crossbar below proclaimed *Stammlager IIIA*.

"The sumbitches're consistent, anyway," muttered Goldman. "Good at *Arbeit*, but they don't know shit about *frei*. Bet my first day's soup we'll be diggin' them Geneva Convention potatoes again in no time."

# CHAPTER 14

▼

# STALAG IIIA

The *Volkssturm* shaped the POWs into their standard five-man-ranks and marched them into the camp. Prisoners wearing all kinds of uniforms—light, dark, multi-colored—spilled out of low, concrete-block buildings and crowded along the fence. One man, his hairless face thin but clean, pointed thumbs up and shouted, "It won't be long now, Yanks. Jerry's on his last leg. Home by summer, lads! Home by summer!"

"Summer time, and the livin' is easy," poured warm and humid across Wilhelm's mind. The little brick house on Yoke Street, dark green spruce trees in front, the cherry tree greening next to the garden out back, quivered before his eyes. He blinked back tears he didn't know he still had.

Some of the new arrivals responded to the strangers' greetings, but most kept their eyes on their feet. The column passed a long building on the left, a sign in German over the entrance, soldiers holding burp-guns on either side.

Goldman stared at the guns. "Looks like the head Kraut's hangout. Plenty a guards, too. Bugger must be 'fraid a somethin'."

The odor of food turned the prisoner's heads toward a small building set back from the path. "The Kraut's chow hall," Wilhelm murmured. "Bet I could eat ever'thing in there before they caught me."

A wooden structure with floor-to-ceiling windows and several tall brick chimneys came into view behind the fence. "Hey, look at the big chimneys! That means there's *stoves* in there! Heat! Remember *heat?*" But Wilhelm's joy evaporated when he saw the gold and silver bars glinting on the collars of the men standing behind the windows. "Oh, hell, that's the officers' barracks! Fuckin' Krauts give the best to our Gentlemen-by-Act-of-Congress! I shoulda known!"

At a long double fence, a *Volkssturm* guard came along, keys jangling. The gate swung open and the column marched inside. Inside the fenced compound, the column stopped and did a ragged left-face. A row of eight long, brown-streaked tents stretched before them. A broad snowfield lay behind the tents, encircled by a fence with guard towers at the corners.

"Tents! They walked us alla way across fuckin' *Deutschland* to put us in a buncha fuckin' tents!" Goldman's words burst above the hubbub of curses and groans surging from the column.

Wilhelm sighed and rolled his eyes. His whole body sagged.

Lumley said nothing, just looked around.

"Look at them camouflage marks. Them's desert tents! Damn things was used in Africa! It's the middle of fuckin' January, and they're puttin' us in *desert* tents?" Goldman stomped his foot. "See, I *tol'* yooz guys we oughtta take off! But nooo, yooz didn't have the guts! So, now we're gonna freeze to deat'!"

"Oh, for chrissake, Goldman. Knock it off, will ya?" Wilhelm scowled at the little man. "Just shut the hell up!"

A guard came along counting the prisoners. The first time since IIIB, Wilhelm realized. Goldman's right, we should've taken off. Ha! And we'd be goners by now, too.

Lumley stood on tiptoe. "Our crowd looks a l'il smaller'n it was, don't it?"

"Yeah, looks like it." Wilhelm's tone said he didn't care one way or the other.

"Yeah, at least some guys had the guts they was born wit' and...."

Wilhelm turned on the little man. "If you had so damn much guts, Goldman, why the hell didn't you take off when you had the chance?" Goldman just stared. "Awright! I don't wanta hear anymore about it. Just shut the hell up!"

"Looks like we got us a new counter-upper, too." Lumley turned to Wilhelm. "'Member that little fella with the iron cross on his chest back at IIIB? Wore them funny-lookin' Worl' War I putees?" His face fell. "Looks like the Rooskies maybe got 'im."

"There you go again, feelin' sorry for some fuckin' Kraut." Goldman's head shook. "You're some kinda Section Eight, y'know that? You belong in a rubber fuckin' room."

Lumley acknowledged Goldman with a squint and turned away.

Divided into seven "companies," the formation broke up, each company going to its assigned tent. Lumley and Wilhelm behind Goldman shoved through the crowd into tent #3. Dodging around the tent poles down the middle aisle, they stopped about half-way down and looked around. "Well! Ain't this wonderful?" Goldman yelled, his voice bouncing around the canvas walls. "Nuttin' but straw to sleep on, horseshit and all! They're treatin' us like a buncha fuckin' ani-mules!"

Prisoners poured into the tent, sighing, groaning, most throwing themselves into the straw and stretching out. Lumley took three big steps toward the side wall and dropped his blanket roll. "This here oughtta be 'bout right. It's 'way from the aisle and outta the wind comin' in at the front." Standing straight up, his head almost touched the canvas. Wilhelm fluffed up the straw next to the redhead and spread his blankets on it. Goldman, cursing under his breath, wandered on down the aisle, kicked at the straw and a center pole, and finally settled in next to Wilhelm.

When Sergeant Sharkey, their old friend from IIIB, came to check on his tent, he found three rows of "beds" on either side of the aisle, the men sitting or lying on their blankets. The tent was full.

Legs crossed, hands stuffed into his armpits, Wilhelm sat looking around. Cold and dark. A roof overhead and straw underneath. Could be worse. "Must be at least three hundred guys in here, Lum." He sneezed and wiped his nose.

"More like four hundred. Ah done a li'l countin' m'se'f." Lumley sneezed, too. "Not gonna warm up much in here with the sides flappin' loose like they are. We aughtta do somethin' 'bout that." He looked up at the canvas. "Looks warm though, don't it, when the sun comes out? Makes ever'thin' look sorta gold-like." His words formed a white cloud in the golden air.

"Think I'll go see what's outside." Goldman got up. "Gotta find the latrine. First-class place like this oughtta have runnin' water somewheres." Stepping over the men between his blankets and the middle aisle, he took the only way out of the tent, the front flap.

Wilhelm, his body stiffening, lay back and watched the canvas ripple. Feeling sleepy, he took off his boots and made a pillow of them. Leaving his overcoat buttoned up, he pulled his second blanket up and slipped into a dreamless sleep.

\*          \*          \*          \*

Wilhelm awoke to the soft wheeze of some four hundred sleeping men. Fingers and toes coming alive, chilblains reminded him of how cold they'd been on the road. Even after walking and freezing for a hundred miles, he thought, they're still alive and kicking. Somewhere down the tent, a moan rose up. "And the rest of the guys are alive, too. Thank you, God," he muttered, "or whoever's been watchin' out for us up there."

The bones in his neck made grinding noises and his hipbones throbbed as he rolled over and sat up. "Damn boots make a lousy pillow," he whispered, rubbing himself. "Damn straw is hard, too, after you lay on it a while." The sounds of snow plopping down off windblown pines beyond the fences brought to mind the sounds of snow falling off the cherry tree next to his window back home. Cold and snowy there, too, I expect, but not like this. It's never this damn cold in Indiana.

He watched Lumley's broad back rise and fall, turned and watched the white cloud above Goldman's mouth swell and fade. In spite of his empty stomach, his tingling toes and fingers, he was amazed at how well he felt. I'm lucky to be out of the fighting, alive and safe in here. No bombs, like at Limburg, and no killing, like what must be going on back in France. Still can't believe the Sarge couldn't get past that damn fence. Nobody up there was looking out for him, I guess.

Morning sunshine tried to warm the canvas atop the tent. Wilhelm rubbed his eyes and scrubbed his cheeks with his palms. He pulled off his wool cap and dug his fingers through his greasy hair and his dry, itching scalp. Goosebumps rose and he shuddered. It felt good to be alive, sooo good. His tongue found his teeth sticky—sticky with what, he wondered. He looked up and asked "somebody up there" for tooth-paste and a toothbrush. There was no response. Now his bladder spoke, sharp, insistent. He pulled on his one and only glove and his boots, and rolled up his overcoat collar. Outside, the wind nearly knocked him off his feet. Head down, he squinted at the snow and shoved his hands deep in his pockets. A Hitler-mustachioed *Volkssturm,* whom Wilhelm recognized from the road, came down the path inside the double fence that separated the new arrivals' compound from the officers'. He opened his mouth to greet the German, but clamped his jaw shut. I'm not playing the Friendly American anymore. I'm gonna be the *tough-sonofabitchin'* American from now on. The thought warmed his insides.

Down the double fence, a group of foreign prisoners in an adjacent compound, heads pulled down against the wind, walked along silently. A guard, bigger and broader than the *Volkssturm* Wilhelm knew so well, stared down from a tower, his rifle pointing down at Wilhelm. "You get a pay raise if you shoot me, you bastard?" he whispered softly, much too softly for the guard to hear.

Bladder threatening in earnest, Wilhelm walked briskly down the side of the tent toward the snowfield behind it. A roughly 12' x 12' freshly dug hole formed a dark blemish in the snow. "Gotta be the latrine," he said, opening his pants. "Biggest damn slit trench I ever saw!" Logs rested on crisscrossed stakes along three sides of the hole. As he urinated, he imagined balancing himself on one of them, his bare butt and testes dangling in the wind. "A man could disappear into this damn thing if he's not careful. 'Specially in the middle of the night."

He studied the broad barbed-wire-encircled snowfield behind the tent row. Guard towers were at each corner and at the center of the long back fence. We're gonna freeze ass out here doing *Appell* twice a day, he thought. The sun hung just above the trees on his right. That's east, he thought, probably southeast, and that open field beyond the fence the other way had to be west, toward France, toward home. *Home.* The word, the thought, made him both sad and happy.

✳    ✳    ✳    ✳

They slept in that first morning. No tea, and no *Appell.* That afternoon, however, they fell out for their first *Appell* at IIIA.

"Oh, shit, look at that," Goldman whispered, his eyes on the *Feldwebel* in front of tent #3's formation. "It's that sumbitchin' Kruger! I was hopin' the Rooskies got 'im." Lips pulled into a grimace, the stocky German's gold tooth flashed in the gray light. Number 3's counter-upper, a small *Volkssturm* from the march, threw up his Hitler salute and reported the count. Kruger did a sharp about-face and shouted the number at the sky. *Der Leutnant*—the officer in charge of the first three tents—swung around and reported to *der Oberleutnant*—Commandant of the American compound—who in turn reported the German equivalent of All Present and Accounted For to a hard-faced *Hauptmannn*—Commandant of *Stammlager IIIA, Luckenwalde.* Prosthetic hand held up in response, *der Hauptmann* turned and limped away toward the gate. The *Appell* was now formally complete, but the prisoners stood in the freezing wind another quarter hour while the junior officers chatted near the center of the formations.

Back inside #3, the three buddies grabbed their dixies and jumped into chow line. As they approached the food handlers, Goldman pointed at the loaves of bread piled behind them. "My God, look at that! The bread's wrapped in cellophane! And, look, there's numbers on 'em! 1938! Burned into the bottom!" He turned to Lumley. "These fuckin' Krauts a yours been savin' up jus' for you, big boy. Jus' for you!"

"If you say so, Goldman. You ain't gonna eat yours, Ah'll eat it for ya." Lumley reached for Goldman's piece, laughing as he jerked it away. "And they ain't *my* Krauts, neither, Goldman, so…."

"Awright, you guys, shut up and eat! You're lucky you got anything." I'm gonna put in for three stripes when I get back, Wilhelm told himself. Finished with dinner, he pulled off his boots, wrapped them in his field jacket, and put them under his head. "I'm gonna digest this here Geneva Convention chow, now, guys, so keep it down, will ya?" Squirming in under his overcoat, he shoved his hands between his thighs, closed his eyes and almost immediately slept. Snow flying, the wind burning his ears, dark hulks crunched along a white path, his boots slipping and sliding on black ice buried in the ruts, he moaned, turned, and twisted, as the dream ground across his mind.

*     *     *     *

Between tents #5 and #6, a pipe stood shoulder-high out of the snow, a rope of ice hanging like snot from an iron nose. Wilhelm stopped in the path and stared. "Look at that. The only friggin' water pipe in the whole place and it's froze solid. Fuckin' Krauts don't give a damn if we die a thirst or not, do they?" He would never have said a thing like that before the war. He was learning, now, to hate them, hate them with a passion.

"Hey, yooz're ketchin' on, buddy." Goldman grabbed the pipe and shook it. "Dis here's the Geneva Convention pipe. Nice ain't it?" Squinting at Lumley, he patted Wilhelm on the back.

Walking along the eastern fence, the three buddies saw a detail of gaunt, dirty-faced men, clothes torn and filthy, picking up fallen limbs and piling them near the fence. Guards stood around watching. "Ah bet them's Russians," Lumley said. "Wonder if they get extra chow for workin' like that."

"Hell, no, Lumley. I bet the Krauts don't give Rooskies hardly enough to stay alive. Way they look, they're prob'ly Rooskies, awright."

Goldman, arms akimbo, stared a while at the ragged workers, then moved on.

At the double fence between theirs and the officer's area, they passed the guard tower in the center and stopped to watch groups of foreign prisoners stroll past. "Them's Polocks, sure as hell. I'd know 'em any-where," Goldman whispered. "And look at that! They're livin' in con-crete barracks, and all we get is tents! Who's winnin' this fuckin' war, anyway?"

"They got here first, Goldman. You coulda beat 'em, if you'd thrown up your hands and shouted, 'Here I am! Come and git me!'" Lumley chuckled. "'Sides, how d'you know if they're, uhhh, Polocks or not? You cain't tell that jus' lookin' at 'em."

"The hell I can't. I went to school with them buggers." He sniffed. "I can smell 'em clear over here." Heads shaking, Lumley and Wilhelm exchanged glances and walked on.

Except for their dead eyes and pale, drawn faces, Wilhelm thought those long-time POWs looked pretty good. Do *I* look that good? he asked himself. Ain't seen a mirror for so long, I don't know *how* I look. He ran his bare hand along his frizzled jaw and tucked some wild hair under his wool cap. I need a shower and a haircut that's all, and, yeah, a piece of Mom's meatloaf with mashed potatoes and gravy and.... He looked around at his buddies: Lum looks okay. Red beard's pretty scruffy, but holds its shape nice. And Goldman, well, Goldman looks like that picture of the Ancient Mariner on the front of my old English textbook.

By now, the sun had dropped to the treetops, and the wind was moaning through the pines. The three buddies finished their hike, went in, and fell on their blankets. Wilhelm, staring up, watched the swarm-ing mites go suddenly gold in a flash of sunlight. What now? He asked himself. What now?

"Guess we oughtta be thankful we got that canvas coverin' over us tonight, huh? Sorta like the man up above coverin' us, shelterin' us from the weather," Lumley ventured.

"Yeah. I guess." Don't tell me he's gonna start spoutin' sermons now that we're settled in, Wilhelm thought.

"Your man up there oughtta put a roof up there, Lumley, and a bed with a mattress down here. Boy, when I get home Rooz–a-velt's gonna get an earful!" Goldman, lips stretched into a grimace, pulled up his overcoat and lay back.

Talk about the war, when it would be over, when they might get home, floated about the tent. But food, food, food was the main topic. No dirty jokes, no girly stories, only reverent words about Mamma's cooking, their favorite dishes, the texture and tastes of them. A voice as husky as a man in heat told how to add chocolate syrup to pancake batter and the outstanding taste of his "masterpee-ayse duh ray-zis-tawnce." Fake French talk really annoyed Wilhelm. When a second voice began to describe the "makin's of Grandma's homemade ice cream," Wilhelm covered his ears, rolled over, and closed his eyes. "I hate this!" he whispered. "I'll go nuts listenin' to these guys the rest of the war." He wished for the chemistry book he'd lost, even tried to remember some of the formulas and reactions, but couldn't remember enough to allay his boredom. Hell, what good would it do me? Probably never get to use any of it anyway. Asleep now, he dreamed of molecules bumping and whorling and flying off in all directions, his body twisting and turning in sympathy.

Wilhelm, for some reason, awoke long before *Appell*. He sat up, draped a blanket over his head and shoulders, and looked around. Somehow the inside of the tent looked strange. He seemed to discover it all over again. No light, no heat, and no *breakfast!* Freezin'-ass cold and nothin' to do, nothin' to eat! He shivered. I'll go nuts sitting around here with nothing to…hell, even the cavemen had fires. And they and went out and killed something to eat. And they had girls there and they would cook up something and then the boys could mess around with them afterwards. But there's *nothing* here but these stinking goddam men and their stupid talk. And how long's this gonna last? How long will we be here? Could be a year! Two years! Three years! The dust mites before him went gold, and the tent poles emerged from the darkness, clean and clear. "The sun," he muttered, wanting to shout, "the good ole sun! Just like back on the road! You make all the difference! Stay Mr. Sun, you make all the difference for all of us!"

A sound, a soft, high-pitched wheeze caught Wilhelm's attention. Behind him, a sandy-haired soldier, three stripes glinting on his sleeve, sat stiffly upright, eyes half closed, the balls of his stocking feet pulled tight against his thighs, palms atop his knees, thumbs and middle fingers touching. Looks like a monk, Wilhelm thought. Seen pictures of them sitting like that. The man's ruddy face, broad forehead, and heavy, dark eyebrows makes him look Indian, but Indians don't grow beards. A scar runs from his ear under his beard and all the way down into his shirt. Shows he's been in a fight, for sure. A knife, or maybe a Kraut bayonet cut him. A stack of pots sat on the blanket next to the man—extra dixies, maybe—several sardine and powdered milk cans, too. The tinkle of metal came from a leather pouch as the soldier breathed. Did he carry all that stuff on the hike? All by himself? And what is it for?

Wilhelm took a deep breath, turned around, and leaned in close. "Hello, Sergeant. How y'doin'?" The soldier's eyelids fluttered, and a pair of steel-gray, red-rimmed eyes appeared from beneath them. His wide mouth, as if spring-loaded, snapped open, then shut. The sergeant spoke in the soft monotone of a man just come from a deep sleep: "Doing okay.

You?" A lax-wristed hand rose almost involuntarily and pulled an empty Klim can from the pile next to him.

Wilhelm, surprised by the sudden movement, dug for something more to say. "If you don't mind my askin', Sergeant, what do you do with all them, uhhh, cans and stuff?"

The soldier's other hand had already extracted a pair of tin snips from the leather pouch. He proceeded to cut the top off the chosen can, as he said, "Make blowers out of 'em," his voice stronger, deeper than before. The tool moved smoothly around the can's circumference, the rippled bottom rising, edges curling.

"A blower?" Wilhelm's eyebrows rose up. "Oh, yeah, I saw one a them back at IIIB. A dixie with holes in the bottom and a fan you crank to blow air up through it to fan a fire." He grinned. "Not much use now, though, are they? Not a helluva lot to cook around here, is there?" The sergeant didn't seem to hear. A miniature ballpeen hammer in hand, he melded the pieces of tin together to form a long flat sheet.

Goldman came in from his trip to the latrine and began turning over the straw beneath his blankets. "Hey, you seen my dice anywhere?" he asked. "You know, the ones I had back at IIIB. Some sumbitch has come in here and stole 'em, for sure!" Eyes narrow, tic twisting his cheek, Goldman poked around in his coat pockets.

Wilhelm turned to watch him. "You had a deck a cards, but I don't remember seein' any dice. Ain't nobody gonna steal your stuff in here. Don't worry about it." The bruised face of the prisoner back at IIIB with "Thief" painted across his back crossed his mind. Never did find out what they did with that guy.

"I catch 'em, I'll kill 'em," Goldman snarled. "Any sumbitch 'at comes near my stuff, I'll kill 'em!"

Wilhelm, grinning, turned back to the blower-maker in time to see him attach a four-bladed fan to the belt-driven wheel that would turn it. Working metal looked easy, he thought, especially the way this guy does it. He remembered the ashtray—a Father's Day present—he'd fashioned from a tin can in shop class. His father had turned it over and over, wondering what it was.

"Dammit, I got them dice for Hanukkah back at the house, you remember? Had 'em in my pocket when we was captured. That Kraut musta stole 'em! The bastid!"

"Well, Goldman, I…" A long shadow fell across Wilhelm's blankets, and he looked up.

"Goldman! Wilhelm! How you doin', guys?" The long, muscular body of Danny Danzig bent down between them, his pearly-whites glowing in the golden air.

Silently, Wilhelm swung around to watch the blower-builder. Danzig's honeyed voice took Wilhelm back to his stay in IIIB's frigid latrine.

"Well, hey, there's ole Tim Jones. How you doing, Sarge?" Danzig leaned across Wilhelm and offered his hand to the sergeant.

"Doin' okay. You?" Jones ignored the proffered hand.

"Fine, fine. See you're back at makin' them blowers again. Good for you. They'll come in real handy now that we ain't got no stoves. You're gonna be one rich POW one a these days, y'know that?"

Same ole Danzig, Wilhelm thought. Same ole bullshit.

"Hotdam, here they are!" Goldman shoved his clenched fist in the air. "I knew they was here somewhere. Now we can have some fun!" He held the dice up between two fingers and shouted, "Get out your cigarettes and D-bars, boys! There's gonna be a little game over here! Come one, come all!" He tossed the dice in the air for all to see.

"Heyyy, Goldman, let's see them dice!" Danzig caught the dice in midair. A hard shake and they rolled out on the blanket. "Seven!" he shouted. "By damn, looks like I ain't lost my touch!" Seemingly mes-

merized by the little black-spotted cubes, the two soldiers went on tossing them back and forth, laughing and whooping like a couple of kids.

Wilhelm, wishing they'd play somewhere else, ignored them as best
he could. "How much do you get for your blowers, Sergeant?" He
loved the sound of the word "Sergeant."

"Oh, usually 'bout eight packs. 'Less it's Chesterfields you're offerin',
then it's gotta be more like twelve."

"Eight packs! Wow! That's twice what we get in a Red Cross parcel.
If we ever see one again, that is."

"You ever try to start a fire out there in that wind?" Jones almost
grinned.

"No. But I...."

"Well, if you do, you won't think eight packs is too much." Jones'
yellow teeth flashed.

An hour later, the sergeant put his hand over his new blower and
cranked it, testing the breeze it made. "I didn't get your name, fella," he
said.

"Jimmy Wilhelm, Sergeant. I didn't get yours, either." He knew it
by now, but thought it polite to ask. When they shook hands, Jones'
calloused palm reminded Wilhelm of his dad's hard, tobacco-yellowed
palm.

"M'friends call me Slim." Jones said, pulling his boots on. "C'mon,
Jimmy, let's take 'er out and give 'er a whirl. Bring your pot and we'll
make some tea." Carrying the blower in one hand, he lifted the tent
wall with the other and dipped under it.

Wilhelm, overjoyed by the invitation from his new friend, pulled on
his boots and overcoat and grabbed up his dixie. They hunkered down
out of the wind in the snowy ditch around the tent, Jones' shiny new
machine resting between them. Jones pulled bits of paper and tree bark
from his pockets and placed them in the punctured dixie above the fan.

He whipped a wooden match across his thigh and, sheltering the little flame behind a glove, said in a voice barely audible above the wind, "Turn the crank real slow, Jimmy, and we'll get this thing goin'." Wilhelm cranked and watched the tiny flame flutter into a full-fledged fire. He looked up at the dark, rushing clouds. To a bird, he thought, he and Jones would look like a couple of Neanderthals nursing a hard-to-come-by fire. The story of Prometheus, the god who stole fire from Zeus and gave it to humans, came to mind. No wonder the Greeks worshiped him. Fire's damned important, a lot more important than I ever thought. Harrah for ole Prometheus!

Jones placed a can full of snow over the fire, watched it melt and then bubble and steam. "Boilin' water already! It's a miracle, Sergeant! A real miracle!" Wilhelm could hardly believe his eyes. "I got some tea and sugar from the parcel we got back at IIIB and…."

"Set tight, Jimmy. I got it." To a Marine sergeant's son, it sounded like an order. Wilhelm put away his things and watched Jones make the tea using a dark powder and some sugar cubes.

Squinting, Jones took Wilhelm's dixie and filled it with tea. "That Wilhelm name of yourn is the same as the German Kaiser's in the last war, ain't it?" Jones grinned. "Relation a yourn, was he?"

Wilhelm chuckled. Nobody'd ever asked him that before. "Well, my grandpaw was born over here in Krautland, somewhere around Munich, I think. Why? You thinkin' I might be a spy, or somethin'?" They both laughed.

The sergeant's eyes went narrow, and his face hardened. "You know that big blond kid inside there, Jimmy? The one said I was gonna be a rich POW?"

"Yeah. That's Danzig. Met him back at IIIB. From Indianapolis, my hometown. Came around when we got in and…."

"Well, that's the kinda crap that really gits to me. Thinks havin' more cigarettes than ever'body else is all there is to this fuckin' life," Jones sniffed. "Acts like he's gonna take ever'thing with 'im when he goes." Jones looked over the lip of his dixie at Wilhelm. "Crazy as hell, if y'ask me."

"Well, yeah, he's a little nuts, I guess." A question had been bugging Wilhelm. "If you don't mind my askin', what is it you're doin' when you sit there with your legs tucked under and your...."

"Meditatin', Jimmy. *Zazen*, the Zen boys call it."

Wilhelm's brows rose. "*Zazen*. Oh." He frowned. "Is that like prayin' or...."

"No. Buddhists don't pray. They don't think or talk about God. They're lookin' to live life on earth to the fullest. They study ways to do away with sufferin', their own and ever'body else's."

"Oh." Wilhelm blinked. Suffering? I know all about that. But how can you have a religion without God? Too many questions to ask and his tea was already gone, his dixie cold. Shoving his bare right hand into his pocket, he balanced the pot on his knee. "But, if they ain't prayin', what *are* they doin'? What's this meditatin' s'posed to do?"

Jones sighed. "It's a long story, Jimmy, and I ain't sure I can explain it so's you can...well, see, they sit that special way and listen to their breath and try to empty their minds—go blank and just *be. Satori*, they call it. They try to understand themselves, try to eliminate their ego and be one with the world, see things as they really are, not all screwed up like most of us do."

"Oh." Wilhelm frowned. "So you're a Buddhist, then, huh?"

Jones chuckled. "No, not hardly. I don't go along with reincarnation and that kinda stuff." His eyes met Wilhelm's. "I been in a lotta POW camps since I got caught down at the Cassarine Pass, in Africa. We was in one helluva fight down there. You prob'ly heard about it."

Wilhelm shook his head, realizing how little he really knew about the war. School, he thought. Classes and grades and girls. Just a stupid teenager, drifting along, unaware all that time that people were fighting and dying over here. Something seemed to open up inside him. He felt ashamed.

Jones dumped snow on the fire and turned the blower upside down. "Back in Italy, a guy gave me a book on Buddhism. Didn't have nothin' else to do, so I read it and started meditatin' like it said. There's somethin' to it, y'know, Jimmy, there really is somethin' to it." He half grinned. "It's a good feelin', listenin' to your breath. Kinda strange, like hearin' your life go by."

"Never heard of it, Sergeant. There's not much meditatin' goes on back in Hoosierland where I'm from." Wilhelm grinned, wondering what *satori* could do for anybody. With all this killing and suffering going on these days, it's not the way *I* look at the world, but it's the way the world *really is.* It's so damn bad, I hate sitting around here thinking about it all the time.

Jones got up. "You ever wonder, Jimmy, why *over here* it's all right to kill a man you never saw before, who you don't even know, but back home you do that and they'll fry you in the 'lectric chair so fast your head'll swim? You ever think about that?"

Shivering all over now, Wilhelm just wanted to get out of the wind, maybe continue their talk inside. "No. I guess I never did, Sergeant. I'm carryin' *Kraut* blood inside me, so I just do what I'm told. Don't think much about it." He grinned. "Went down and joined up like all my buddies did! And here I am. God, if I'd refused to go, Dad would've killed me right on the spot! I find it hard even now to hate the Germans. When I came over, I wasn't at all sure I could kill one." He thought of all the dummies he'd bayoneted and targets he'd shot holes

in. "Course, when they started shootin' at me, I shot back. It was automatic."

"Yeah, well, that's just it. Jimmy. That's the way the big shots set it
up. Somebody shoots at you and you gotta shoot back. All because
some sonofabitch runnin' the show wants to take over somebody else's
country. Animals don't do that. Only humans. We're the rottenest
fuckin' animals on the face a the earth." He got up, ducked under the
canvas wall and disappeared into the tent.

Wilhelm, eyes blinking, sat watching the wall of the tent flap back
and forth. Me? A "fuckin' animal"? Jones is a little nuts from sitting
around these camps so long. Maybe it's all that meditating he does.
Wilhelm imagined sitting on his legs, palms up and forefingers touching his thumbs. "Forget it," he muttered, getting up. He shook the
snow off his shoulders and followed Jones.

Inside, the sergeant stood over a circle of men intent on a pair of rolling dice. When the little cubes stopped, some men moaned. Some
laughed and clapped their hands. Goldman, a big grin on his face, sat
before a pile of cigarettes, sugar cubes, and bits of bread. "Okay, yooz
guys! Make your bets!" He was shaking the dice in his fist when Jones
stepped into the circle.

"Awright, you guys! The game's over! There's no gamblin' 'round
here! Pick up your crap and move out!" He stared directly at Goldman.
"Yes, you! Clear out!"

Tic twisting his face, Goldman looked at Danzig, the unannounced
bouncer at all the small one's games. Danzig grinned and turned slowly
toward Jones. "C'mon, Sarge. We're just havin' a little fun here. We
ain't hurtin' nobody, least of all you."

Jones covered the dice with his foot. "I guess you don't hear good, *Corporal*." He continued to stare at Goldman. "I said take your shit game and

git the hell outta here!" A white cloud containing his words condensed above Goldman's head.

Lips pursed, Goldman unwound his legs and got up. "Well, shit," he said softly. "Okay, yooz guys, let's go down to Danzig's place." Jones moved his foot away, and the small soldier picked up the dice. "Your rank don't mean shit in a POW camp, *Sergeant!* We'll be back!"

Wilhelm stood behind Jones watching, trying to decide whether he agreed with Jones or not. He'd played nickel blackjack back at Fort Benning and usually won enough to buy a Coke at the PX. What was the big deal? Never mentioned that in his letters home, knowing how his mother felt about gambling.

Jones sighed, sat down, pulled off his boots, and assumed his favorite position. "They wanta lose their shit to that little crook, it's fine with me. But they ain't gonna do it 'round here." His eyelids went to half-mast and slowly, very slowly, he murmured, "Not as long as I'm here, they ain't."

A strange guy, Wilhelm thought, older than most of us and smarter, too. Wonder what he did before the war.

▼

# CHAPTER 15

# THE CASINO: TROUBLE

Around the middle of February, the skies south of Berlin, which lay some twenty miles north of *Lukenwalde*, cleared, and the *Appell* field behind the tents glistened like wet glass in the warm sun. Some of the prisoners, like the young men they were, took off their overcoats, hats, and gloves and threw snowballs at each other. But most just walked the slushy path around the compound, taking the air, talking about the war, the soup, the bread, and home—blessed home.

"D'you hear them guys down at the other end of the tent cussin' and goin' on about somethin' last night, Lum? One of 'em had his pants down scratchin' or maybe playin' with himself." Wilhelm and Lumley stood at the western fence, their favorite spot, looking toward home.

"No, Ah went to sleep soon's my head hit my boots." Lumley squinted at the muddy field before them. "Sure was good news this mornin', wudn't it? Our guys comin' across the Rhine and all. Wonder how fur they are by now." He sighed. "Wisht they was comin' cross that field out there. I'd join up with 'em quicker'n a gnat's eye."

"Yeah, well, I'd like to see 'em out there, as long as they didn't give me a rifle and 'spect me to get in the fight. I don't need anymore a that." Wilhelm sighed. "I hear the Rooskies do that, y'know? Join up and start shootin'." Wilhelm's head shook. "I just hope they know we're here and don't throw any a that heavy stuff at us. These damn tents...." Wilhelm swung around and stared. "These tents ain't much cover, that's for sure."

"Guy I was talkin' t'other day said he'd jump in the latrine, if artillery comes in." Lum chuckled. "Would you hit the shit with me, Will?"

"Depends on how deep it was." Wilhelm grinned. "And how much and what kinda artillery we're talkin' 'bout." His eyes followed a squadron of bombers across the sky. "I just hope our boys beat the Rooskies in here, that's all. I bet they blew hell outta IIIB after we left."

"Yeah, Ah do, too."

As they walked on down the west fence, Wilhelm's thoughts slipped back to the night before. "What do you s'pose that guy was doin', Lum, the one I saw last night?" Weehunt came to mind. "I hope that ain't some nut beatin' his meat in the middle a the night. Some guys're nuts that way, y'know? Don't think we're gettin' enough to eat to be doin' that. I sure as hell ain't."

"Maybe it was bugs bitin' 'im." Lum, embarrassed, looked away.

"Bugs! It's too damn cold for bugs. Ain't it?"

"Bugs? Who's got bugs?" Goldman shouted, his head jutting between the two men. "There's a buncha guys got lice down at Danny's bed, y'know. I seen 'em scratchin'."

Danzig, standing alongside Goldman, held some broken Red Cross boxes under his arm and a blanket roll in his hand. "Yeah, they got 'em awright. Them lice come down the tent like a wave. Been a lotta scratchin' down there."

Wilhelm's jaw dropped "We got lice in the tent? My God! My mom would…my God!" He looked away quickly. Men, real men, don't worry about what their moms would think, not out loud, anyway.

"Well, for crissake Wilhelm, it ain't no big deal. They itch the hell outta you, but big tough guys like you oughtta be able to handle that." Goldman chuckled. "Back in Jersey, lottsa kids had 'em. Teachers'd send you home if they caught you scratchin'. I used to get myself caught 'bout once a week so's I could go down to Joe's and shoot some pool." He laughed, looked at Danzig, and nodded. The big Hoosier hitched up his load of cardboard and, as if on some kind of mission, he and Goldman stepped off together.

"You know 'bout lice, Lum?"

"No, but Ah knowed kids that did. Hadta wash up real good to get rid of 'em. Ah know that."

"Well, we ain't gonna be 'washin' up' 'round here, that's for sure." Wilhelm massaged his hairy chin, as they walked on and turned along the back fence. Halfway down, Goldman and Danzig were laying these sheets of cardboard on the ground. The guard in the center tower leaned into his window, watching.

"Well, wonder what that's all about."

"God only knows, Will. God only knows."

"And why'd they carry that cardboard all the way around the compound, when they coulda walked straight across and…."

"Maybe Goldman wanted us to see it. You s'pose?" Eyebrows up, Lumley's head shook. "He's always up to somethin'."

When they arrived at the cardboard-covered patch of wet earth, Wilhelm placed his right forefinger across his upper lip and threw his left arm in the air. "Hey, Americanischa dogfaces! Dee terd Rike don't allow dee Fadderlandt up to be covered like dat!"

"Ahh, go screw yourself, Krauthead! Us Americans're goin' inta bidness out here, so fuck off. Yooz ain't got nuttin' to say 'bout it!" Squatting, Goldman unrolled the blankets, pulled a corner of one over the cardboard and piled snow on it. Across from him, Danzig did the same.

"Business, huh? You're startin' a game out here, ain't ya?"

"Right! But, yooz guys don't roll 'em, so yooz ain't got nuttin' to do wit' it."

"Okay, okay. We thought we might wanta make a little investment, but I guess if you don't want us in on it, well...you *do* know the war's gonna be over pretty soon, don't ya?"

"Yeah, yeah, we know, we know," Goldman sneered. "I'm just tired a takin' the same shit off the same ol' guys alla time, 'at's all."

"I" instead of "we," Wilhelm noticed. Poor Danzig. I ought to feel sorry for him, but somehow I can't seem to.

It was true that the indoor game had become a desultory thing in which only matches and bread were wagered. But now that Red Cross parcels had come in—the first, it was said, ever seen at IIIA. Goldman, ever shrewd, ever wanting, had decided the camp's gamblers were ripe for the picking.

That afternoon, Danzig's voice, bouncing off tents and pines alike, boomed across the *Appell* field. "Casino IIIA! Now open for business! Come one, come all! Come one, come all! Come on out and roll 'em! Come on! Come on!"

Goldman, on his knees at the tall man's feet, blew on the dice and tossed them against a large Red Cross box. "Seven! See? A seven! A seven!" He held the dice in the air and then threw them against the box, over and over. Prisoners gravitated, albeit slowly, toward the "casino," their eyes large.

A circle formed, the dice bounced and rolled, some men shouting and some groaning. Goldman, hands shaking, cheek twitching, collected and sequestered the house winnings in the cardboard "bank," while Danzig, magnificent in voice and stature, congratulated or consoled the winners and losers, simultaneously maintaining order. By time for afternoon *Appell*, a mixture of Lucky Strikes, Camels *and* Chesterfields, cans of Spam and "liver patty," and boxes of sugar cubes and D-bars filled the casino's bank. Goldman carried it, while Danzig hauled the cardboard rug inside. Both men barely made *Appell* in time to be counted.

After soup and bread, extended by Red Cross Spam and D-bar chocolate bars, jubilation reigned. In voices not heard since France, the men sang "I've Been Working on the Railroad," "Ninety-nine Bottles of Beer on the Wall," plus a mixture of venerable and brutally obscene marching songs. Suddenly, a short, dark-eyed, black-haired soldier stepped into the center aisle and began to dance, his hands high, fingers snapping. The crowd clapped and moved with his rhythmic dance.

"Ain't never seen a *man* dance by hisself like that, have you, Will?"

"No, but I think it's some kinda Greek thing he's doin'. Saw one like that in a movie once."

"That's Stavros," Jones said, standing behind Wilhelm. "Dance like that goes with his name."

Now, a short, swarthy corporal, his lips white with powdered milk (Red Cross Klim), joined Stavros and began to circle with him. "Oh, oh, that's Galapo. I been watchin' him," Jones said. "Dumb-ass has ate a whole can of Spam and poured a can a sardines on top of it. He won't last long."

"He's jus' hungry," Lumley mumbled. "Like the rest of us."

Several men jumped into the circle, the whole tent now clapping, shouting, stomping. Stavros' voice rose high above the chaos, other voices trying to follow. The tent seemed to swell and shift, as if preparing to rise up and float away, Wilhelm thought. Suddenly, a loud belch.

Galapo bent over and pulled out of the circle, a broad, green fountain spouting from his mouth. A gasp rose up, a roar of laughter following him through the front flap.

"Scoop it up and save it, Galapo!" someone hollered. "You can eat it again later!" another voice chipped in. "Better pick the straw out of it first!" somebody else yelled. The tent rocked with more laughter.

"I told you that fuckin' dago was brain dead." Jones, hardfaced, dropped back onto his blankets.

Wilhelm, along with many others, stared at Galapo's leavings steaming there in the aisle. Maybe they could be salvaged somehow, he thought. He knew better, but the thought lingered on, and on, and on.

$$* \qquad * \qquad * \qquad *$$

The following day, a cold rain followed by snow and a bone-chilling wind moved in. The casino moved inside and shrank to its original size, the owners' winnings shrinking to match. Tea and black bread in hand, Goldman, face positively glowing, came back to his blankets one morning after eating morning chow with Danzig in order to begin the game early. "Ain't seen much of yooz guys. We been 'spectin' yooz out at the game sometime."

Wilhelm noticed the "we." Danzig, he thought, must somehow have become a valued addendum to the enterprise. Wow and wow again!

"Stopped and watched some yes'dee." Lumley pursed his lips. "Cain't see losin' my dinner for half a chance a winnin' somethin' Ah don't need."

"Ahhh, you're nuts, you are." Goldman turned to Wilhelm. "Could win yourself a nice big D-bar, Will. Whyn't you c'mon out and try it?"

*Will?* This guy's starting to sound like some kinda salesman. "I'm like Lum, Goldie." He saw Goldman's cheek twitch. "I *eat* my Spam and *trade* my cigarettes. Don't need nothin' else, much."

Goldman scratched his crotch. "Too bad. I forgot neither one a yooz has any guts." Goldman looked over Wilhelm's shoulder at Jones snipping tin.

"Got any blowers for sale, there, Jones?"

The sergeant didn't look up. "Sold my last one. You can have this'n, though, soon's she's finished."

"How much?"

"Twelve packs. Luckies or Camels."

"Twelve packs! Shit, man, I'd make one myself 'fore I'd pay twelve packs!" Goldman sat motionless for a moment, waiting, apparently, to do some bargaining. Finally, he leaned in close. "Gone up a lot, ain't they? Since back at IIIB?"

"Some." Jones said, lips barely moving.

Behind his hand, Goldman whispered, "Cocksucker's trying to steal me blind 'cause he thinks I'm rich. Must be one of them goddam tee-totallin' Baptist holyrollers like lived down the street from me back home."

"Now just a damn minute there, Goldman! There ain't no *Baptist* holyrollers Ah ever heard of." Lumley glared.

Goldman chuckled. "Ha! Woke up the Bible-readin' good-ole-boy, there, didn't I? Don't get your balls in a uproar, Lumley. I didn't mean to...."

"Yeah, well, prices go up when there's a buncha *rich* gamblers like you around." Wilhelm's eyes narrowed. "Business man like you oughtta know that." He waited for the small soldier's response, but got none. "Tried to buy a D-bar yestidy, and the guy wanted *three* packs! Three fuckin' packs for a D-bar! Used to buy 'em for one!"

"Yeah, well, that's another reason yooz oughtta come out and roll 'em. Buy all the damn D-bars you want then!" Goldman snickered. "Had one m'self last night."

\*     \*     \*     \*

That afternoon, Wilhelm lay on his blankets, wondering if his folks had received the letter he wrote back at IIIB. Thinking about what Jones had said about the Buddhists, he suddenly realized the tent had gone very quiet. *Feldwebel* Kruger stood just inside the front flap, four guards, rifles up, standing behind him. Escort close behind, the stocky German stepped off down the aisle, his eyes sweeping the tent right and left. A burst of laughter from the far end of the tent brought a gold-toothed grin to the German's face. Goldman, unaware of the *Feldwebel's* approach, sat with his back to the aisle.

Kruger stopped and pointed down at the small American. "*Du! Komm mit mir!*" Two of the guards kicked their way into the surrounding blankets and stared down at Goldman.

Tic almost closing his left eye, Goldman swung around and found Kruger pointing at him.

"*Hier!*" Kruger shouted, jabbing at the ground. "*Komm hier!*"

Cursing softly, Goldman got up and stepped into the aisle. Kruger pointed at other men in the game. "*Du! Und du! Komm! Hier!*" Corporals Berger and Rosen got up and joined Goldman, while Danzig, his ethnicity disguised by blond hair and blue eyes, escaped the *Feldwebel's* finger. Coatless and hatless, the three Americans were herded down the aisle into the February afternoon.

"Good God, Lum. What's that sonofabitch doin' with those guys? Y'don't s'pose he's gonna...." Wilhelm imagined Kruger shouting, "Fire!" and a little man with a rope around his waist hauling the Jewish guys' bodies away.

"Cain't be nothin' good, thet's for sure," Lumley whispered. "Maybe, we oughtta go out and see where he's takin' 'em." Wilhelm was already pulling on his boots.

Blowing snow and a face-scouring wind met them when they stepped outside. The path around the compound and *Appell* field lay empty, the gray winter sky throwing snow against the tents. They went back inside and waited. Three hours passed before Goldman and his friends burst into the tent, wiping snow off their heads and shoulders. Eyes averted, they walked down the aisle and dropped onto their blankets.

"Well, I'll be damned! He acted like he didn't even know us! Has to get back to that fuckin' crap game, I guess." Wilhelm, annoyed but glad, lay back and covered himself. "He's nuts, you know that, Lum? Just plain nuts about them damn dice!"

Lumley looked up from his little red book. "Well, Ah 'spect he's feelin' kinda embarrassed, Will. Bein' called out like that and all. Jews been treated bad like that all through history, y'know. What my daddy says, anyway."

"Yeah, I s'pose, Lum. You're prob'bly right about that."

After *Appell* that evening, Goldman, soup and bread in hand, dropped onto his blankets next to Wilhelm and began to eat. Wilhelm said nothing, and Lumley did the same. Finished finger-licking their dixies, the three men sat, scratching and snuffling, avoiding each other's eyes.

Wilhelm's left hand, without his direction he later realized, wandered across to Goldman's shoulder. "Glad to see you're back in one piece, buddy." His voice was husky. Looking away, he waited. For what? A report? "C'mon, dammit, and tell us what that Kraut sonofabitch did do to you guys."

"Don't worry about it, Wilhelm," Goldman snarled. "It ain't got nuttin' to do wit' yooz. So fuggit it."

"Well, we thought maybe...."

"I said *fuggit it!* Drop it! Just drop it, dammit!"

Wilhelm sighed. "Okay, Goldman. That's the way you want it, that's way you get it." He lay back and closed his eyes. Lumley had already stretched out and covered himself.

Soon the rumor mill had the Jewish guys burying dead Russians, emptying Kraut latrines, or waiting on the Kraut officers hand and foot. The next time the Germans came and collected the Jewish boys, Wilhelm and Lumley were bundled up outside waiting for them. They watched Kruger march his detail down to tent #8 at the end of the row.

"So that's it," Wilhelm said. "They're cleanin' shit in the sick tent." He made a face. "Ain't any of 'em medics, are they, Lum?"

The redhead shrugged. "When they get back, ask Goldman 'bout it."

"*You* ask him." Wilhelm chewed a wad of imaginary gum for a moment. "I don' really give a damn what they do in there. Whatever it is, they could be in for a lot worse." He imitated Goldman's snarl: "I ain't got nuttin' to do wit' it. So t'hell wit' it."

Later, when the small soldier finished his evening chow, Lumley belled the cat. "So, what did y'all do down at the sick tent t'day, l'il buddy?"

Goldman's brows slammed together, the valley between them deep and dark. "Well, we didn't sit around playin' wit' our cocks all afternoon, like yooz guys did." He squinted maliciously at both men. "Tell you what, Lumley. You bein' a big fuckin' medic and alla-time Bible-reader, you'd be in Baptist heaven down there. I'll tell Kruger you're dyin' to join up wit us." He rolled over and pulled his coat over his head.

Next morning after tea, while Goldman played cards with Danzig, the investigators put on their coats and hats and, in spite of the huffing blizzard outside, hiked down to tent #8. The wan faces of some eighty men turned their way as they entered, some coughing, a few sneezing. The patients lay on straw-filled pallets under blue, POW-familiar German-issue blankets, the air, a colloidal suspension of dust mites and redolent of barnyard straw, disinfectant, and the odor of urine and feces.

"Hey, look at this!" Wilhelm shouted. "A little stove like the one we had in the Quonset hut back in England. Puts out about as much heat as a kitchen match." His face lit up. "And, hey, look! There's pillows on them empty beds down there! God, I'd give my eyeteeth for one of...wonder if...."

"Nah, Will, if Kruger sees you with a pillow, he'll have you workin' down here for sure."

"Yeah. Prob'bly would." Wilhelm shook his head sadly. "I bet he's wantin' those guys, the Jews I mean, to catch somethin' and die off."

"Well, he ain't doin' 'em any favors, that's for sure." Lumley stared at a man in a white coat sitting in the far corner. "Ain't *nobody* in here watchin' out for these guys, but that fella sittin' down there sleepin'." Shaking his head, he turned toward the entrance. "C'mon. Ah hate seein' these guys layin' here and not be able to do anythin' for 'em." Sad-faced, he and Wilhelm walked out of the tent.

A couple of days later, the two buddies were walking around the compound when Lumley suddenly piped up: "Hey, I just remembered, Will, yest'day Ah was talkin' to Rosen, one of the Jewish guys? One that goes down to tent #8? And...."

"Yeah, Lum, I know who Rosen is. What about 'im?" Lumley's slow, syrupy talk was getting on Wilhelm's nerves.

"Well, he says they don't always go to the sick tent."

"They don't?" Wilhelm's voice sounded unintentionally sharp.

"No, they don't." Lumley, having detected Wilhelm's mood, walked along for a while, watching the mud squeeze up around his boots. "Well," he squinted at Wilhelm, "they take 'em over to where the Rooskies live."

"Where the Rooskies live?" Wilhelm's eyes went wide. "Where's that? Did he say?"

"Says they're in another compound, in sorta like a dungeon with li'l bitty cells and the windows're way up high and the tar-paper roofs leak alla time and...." The redhead swallowed hard, coughed and wiped his mouth, almost unable to go on "and they sleep on li'l bitty boards, too, hardly wide enough for a child to lay on."

"I figgered they were prob'bly worse off than we are."

"The Jewish guys go over and empty the shit cans and swab the floors. Said the place stinks somethin' awful."

"Strickly against the Geneva Convention, y'know, Lum, making our guys work like that. Them Jewish guys are all corporals. They ain't s'posed to have to work." Wilhelm joined Lumley's study of mud on boots. "Just shows the Krauts hate the Jews even more'n the Rooskies. Hard to believe."

"Yeah." Lumley sighed. "It's awful the way these people over here hate each other. Ah jus' cain't understand it." He sighed again, long and deep. "Ah shore will be glad to git home."

∗     ∗     ∗     ∗

The weather had turned blustery, a little rain, a little snow, lots of wind, bad for the casino business. March had slipped into the American compound. Lumley slept or read his Bible. Goldman played cards and rolled dice in the mornings; he and his Jewish friends spent afternoons in tent #8 or the Russian compound. Wilhelm slept when he wasn't talking history or religion—things he knew little about—with Jones. He was amazed when the tall Tennessean mentioned entropy one day, connecting it to the slow disintegration of the canvas over their heads.

Suddenly, Sergeant Carter, the new tent boss, came in and, smiling big, announced that Red Cross parcels, *one whole box* per man, had just arrived! Spirits rose, bellies filled, and, as usual, some emptied themselves almost immediately.

Wilhelm came in from the latrine that evening shaking his head. "Must be a lotta Galopo's 'round here. Puke's so thick out there, I thought I was back in my Uncle Hoop's bar." He snickered, sat down, and pulled his Red Cross parcel on his lap. "Some guys don't have any damn sense at all, y'know that, Lum."

"It's hard to keep from eatin' when there's a box a goodies sittin' right there in front a ya."

"Yeah, sure it is. Makes me hungry, too. Don't it you?"

"Yeah, but even back home Ah was always hungry. Cain't tell much difference 'tween now and then." Lumley chuckled. "It's 'cause my stomach's all shrunk up now. Eatin' more stretches it out and makes me hungrier."

"Sounds right, Lum. Might be." Lum's brighter than I give him credit for, Wilhelm thought. Thinks a lot faster'n he talks. I oughtta listen better to what he says, even if it does take him all day to say it.

Day and night, now, British and American bombers and fighters filled the sky, their contrails crisscrossing above the camp. German planes were seldom seen. One clear night, the men stood along the double fence looking north. Berlin was burning. Tall flames reached for the sky. Every time an especially bright one stabbed the clouds, they hurrahed. It won't be long now, they told each other. It won't be long now.

Wilhelm watched, too, but the same old questions bugged him: Will there be artillery, tanks, and small-arms fire when they—They? Who? The Russians? The Americans?—get here? And what about the planes? Will they bomb *Luckenwalde*? *Limburg* all over again? It was scary, just thinking about it. Damned scary.

# CHAPTER 16

▼

# THE STORM

During evening *Appell* a few days later, a warm, wet wind buffeted the formation, and the sky turned the color of green peaches, dark, heavy clouds rumbling in the northwest. "That's a tornado sky, Will," Lumley whispered. "Ah've seen 'em back home. We're fixin' to have us a big blow. Ah can smell it."

"Yeah, I've seen skies like that over Indianapolis, too. Looks bad."

"We get us a tornado and we'll be sleepin' out here by the shithole for the doo-ray-shun."

Wilhelm had to laugh. "Yeah. Won't that be fun! Just what we need." *Appell* over, everybody, including the German officers, checked the sky and headed for shelter. Voices sounded weak and high-pitched in the tent that afternoon, the air warm and wet. As the wind picked up, the woods began to hum, limbs and pine needles bouncing off the tent, its sides snapping. As darkness fell, the hum rose to a constant moan, then a roar. Thunder rolled and lightning stung the darkness, on and off strobing the white faces of the men.

"God's takin' our pitcher," Lumley mumbled. "What my Momma allus says." The poles down the center aisle danced and whirled, the wind shaking the tent relentlessly.

Wilhelm rolled into the fetal position—his nightly favorite—pulled up his overcoat and closed his eyes. I'll just wait it out, he thought, just like back home when it stormed. Goldman disappeared under his overcoat, too, but Lumley, grinning, watched the poles. "That's God's music," he said above the storm.

A lightening flash illuminated Sergeant Carter, holding onto a pole in the aisle. "C'mon, you guys! We gotta get out and check the guy poles! See if we can shove some mud on the sides to hold 'em down! C'mon, let's go, let's go!" He turned, stopped and looked around. Only a few men, the perennial volunteers in every crowd, got up and joined him. Lumley shoved his Bible beneath his blankets, pulled on his field jacket, and joined the sergeant. Carter, cursing loudly, ran among the beds kicking and yanking at the men.

Wilhelm, feeling guilty, wriggled deeper into his nest. I will *not* get soaking wet and die in that stinking sick tent. I won't. I just won't, he told himself.

A whoosh and the far end of the tent rose up, guy ropes snapping, attached stakes whipping wildly. Blankets and Red Cross boxes came tumbling down the tent, their owners in hot pursuit, yelling and cursing. Chaos, obscene and loud, reigned until several men grabbed the canvas, pulled it down, and stood on it.

Wilhelm found Carter's cold eyes glaring down at him. He proceeded reluctantly to pull on his boots and field jacket. He grabbed a center pole next to Lumley and waited for the sergeant to finish his search for "volunteers." Sergeant Carter finally headed for the front flap, his workers close behind. Seeing the group disappear outside, Wilhelm hung on tightly to his pole, pulling it down hard against the ground. He would stay and make sure the pole did not fail.

A flash of lightening illuminated Jones sitting upright in the monk's pose—a strange sight in the middle of a thunderstorm. "Sergeant Jones!" Wilhelm shouted. "Hey, Sergeant!" The tall man's eyes fluttered open. "What do you think, Sergeant? Should I just sit back and let this pole go?" A dumb question. What should a Buddhist do in this situation?

Jones' flat face flared chalk-white in the next lightning flash. "Take it like it is, Jimmy." The high, thin voice cut through the rush of wind. "Roll with it. Have fun with it. It'll be over 'fore you know it. All is change, Jimmy. All is change."

Wilhelm, the pole slamming against his chest, smiled in disbelief. "Yeah, Sarge, I'm gonna roll, awright. Roll and hope!" Philosophy in the middle of a goddamn tornado! He's no better'n Goldman lying there rolled up in his blankets. "You just gonna sit there and let the tent take off, huh?"

"Nah! Tent comes down, we'll put 'er back up." He grinned. "Don't get all uptight, Jimmy. Storm'll be over 'fore you know it." Water had begun surging under the walls, Jones' blanket going wet beneath him. Slowly, as in a dream, he began to rummage through the leather pouch. He pulled out a wrinkled, black poncho, stuck his head through the center hole and, barefoot and bareheaded, bent under the side wall into the storm.

Wilhelm watched the water seep into his blankets and looked at the lump that was Goldman. I hope the little Jew-boy gets his ass soaking wet. He's such a goddam goldbrick. At least, I'm doin' my part! "Dammit, Goldman, get your ass outta there and grab one a these poles!"

"Help yourself, pal!" A voice squeezed from under the blanket. "Yooz don't need no little bitty guy like me hangin' on there."

The pounding of guy stakes into the ground could be heard, the rear of the tent now tight to the ground. Wilhelm's pole steadied a bit as the wind slowed. Rain, however, attacked the canvas with such force that tiny droplets appeared on the underside. "Just like a fuckin' pup tent," Wilhelm shouted. "Goddam Krauts don't have any better tents than we do." The inward flow of water was slowing now, invisible hands battening down the sides. The storm gradually abated, Wilhelm, feeling simultaneously proud and a little ashamed of himself, let go of the pole and went to his blankets: one wet and one dry. He sat down on the dry one and looked around. "God and the Devil have made up," he mused, "and the tent and the rest of us are still here. Not too damn bad. No sir, not bad at all."

The woods still hummed when sleet began to peck at the roof. Exhausted prisoners—the mud slingers and stake pounders, every one soaked to the skin—straggled in, some of their beds wet and some dry. They cursed the crowd of slackers, some of those answering with equal vehemence. "Maybe the Krauts'll get us some dry blankets in the mornin'," someone shouted. Silence and then a burst of laughter, the tension broken. The speaker, shouting and laughing, disappeared under a pile of men, pummeling him good-naturedly.

Lumley, wet clothes spread across his dry overcoat, lay asleep, naked beneath it. Wilhelm slid over against the big man, offering a bit of warmth. He saw Jones, pancho-less, slip silently under the side of the tent, strip naked, and roll into his wet blankets. The man seemed to fall asleep immediately.

$$*\qquad*\qquad*\qquad*$$

Morning. The sun bright, the golden light in the tent warming the eye, if not the blood. Blankets, coats, pants, and underwear, all had frozen stiff. All day, clothes stretched along guy-ropes, draped across the log seats around the latrine, their semi-naked owners inside the tents trying to stay warm. Even the warning wires along the fences, normally off limits, accommodated prisoners' clothing without incident.

"Heyyy, I can't believe this," Goldman said, shaking crumbs of bread into his soup. "No *Appell!* Bread and *barley* soup for breakfast! The bastids're goin' soft." He grinned and leaned in close. "Y'know, we coulda took off in that storm last night. They never woulda...." The looks on his friends' faces stopped him. "What's a matter wit' yooz guys?" The groove between his eyes deepened. "Oooh, I get it. Last night, huh? 'Cause I didn't go out and get soaked to the nuts wit' the resta them jerks!" He looked down toward Danzig's bed and licked his lips. "Well, well, ain't dat just too damn bad!" He jumped up. "Okay! Fuck yooz guys! I don't need yooz! There's other places I can sleep!"

"What's a matter, Goldman?" A little smile crept across Wilhelm's face. "You got some kinda problem?"

"Fuck you! Bot' a yooz. Jus' go to hell!" Goldman tipped up his dixie, drank the last of his soup and, resting on his knees, wadded up his damp blankets and gathered up his Red Cross box. He stood and looked down at Wilhelm and Lumley. "I'm leavin'—I'm goin' and..." He hesitated, "And yooz ain't gonna stop me." He waited for one of them to...to ask him to stay?

Wilhelm squinted up at the little man and grinned. "Go ahead, buddy. Ain't nobody gonna stop you." Voice weak and a little sad, he had wanted to sound tough.

Out in the aisle, Goldman hesitated again, looked back and marched off. Damn if he ain't as stiff as Kruger, Wilhelm thought, stiff as the damn Kraut he hates so much. Dixie wiped clean, he licked his forefinger clean. "Well, whattaya think a *that*, Lum? Our old buddy's done gone off and left us."

"Yeah. Ah give 'im a week. Him and Danzig ain't gonna get along that good. Livin' with Goldman ain't the same as rollin' dice with 'im." Lumley sniffed and picked up the overcoat he'd so wisely left inside the night before. "I'm purty well dried off, Will. Let's go take us a little walk. See how t'other tents made out. Ah need to get my blood movin'."

"Your blood oughtta still be movin' from last night, boy." Wilhelm chuckled. "You looked pretty pooped when you came in."

"Yeah, Ah was. But back home Ah used to play all four quarters, sometimes in rain heavier'n that. Course, I was getting' a little more to eat, then, but...."

"Yeah, I bet you were!" Wilhelm pulled on his overcoat. He looked down the aisle toward Danzig's hangout. Goldman, spreading his blankets, looked up just then. Their eyes met, but absolutely nothing passed between them. The end of an era, Wilhelm thought. What'll we do for fun now?

# CHAPTER 17

▼

# STORIES AND A BIRTHDAY

Finally, the temperature edged above freezing and the woods sang a softer tune. Moods rose and the men began to talk more about girls than about food and spend more time than before at the fences, looking and listening for guns. A crew of Russian prisoners came into the American compound, cleared the ditches, and tightened the guy stakes around the tents. The Americans marveled at their energy, sure that they, ragged and dirty as they were, must be eating better than themselves. By the middle of March, snowballs made of soft, mushy snow flew about the compound, and the ice melted from the "Geneva Convention" water tap. As evidenced by bloody cuts on some faces, some men attempted to shave.

Kruger and his backup came either to the tent or the casino every afternoon and collected Goldman and then his Jewish buddies. One day, Goldman finally stood up to the German, refusing to go. "I'm too busy," he shouted. "Can't you see all these guys here?" Kruger's bayonets quickly convinced him otherwise, and he was hustled off to work.

Several days later when Goldman, morning tea and bread in hand, stopped by his old haunts, Wilhelm and Lumley sat on their blankets, eating.

"Well, how yooz guys doin'? Ain't seen mucha yooz since we got the game goin' good." Goldman's face fairly glowed. "There ain't nuttin' to it, y'know. You can count to twelve, you can shoot craps. Whyn't yooz c'mon out?"

"Nah. Like I said before, I *eat* my Spam and *trade* my cigarettes. Just like Lum, here. I got no interest in rollin' dice."

Goldman twisted around, picked up Jones' bag of tools, took them out one by one and examined them. "Where's the old man this mornin'?" He held the tin snips up and smiled. "I bet you could cut your way outta this dump wit' these damn t'ings." He put the snips back, his grin widening. "Believe it or not, Jones was out at the game yestiday. Not playin', just watchin'. Got hisself pushed around by Kruger's boys when they come after me. Ole Jones has got one helluva temper, y'know that?"

Wilhelm stared as Goldman handled Jones' things. "You better not let him catch you playin' with his stuff, boy. You and him ain't zactly friends, y'know."

"Yeah, yeah, I know." One by one, Goldman put the tools back. "Sure is a nice buncha stuff he's got there. Don't s'pose there's much chance a him lettin' us use any of 'em." Chuckling, he got up and ambled off down the aisle.

"Well, what was that all about?"

"Just bein' friendly, Ah guess."

"Friendly? Goldman? Bein' friendly? You gotta be kiddin'." Wilhelm lay back and closed his eyes. "Sure he was."

\*     \*     \*     \*

A couple of days later, the small soldier came up the middle aisle with a blanket full of loot from the casino.

"Lookin' like Santa Claus there, Goldman," Lumley shouted. "Givin' some of your winnin's to the kiddies in town, are ya?"

"You're nuts, you know that, Lumley?" Goldman stopped in his tracks. "I'm goin' out and do some *tradin'*, buddy. Some *serious* tradin'." Standing, he could look down his nose at the redhead.

Wilhelm came up on one elbow. "You got yourself a guard that deals in broad daylight, Goldman? Could be dangerous, y'know."

"Nah. Nuttin like dat." Goldman came over and hunkered down between his old buddies. His eyes flashed around before he whispered, "See, me and Danzig has got us an idea. I go across the fence into the promised land, buy up a lot of stuff cheap, and t'row it back to him. He sells it here for more loot and then...." he chuckled. "Come on out and watch, if you don't believe me!" He shot up, jumped back into the aisle, stopped at the flap, and waved daintily.

"Well, wherever he's goin'," Wilhelm said, scratching his crotch, "I wish to hell he'd take these goddamn bugs with him."

"Yeah, me too!" Lumley, also scratching, laughed. "Me, too."

Walking down the double fence half an hour later, the two buddies found Goldman, blanket-sack in hand, standing next to Danzig across from the "Polock" compound. The guard between the fences got a nod from the tower guard, so he opened the wire door in front of Goldman. The little man, bag of cigarettes and cans of food across his back, stepped over the warning wire and hurried into the path between the fences. He handed the guard something and followed him down the path to a second door, now open, in the opposite fence. Goldman stepped quickly through it, bounded over the warning wire, waved to

Danzig, and took off across the open field. Puffing white clouds of breath, he disappeared into a one-story, concrete-block building.

Wilhelm stopped next to Danzig. "Well, I guess he wasn't kiddin' when he told us he was goin' over there."

"Nah. Goldman don't kid around when it comes to business." Danzig smiled and sat down in the mud to wait.

"So *that's* his promised land." Wilhelm looked around at Lumley. "Wonder what the Polacks got that we ain't got over here."

"Prob'ly not much. But he thinks he can buy whatever it is cheaper than here. Li'l bugger's got the guts of a wild dawg."

Wilhelm, remembering Christmas Eve when "the li'l bugger" climbed out of the boxcar and opened the door, chuckled softly. "Wonder what them Polacks'll do when he walks in there with that bag a stuff on his back. Li'ble to take it away from 'im and beat hell outta him. Couldn't call the cops, could he?"

They walked on around the compound, looking often at the empty Polock compound. Each time they passed Danzig, waiting there for his itinerant partner, they nodded and kept going. An hour later...what was going on over there? And how much would the guards extract from the little man's take when he came back? They finally stopped and waited with Danzig.

"Hey, there he is!" Danzig, clapping his hands, jumped up. "Look! The bag's so full, he's draggin' it! Woweeee!" The man in the tower shouted, and the guard between the fences went to the far door.

Goldman, puffing, stopped at the warning wire on the other side. "These damn Polocks're some tough sonsabitches, let me tell ya! Argue like a buncha fuckin' Ay-rabs. Talk funny, too." He dumped some cans, bottles of something white, raw vegetables, and cigarettes on the ground. "Okay! Stand back and I'll t'row it over!" The half-empty blanket, its corners securely tied, flew up and over the double fence into Danzig's arms. He dumped it on the ground and threw it back.

"Awright! Good! I'll bring the rest a the stuff over with me." Goldman, the sack now on his shoulder, stepped over the warning wire with the demeanor of a "member" of some through-the-fences private club and joined the guard between the fences. He grinned big and handed the guard a half a dozen packages of cigarettes, the joy of wealth on his face. He trotted down the path, popped through the American-side wire door and leapt over the warning wire into the American compound. He hugged Danzig and shook hands with Wilhelm and Lumley, laughing as if he'd just made a million dollars. When the casino opened that afternoon, a store offering "fresh" vegetables, cow's milk, beets, and "Polock" bread opened next to it. Business boomed.

After evening soup, Wilhelm lay on his blankets scratching his belly. "Dammit, Lum, we shoulda thought a that ourselves. Goin' over there and selling some of our stuff like Goldman did."

Lumley shook his head. "We jus' ain't got 'em, Will. And that ain't the half of it, neither, we ain't never gonna git 'em."

"Get what?"

"Guts, boy! Guts! Like that hungry dawg I keep tellin' you about. You know!" Lumley laughed and slapped Wilhelm on the shoulder.

*      *      *      *

A couple of mornings later, the two buddies sat smiling at a dirty joke one of the men on an adjacent bed had just told. "I heard that one back high school. Do guys down in Jawja tell them kinda jokes, Lum?"

"Yeah, sure. Always' 'joyed 'em, m'self." Lumley stopped and studied the canvas overhead. "I 'specially liked the one about the...." Wilhelm had lain back and closed his eyes. "Hey, Will," he leaned in close and whispered, "you ever *had* a girl?"

Wilhelm's eyes popped open. "Had a girl?" He sat up. A little smile formed on his lips. "You mean *really had*...one?" He squinted as if trying to remember. "Well, no, I guess I ain't." It's okay, he thought, Lum won't tell anybody I'm a virgin.

Lumley's eyes flashed around, his face going almost as red as his beard. "Well, if you wanta hear it, Ah got a story Ah could tell."

"You mean a *real* story about...?"

Lumley nodded. "Yeah. Me and my girl did it at the spring dance jus' before Ah joined up. She was wearin' one a them fancy formal dresses, too."

Wilhelm, head tilted, squinted skeptically at the big man. "Kinda tricky, wasn't it? With that big dress, and all? Wasn't it?"

"Well, yeah, it was. But a course, we didn't do it on the *dance* floor. It wasn't like that."

"Well, hell, Lum, I didn't think you did." Wilhelm smiled up at the canvas, his thoughts going back to Ray's drugstore and the Coke delivery he'd made one time. "Come to think about it, Lum, I came mighty close once, but...no, you go ahead. I'll tell you about it some other time. The war ain't gonna be over right quick."

"Now, one thing you gotta understand is, none a this was *my* doin'. It was *all* Marylou's." Lumley's eyes dropped to his crotch. "You know's well's Ah do, they's times when a man cain't he'p himself, and, well, see, we was at this country club dance, where the guys buy the girls a corsage and git to stick 'em on their chests? You know."

"Can't say I ever been to one, but that's okay. I know what you mean."

"Well, that's too bad, buddy. They're lotsa fun. My dad's a member of the club, so we go ever' year." It was clear from the warm glow on Lumley's face that the band was playing and Marylou was already in his arms. "It was one a them hot Jawga nights and we both got het up purty good dancin', so we went out by the lake to cool off. Well, 'steada coolin' off, we got het up even worse. We was kissin' and smoochin' to beat the band. Well, before Ah knowed what was goin' on, Marylou spreads out that big ole dress of hers and sets herse'f right down on my lap. Her hot lips stick in my ear and whisper, 'Honey, ah've gone off and lef' my panties at home. Jus' for you, Honey. So you could....' Ah swear, ah'll never forget them words 'slong as Ah live!" The redhead took a deep breath. And so did Wilhelm.

"So, you did it right there by the lake? You put it in her right then?" Wilhelm licked his lips and moved in closer. "Hell, boy, *she* had you, you didn't have *her!*"

Lumley leaned back and laughed straight up so hard the men all around grinned. He stopped, straightened himself and went on. "Ah still don't know how Ah did it, but, well, Will, Ah ain't never felt *nothin'* like it! Not in my *whole* life!" He took a deep breath.

"Awright, c'mon, Lum, there ain't nobody listenin' but me." Wilhelm scooted even closer. "What d'you do then?"

"Well," little drops of perspiration stood on Lumley's forehead. "We was just getting' into it real good," he giggled, "when we heard the band stop playin' back inside. So we knowed what was comin'."

Wilhelm frowned. "What?"

"Intermission. The crowd allus goes out to the lake to cool off and...." Lumley wiped his forehead on his sleeve—"we knowed we oughtta stop, but we couldn't, we jus' couldn't." He shook his head. "She stopped movin' and jus' sat there on my lap real quiet like and Ah held still tight as a drum and, well, my heart was athumpin' so hard, Ah was 'fraid Marylou'd bounce right off my belly."

Wilhelm snickered, then laughed straight up. "Damn if that girl a yours don't have her nerve, stayin' up on you like that." The men around them smiled at them again.

"Yeah, she sure does. She's a good 'un, she is. So, purty soon folks came mosyin' by, and we just nodded and said 'Hey' to 'em like always. Some of 'em looked at us a li'l funny, but most didn't pay us no mind a tall." Lumley sighed deeply. "Then her momma and daddy come along. A course, her momma stopped and looked and went all white and Ah thought, for sure, she was gonna be sick. Ah was worrin' how Ah wouldn't be able to get up and he'p her and Marylou's daddy would be mad and wouldn't let me see her any more. Ah cain't believe, now, that Ah was thinkin' about *that* and not what we was *doin'!*" Chuckling, he shook his head.

An image of Cindy, Wilhelm's old girlfriend, sitting on *his* lap with her dress all spread out rose in his mind. Why didn't *I* think of that on the porch that night? We'd have had it made! "So, did she faint, or what?"

"No, she just drew herself up stiff-like and stared. She's a tall, thin woman, anyway. Looks sorta like a big white stick—more like a sword that night." Lips pursed, Lumley stared up at the canvas again. "So Marylou pipes up and says, "Hey, Momma. Hey, Daddy. Enjoyin' the dance?" I tell you, Will, that little gal's got more damn gumption than Ah don't know what. She rode me through that storm 'thout a slip or a slop."

"Or underpants!" Wilhelm shouted. They laughed and fell into each other's arms. Men all around, still smiling, shook their heads.

"So what happened then?"

"Well, her folks moved on and the band started playin' again and the crowd left. But not her momma, she…."

"That's a helluva story, you got there, Lumley!" Jones thrust his head between the two boys. "'Specially for a Bible-readin' fella like yourself."

"Uhh, yessir, I guess it is at that." Lumley smiled sheepishly.

"Don't 'Sir' me, soldier. I ain't no officer." Jones' eyes went narrow. "What I was gettin' at, boy, was you fuckin' your girlfriend like that. And right in front a her folks, too."

Lumley, eyes batting in the smoke from Jones' burning words, frowned and reared back.

Head canted, Jones moved in closer. "Don't seem like it matches up with all that Bible-readin' a yours does it, Red? Ever come into that big fuckin' head a yourn that them two things don't match up?"

Lumley looked at Wilhelm for help, but got only a slow smile. "Well, Ah guess Ah never thought 'bout it like that, Sergeant. Don't really see how it...."

"Yeah, that's just it, Lumley. You don't *really see* anything. You think all you gotta do is read your little red book and pray real good and God'll forgive you for fuckin' your girlfriend any time you want. Right?"

Lumley took a deep breath and his face darkened. "No, Sergeant, that *ain't* it!" He hesitated. "But...."

"But?" Jones' eyebrows rose, his head canting even further. "Tell me, Lumley, whaddya read about in that Good Book a yours. What's your favorite part?"

Lips pursed, Lumley stared down at the blankets and shifted his bottom. "Nothin' special, Sergeant. Mostly the Gospels and, well, Ah been readin' a lotta Job since we got caught."

"Oh, so this here's a test! God's testin' you, is he?" Jones chuckled. "Well, tell me, what about Hayzoos—that's what the Mexicans call 'im, y'know—what about him bein' the Son of God and his mother bein' a virgin? You believe alla that?"

"Well, sure, Sergeant. Sure Ah *believe* it!"

Jones leaned back, his face split with a wide grin. "So how 'bout the Big Man up in the sky? The one that answers alla them prayers you're always sendin' up? You believe he can save people from goin' to hell and so on?"

"Yessir, Ah do!"

"You *also* believe the world is flat, and the sun drops over the edge of it ever' night and somehow comes up on the other side next day? Like Hayzoos and his buddies did in the good ole days?"

Lumley's face almost glowed with the strength of his beliefs. "No, Sergeant, Ah don't b'lieve all that, but...."

"Hey, Lum, I think it's time for us to take our walk." Wilhelm had put his boots on and was up pulling on his overcoat. Head shaking, he looked down at Jones. "I don't think it's any of your business what Lum believes, Sergeant. It's *his* business, and he don't owe you nothin' about it."

"Ohh, c'mon, Jimmy," Jones smiled contemptuously. "You're smarter'n that! You don't go along with Big Red, here, do you? You don't believe in Hayzoos and all that crap. Do you?"

Wilhelm stared, his mouth a tight line. "I ain't decided yet. Like my dad always says, that's private and nobody's business but mine."

"Your *dad* always says! Shit, boy, when're you gonna grow up and start sayin' what *you* say? Tellin' people what *you* believe?"

"C'mon, Lum, let's go. It's gettin' stuffy as hell in here. I need some air." He led his buddy out of the tent.

Halfway to their favorite spot at the western fence, Wilhelm stopped and studied his friend. "I'm sorry, Lum. I had about enough of Jones and alla his shit in there. I hope I didn't...."

"It's okay, Will. It's okay. Ah was gettin' kinda tired of it m'self." Lumley's head was shaking. "Allus did hate arguin' with older guys."

They stood at the warning wire looking west at the trees across the field, both thinking about what had and what had *not* been said just now. "Y'know, Will, I was really s'prised when you got up and told Jones off, like that. Ah thought you and him was...."

Wilhelm chuckled. "I was, too. Don't ever remember using that tone of voice with a sergeant." He was thinking of his dad. "He hit me just right, I guess. It just popped out."

A few quiet moments passed. "I guess I oughtta start thinkin' more 'bout what I *do* believe." Lumley looked up at the dark, scudding clouds. "It was bad wrong of me and Marylou to do what we did, but—" he hesitated. "Hell, Ah'd prob'ly do it again right now, if Ah could." Their eyes met and they laughed and punched and slapped each other around like a couple of schoolboys.

∗    ∗    ∗    ∗

Three uneventful days later, Wilhelm and Lumley sat, after morning *Appell* and tea, picking the latest crop of lice eggs from their shorts. "Hey, Will, ole buddy, ole pal," Lumley smiled broadly. "Remember you said you had a story 'bout how you and your girl one time...."

"Well, c'mon, Lum, you never even finished your story. You gotta finish it before I...."

"Well, there ain't nothin' much more to tell, Will. Her momma stared real hard and went on inside. That's all there was to it."

"Well, did you, you know, finish it off?"

"Wasn't nothin' to do but finish if it off after all that." Lumley grinned sheepishly.

Wilhelm giggled. "Well, I guess you know by now you're prob'ly gonna be a Poppa." Wilhelm was trying to imagine big old Lum as a father.

"Nah. I ain't. Heard from Marylou back in England and ever'thing was awright." Lumley grinned. He settled himself on one elbow.

"C'mon, Will, tell me about your girl. Ah hate t'think my best buddy's still a virgin."

"I never said I was…or I wasn't." He couldn't bring himself to say it.

Lum frowned. "Well, c'mon, then. Fess up. Ah told you mine, now you gotta tell me your'n."

Wilhelm felt as if he were back in high school listening to stories the guys were telling about what they'd "got away with" on dates. He took a deep breath and dived in. "Awright. But you'll be sorry. It ain't near as…." Lum's dark frown intimidated him. "Okay, okay. See, my Uncle Ray owns this drugstore where I worked jerkin' sodas and deliverin' stuff on my bike the summer before I joined up. Well, one day, I noticed Ray and Seamon, the pharmacist that worked there, and Ole Cap, Ray's dad, sittin' around the marble-topped table in back whisperin' about somethin'. They always whispered when they didn't want me to hear, so I slid down, and pretty soon I heard 'bawdyhouse' and '128 Flagler.' Well, I thought, I gotta look into this."

"A whorehouse, huh, right there in the neighborhood? Don't think there was ever one in Tallapoosa. No, wait." Lumley's thinking finger rose up. "Yeah, there was, too. Ole Essie's place. Coach allus took us there when we won our games. But Ah don't think that was really a…." He realized something had slipped out. "Four-quarters-Red-Lumley," the 1941 All Conference Tackle, blushed and looked down at his crotch.

"Well, shame on your coach, Lum. And shame on you, too." Snickering softly, Wilhelm continued. "So, as I was gonna say, next day when Seamon told me to take some Cokes down to number 128, I couldn't help but smile. He knew right away that I knew about the whorehouse." The tobacco-stained teeth, fat, bald head and pink cheeks of the small druggist rose in Wilhelm's mind. "Seamon drew himself up big as he could—he was a sergeant in WWI, that's what he said, anyway—and told me I was *absolutely not* to go inside #128! To stay outside till I got my money and then get back to the store toot sweet. Always said 'toot sweet' with a French accent to prove he'd been there. He was serious, awright. *Real* serious!"

Grin splitting his face, Lumley scooted in closer.

"I was excited ridin' down there. Hell, I'd never even seen a naked girl, and, a course I didn't think I'd see one just takin' Cokes to 'em, but...."

"But you were hopin'. Right?" Lumley's eyes glowed.

"Well," annoyed by the interruption, Wilhelm continued, "when I rolled the bike up the driveway at 128, the whole place was lit up like a damn carnival, like the ones at the fair grounds ever' summer. Anyway, I went up on the porch with my hands full of Cokes and kicked the screen door real hard. Well, pretty soon a cute little blonde appeared behind the screen and damn if I couldn't see right through her shirt. And she was wearin' the shortest damn dress I ever saw in my life." She seemed to be standing on his blanket right there in front of him.

Lumley laughed. "So, you dropped the Cokes and run like hell!"

"Nooo, hell, no, Lum! I was petrified. Those little pink nipples winkin' at me like that, I couldn't a run six feet! Honest to God, Lum, they winked at me! They really did!" Still staring into the distance, he sighed. "You ever been shocked, Lum? By electricity, I mean?"

"Yeah. I got onto a old shorted-out lamp one time. 'Bout knocked me on my butt."

"Well, that's what it felt like. Like grabbin' a bare electric wire. She laughed and said to bring the Cokes on inside and she'd get me my money. Well, I opened my mouth to say no, but before I knew it my feet had carried me right in the door. My damn feet did it.

Lumley laughed again. "Your feet, huh? I heard a lotta 'scuses in my time, Will, but I ain't never heard that one before."

"It's true, Lum. It's the God's truth." Wilhelm's face went a rosy pink. "I remember it was kinda hazy in there, but I could see some more girls wearin' them short dresses and see-through shirts sittin' on a couch in there. Some kinda uniform, maybe."

"Uniform?" Lumley snickered. "Ah doubt that, Will. They didn't have no uniforms on at Essie's back home."

Wilhelm seemed not to hear. He kept looking off across the tent. "Well, I stood there waitin', smilin' at the girls while Cloe (that was her name, she said) was gone. I was getting' edgy about bein' in there, but, enjoyin' the view so much, I didn't let it bug me. When Cloe came back, she said we'd have to go upstairs to get the money from Marge, the boss, and to come on with her. Well, Seamon's fat, red face jumped up sayin' 'Don't you dare go up those stairs,' but my feet took over again and I followed Cloe over to the stairs."

Lumley guffawed. "Your feet again, huh? Them damn feet a your'n knew what they were doin', that's for sure!"

"Yeah, I thought about it, but once I got to watchin' Cloe's twitchin' butt goin' up them stairs, I couldn't stop 'em."

"We git back, you gotta git 'them feet a yourn checked out by a doctor, or somebody. You don't, they're gonna git you in some *bad* trouble one a these days."

"Yeah, well, they ain't had a lotta chance since I been in the army. Hardly ever had a pass into town." Wilhelm leaned back, thinking. "So, anyway, when we got upstairs, Cloe put her ear up to a closed door and listened. Said Marge was busy in there and we could wait for her down the hall. Well, by that time, I was gettin' pretty nervous. Cloe was smart, Lum, real smart. She had me down the hall to another room before I knew what was happenin'. *Her* room, she said."

"Ah understand, Will," Lumley murmured. "In a sitchiation like that, a man's body does everwhat it wants, and he ain't got nothin' to say 'bout it." Nodding, he smiled softly.

But Wilhelm was frowning. He didn't like not being in control, but, looking back, he knew he really wasn't. "I remember there was a big window at the end of the hall. As I looked out, two guys were walkin' by, smilin' up at the window. That's when it hit me: I was in a *whorehouse!* What would Mom think? And Dad! But, before I knew where I was, I had a naked girl sittin' next to me on her bed."

"Happy birthday, buddy! Happy birthday!" the shout broke across Wilhelm's thoughts like a sledgehammer. "April Fool's Day, buddy! Your birthday! Ain't it?" Goldman's scruffy grin hung directly above Wilhelm, his arms holding a Red Cross box tight against his belly. "Ain't that what you told that Kraut when we checked in? April first? April Fool's day?"

Wilhelm, jaw slack, blinked and looked up. "Uhh, yeah, sure, but." He squinted. "Is this the first?" A strained laugh, then: "Gosh, Goldman, hows come you remembered?"

"Oh, I don't know. Rain's got the casino closed and we was lookin' at the calendar and saw it was April Fool's Day, your goofy birthday, so here we are." Goldman looked around at Danzig. "We mashed up some crackers and Klim and sugar together and made you a *Stalag* pudding." Chest swelling beneath his field jacket, Goldman laid the box gently in Wilhelm's lap. "Happy birthday, Will! How the hell old are you, anyway?"

"Well, let's see, born in '25, so I guess I'm about twenty years old." Wilhelm smiled. "And damn glad to make it, too!" The dense tan solid in the box reminded him of his mother's brownies. "God, Goldman, it's so big! I saw a one a these back at IIIB once, but it wasn't near this big. Golly!" Golly: a throwback to my civilian days. Haven't said that in a long time. He put the box aside and pulled up his shorts and pants. A thought clouded his mind: Is this some kind of trick? Do these guys *want* something, want me to *hide* something, a rifle, a grenade, or…oh, no, not another *radio!*

Danzig, a quart of white liquid in his hand, stepped in, picked up Wilhelm's dixie, and poured it half full. "That's real cow's milk, buddy, but that ain't all we got for you." A purple-gray sphere the size of a bowling ball dropped into Wilhelm's lap. "A present from the Polock compound."

"What…what the hell is this?" As he hefted the ball, Wilhelm noticed Danzig's use of "we" and "buddy."

"It's a beet. Oughtta be good eatin'."

"Well, thanks, guys." Wilhelm, still a little suspicious, couldn't believe this was happening. "This stuff musta cost you a whole *carton* of cigarettes!" He drank deeply of the milk, a little warm and a little sour, but he licked his lips and expelled a long "Ahhhh." Warmed by all this special treatment, by the "love of his fellow men," he pulled his dad's knife from the straw beneath his blankets and held it up. "Ta! Da!" They all reared back.

"God damn, Wilhelm! Where'd you get that?" Goldman immediately reached for the knife. "How'd you get it t'ru duh search? You know, when we was captured?"

"Had it down in my leggin'. Remember? I had wet pants and that Kraut didn't wanta reach in there." Wilhelm grinned. "You guys thought I peed myself 'cause I was scared, but actually I was just protectin' this here knife." They all laughed.

"Yeah, sure you was." Goldman couldn't take his eyes off the knife. "Boy, she's a real beauty, ain't she! Whaddaya want for it? I'll buy it from you right now!" He took the knife blade between thumb and forefinger, pulled it away, flipped it over and swished it around. "God, Wilhelm, I *love* it. C'mon, buddy, sell it to me. I *gotta* have this thing!"

Wilhelm grinned. "No. It's my dad's. I can't sell it to you!" Feeling a little beholden to Goldman for the presents, he wished now he hadn't shown the knife. "Dad had it in the Marines. He had it a long time. I couldn't possibly sell it."

Goldman scowled. "Christ, boy, I'd a known you had this thing, we coulda cut our way outta here a long time ago."

Smiling thinly, Wilhelm took the knife and, frowning menacingly, said, "So, pal, it's a damn good thing you ain't tried to give me a hard time lately."

Goldman threw up his hands and looked scared. Everybody laughed.

Wilhelm sliced his big tan present into four pieces and handed them out. Face aglow, chewing the sweet, crusty "pudding," he wished he could express his joy, his gratitude to Goldman, the bitchiest, crabbiest human being he'd ever met. The flashing candles on the big three-layer chocolate birthday cake his mother always baked came to mind. Dismissing the phantom, he murmured, "This is the best damn birthday party I ever had, you guys! I'll never forget it! Or you guys, either!" He coughed and blinked away the tears welling up.

# CHAPTER 18

▼

# SHOOTING AND HATING

"Well, I'll be damned!" Wilhelm shook his head sadly. "I knew he wasn't too healthy, Lum, but I didn't think he was that sick."

"Wonder who's the Vice President?"

"Well, whoever it is, he's president now. Never paid much attention to politics back home. Dad always says all politicians are crooks." Wilhelm lay back and closed his eyes. Jones' words: "Say what *you* think, boy, not what *your dad* thinks," crossed his mind. "I just hope he keeps things goin' over here. I'm ready to get the hell outta this damn place."

"Ah saw him oncet, President Roosevelt. My daddy took us over to Warm Springs one time, and we saw 'im drive by in that little flivver car a his, jus' a-smilin' and a-wavin' like a reg'lar fella. Had a big ole cigarette holder in his mouth. Looked just like his pitcher in the paper. Grand, he was. Looked like a king."

"Golly"—there it is again—"musta been nice to see the actual President. Went there for some kinda treatments, didn't he? Had polio when he was a kid, I think."

"Yeah. Took the waters at Warm Springs for that, papers said. Not but a little piece from Talapoosa, y'know. Y'all come see us sometime, we'll ride over there. Ah'd like to see the place again, m'se'f."

"Take you up on that sometime, Lum." If we ever make it home, that is, he thought.

Walking around the compound that afternoon, they found Danzig at the corner watching Goldman swagger down the path between the fences again, a blanket of goodies slung across his shoulder. He stepped over the warning wire into the Polack compound, smiled, and held up both thumbs.

"Wonder how come the big guy stays here, and the little guy goes over and takes all the chances. Why is that, Lum?" Wilhelm looked sideways at the big redhead.

Lumley grinned, turned, and walked on.

As they came around again, they saw Kruger go up the ladder into the guard tower next to the Polock compound. "Wait a minute, Lum, let's...." Wilhelm stopped and cupped an ear. He could hear quick, guttural German passing between the *Feldwebel* and the tower guard. "Bugger's mad about somethin'. But I can't tell what."

"Prob'bly wants part of the guard's take from Goldman's crossin' over." Lumley stood looking through the fence. "Maybe we oughtta tell Danzig Kruger's up there now and...."

"No, Lum, let's stay out of it." Wilhelm turned and moved on.

Next time around, Goldman stood grinning on the Polock side of the fence, a half-full bag on the ground next to him. He picked it up and heaved it across to Danzig, then called the guard to let him in. As Goldman started down the path, the guard stayed back, his eyes on the guard in the tower. The German up there lifted his rifle and took aim.

"Goldman! Goldman! Watch out! Kruger's up in the...."

The shot erased Wilhelm's last words, reverberating again and again off the woods and the Polock barracks. Goldman jerked, grabbed his thigh and went down. Two more rounds spurted mud in the small soldier's face as he lay screaming. Kruger, silhouetted alongside the tower guard, grinned down at the American, gold tooth glinting in the western sun. A broad guttural laugh cut the air. A fourth shot fired from his black heart.

"Why, you dirty sonofabitch!" Wilhelm shouted, waving his fist in the air.

Lumley jumped the warning wire and slammed through the fence door. He ran down the path, lifted Goldman into his arms and, in seconds, had the wounded man back in the American compound. Wilhelm helped place Goldman on the ground and helped Lumley tear his pants leg open. Danzig rushed over and stood by, watching.

Goldman cursed and squirmed, his leg held high in the air, hands squeezing his thigh. "C'mon, put your leg down," the redheaded medic shouted. "Ah gotta see what kinda trouble you got in there." The hole in Goldman's hamstring bled profusely. Lumley pressed on the femoral artery and felt the thigh up and down. "Ain't no bones broke, anyway. We git the bleedin' stopped, you'll be awright. You're a lucky man."

"Lucky! You call gettin' shot in the ass lucky?" Goldman's whole body twisted. "Always said you was nuts, Lumley. Nuttier'n a goddam…."

"Does it hurt bad, buddy?" Danzig, face twisted in mock pain, squatted down next to Lumley.

"No, you dumb shit-Hoosier, it don't hurt at all! Just feels great!" Goldman stopped rolling his head back and looked up at Wilhelm. "That sumbitchin' Kruger was up there, wasn't he?"

"Yeah, he was up there, all right. But don't sweat it, buddy. We'll see about him later." Wilhelm heard himself say "we." A voice in his head said almost simultaneously, 'Jimmy, you stay out of it! I mean it!'

Lumley looked around at tent #8. "Let's take him inside there and git him a bed." A grim-faced German with a white band on his arm had come out of #8 and was standing over the wounded man. "*Ya.* Ve take him inzide. Here." He held a heavy wool strip out to Lumley, who tied it above the wound and twisted it tight. Wilhelm thought the little man's scream probably reached the outskirts of Berlin. Lumley, Danzig, and some of the men who had gathered around carried Goldman into the sick tent. Wilhelm, remembering the stench and the dreams he'd had of lying in there himself, waited outside. He stood, legs apart, and stared up at the tower guard. Wonder what that Kraut's thinking after shooting down an unarmed man like that. Orders from Kruger, I bet. Wonder he didn't shoot Lum, too, the bastard. Wilhelm sighed. But then, maybe he's just like the rest of us, wishing this stinking war was over so he could go home. If he still has one.

Lumley came out, rubbing his hands together. "If the little bugger ever shuts up, the bleedin'll stop and he'll be okay. Knowin' him, he'll be back in #3 bitchin' his head off in a couple a days."

"What do you think, Lum?" Wilhelm frowned. "Did Kruger get him shot just 'cause he's a Jew?"

"Prob'bly. Cain't think a no other reason, can you?"

"Well, I guess he was askin' for it, goin' through the fence like that." Wilhelm sighed. "From what I've heard, bein' Jewish over here ain't never been a bed a roses." Wilhelm watched the mud squeegee from under his boots as they walked back toward #3. "My grandpaw runs the Jews down all the time. He came to the States about 1890, I think. As a kid, I never understood why he said the Jews were so bad. I went to school with Jewish kids every day and never saw anything wrong with 'em."

"Yeah, well, the Baptists back home don't think too much of 'em, neither." Lumley shook his head. "Y'know, t'other day, when that Kraut was carryin' the Jewish guys off, it come to me what my daddy said one time. Said the Jews was prob'bly the next step up the tree."

Wilhelm's brows jumped. "Tree? What tree?"

"You know, the *evolution* tree."

Wilhelm chuckled. "Hell, Lum, I didn't think you-all Christians believed in evolution. Let alone an evolution *tree*."

"Well, we don't when we're in church, but, see, my daddy went to medical school up north, and he says all of 'em up there believe in it."

"Really!" Wilhelm stopped and turned to his friend. "So what's that got to do with the Jews?"

"Well, Daddy says they's so many of 'em that's smart, you know, good at business, and music and math and science—like Einstein, you know, and stuff like that. That's why he thinks maybe the Jews're on the next branch up."

"Well, I never heard anything like *that* before! My Grandpaw'd dirty his pants if he heard you say that!" Eyes bright, Wilhelm snickered. "And so when the rest of us catch up with 'em, we'll all be short and have ugly noses like Goldman?" Wilhelm guffawed and slapped Lumley on the back. They walked on, thinking, watching their feet in the mud. "Oh, yeah! Lum! I almost forgot."

"Yeah? What?"

"I just wanted to say that was a helluva chance you took runnin' in there and haulin' Goldman out like that. That guard coulda dropped you right on top of 'im."

"Awww, hell, that warn't no big thing. Back at Bennin' they told us the Krauts don't shoot medics."

Wilhelm's eyes went wide. "Well, shit, Lum, that guard didn't know you were a medic! Besides, there's plenty a medics been shot dead over here."

Lumley shrugged. "Well, it's all over and Ah ain't shot. Not yet, anyway." He smiled and looked hard at Wilhelm. "But Ah 'preciate the thought, Will. Ah really do." He swallowed hard. "C'mon, buddy, let's git along. Soup'll be comin' in purty soon."

✳    ✳    ✳    ✳

Three days later, a limping, snarling Goldman stumbled into tent #3, his wound oozing, his face twisted in pain. Between vows to "take care of Kruger, some way, some how," he plopped down next to Wilhelm and moaned how dumb "that fuckin' Kraut doctor was" and how he'd be getting "the hole in his leg" cleaned and bandaged every day.

That afternoon the casino reappeared at the warning wire out back. Goldman was there, too, collecting the winnings and operating the "store." Danzig, as usual, stood guard over it all.

"Looks like Goldman's strong enough to shoot craps and sell stuff, anyway." Wilhelm and Lumley walked around the compound. "Got a nice big crowd, too,"

Lumley nodded. "Hey, and look! Ain't that Jones standin' there watchin'? Never seen him at the casino before. Ah thought you said he was down on gamblin'."

"Oh, yeah, he is. Ran Goldman and his game off my bed one time. Sounded like some kinda old-time preacher." Wilhelm frowned. "He's a funny duck, y'know? Smart, but strange. Wouldn't s'prise me a bit if he sold one of his fire-makers and jumped into the game."

"Boy, look at the planes." Lumley pointed up. For a moment, they stood mesmerized by the flashing wings, whining engines, and peck-peck of machineguns in the sky. "Sound sorta like woodpeckers, don't they?" Wilhelm ventured as they went back to their walk. "That was some show we saw last night, wasn't it? Biggest flames I've seen since we got here. Berlin must be about burnt up by now. Wonder how far we are from there, anyway."

"From the map Ah saw t'other day—guy in tent five has a map overlay—looked to be twenty, maybe thirty miles." Lumley reached down and picked a lump of mud off his shoe. "Y'know, Will, I feel sorry for them people up there. All their homes and their stuff burnt up and them with no place to go. It's a dirty shame, what happens to the civilians in wartime. They're the ones pay for what their leaders get 'em into."

"Yeah, that's true, Lum. But don't forget, those same people made Hitler their president or whatever he is and thought that 'Turd Rike' a his was the cat's meow. I can't feel too damn sorry for 'em."

"Well, in one way, you're right, but, when you think about it, they jus' did what the people always do. Like me and you did, y'know, we joined up, and came over here to fight and we didn't really know what it was all about."

A sudden hollow roar. Everybody ducked and looked up.

"What the hell was that?" Wilhelm's eyes followed three swept-wing fighter planes disappear into the eastern sky. "Oh, I bet I know. They're jets. Newspapers back in England said the Krauts were buildin' jet planes. Said we're bombin' their factories to stop 'em. Make a helluva racket, don't they?"

"Yeah, Ah'll say. Fast, too. Run rings around our planes, I bet. Ah see why we'd wanta stop 'em from buildin' 'em." Suddenly, the ground jumped, a ripple in the soil passing beneath their feet. "And back here on the ground," Lumley said in his radio announcer's voice, "Rooskie guns're shakin' us up."

"Yeah. Must be gettin' close. Them's the first ones we've felt so strong." Wilhelm, thinking of the night Charko went out to dig himself a foxhole and got stuck, wished for a shovel to replace his only tool, his tablespoon. To ease away from these negative thoughts, he grabbed Lumley and shouted, "War's gonna be over purty soon, buddy, and we'll be goin' home! Home, buddy! *Home!*"

"Hey, c'mon, we ain't goin' no place yet! " Lumley, smiling, pulled away.

"Oh, oh, here comes Kruger. Don't tell me he's gonna haul Goldman off to the sick tent again. Not after the bastard got him shot!"

The *Feldwebel* and his backup guards shoved through the casino crowd, prisoners falling away in all directions. "Damn if he ain't...why that dirty...hey, even Jones got knocked down! Boy, is *he* mad!" Wilhelm clapped his hands, but softly.

"Yeah. Ain't never seen his face look so purpley like that." Lumley started toward the melee, and Wilhelm followed.

Goldman, tic squeezing one eye almost shut, stepped forward and would have met the German face to face if he'd he been a foot taller. Kruger kicked the box that was the casino's "bank" up and over the warning wire. He grinned as it bounced against the outer fence and fell open. A guard on his rounds stopped to watch the cans of Spam and sardines, the cubed sugar and packages of cigarettes spill into the snow. Kruger's biggest guard stood next to Danzig, while the other two yanked the canvas up and tossed it, dice and all, over the warning wire into no-man's-land next to the box.

Cursing, Goldman limped over to the wire, dropped to his knees, and stretched one arm under the wire. He looked up at the tower guard, who, rifle at the ready, grinned and nodded. Was that a go-ahead, or what? Goldman slid under the wire on his belly, retrieved his beloved dice, and, laughing aloud, waved the precious cubes in the air.

"Oh, for chrissake! He's like a kid stealing candy from a drugstore. He's nuts, you know that, Lum? Nuttier'n a damn fruitcake!"

"Looks like he's tryin' to get hisself shot again. He does, Ah ain't goin' in after him. Nossir."

Danzig and Goldman stood at the warning wire nodding at the tower guard and pointing at the rest of their stuff. The guard didn't move, his rifle still at the ready.

"Look. Kruger's leavin'. Just came in here to tear up Goldman's casino. The dirty SOB!" He and Lumley watched the Germans cross the compound and pass through the east gate. "You watch, Lum. One a these days Goldman's gonna get even with that Kraut! Maybe after the Rooskies finally get here."

# CHAPTER 19

▼

# DEATH AND RETRIBUTION

A few days later, the Russian guns sounded closer, much closer. Questions filled Wilhelm's thoughts: Do they know we're here? Will that wheel-to-wheel Rooskie artillery dump on us? Will they come rolling in here behind tanks like the Germans did back in Belgium? Depressed, he frowned a lot and walked around the compound by himself, stopping and listening at the eastern fence. Contrails filled the sky, their non-Euclidean loops smearing in the wind. It's spring, he thought, a happy time back home, softball and hardball, tennis and swimming, and…to hell with it, I ain't there. He lay about, long-faced, wishing it was over, *all* over.

Lumley let Wilhelm be. He read his Bible and kept to himself. Several days passed, the sounds of war coming on. One night Wilhelm, sleeping badly, was awakened by the sound of footsteps at the front flap, not uncommon; there was always traffic in and out. He reared up and looked. A man, just inside the tent, stood shifting from one foot to the other. A long second passed. "Hey, you guys," the figure said, his voice too weak to wake anyone. No response from the black hole before him. "Hey, you guys," the voice louder, stronger this time. "Hey! You guys! There's a body in the shithole out back!" The man waited. "There's a body in the shithole and," he swallowed hard, "it looks like a Kraut!" The word *Kraut* bored a hole in the snoring darkness.

"My God!" Wilhelm elbowed Lumley. "Lum! Did you hear that?" The redhead rolled over. Other men were up and stirring. "C'mon, Lum! Let's take a look. If there's a Kraut in the latrine, there's gonna be hell to pay!"

They didn't want to believe what they saw. In the cold gray dawn, they squeezed their noses shut against the stench and stared into the pit. Bits of human excrement bobbed against a dark uniformed body turned on its face, one chevroned arm reaching for the round-handled instrument buried in its back. Like a waterlogged shipwreck, the body bumped against the far shore of the latrine. "Dead man's float," somebody ventured, the voice cracking. Every prisoner knew of the terrible reprisals the Krauts would take for an offense like this.

"Jeez, Lum. It looks like Kruger! I think that's a screwdriver in his back!" Jones' fury at being knocked down by Kruger's men rose in Wilhelm's mind. "Jones has a coupla screwdrivers like that, but he wouldn't...I don't think he would...." Then he remembered Goldman's handling Jones' tools the other day. Yeah, it was Goldman that killed him! Sure as hell! Why didn't the dumb shit wait till the Rooskies got here? Damn him! He's gonna get us all shot!

Somebody found a guy stake and rolled the body over. A gold tooth peeked from the slime-choked mouth. "Christ-a-mighty," somebody shouted. "It's Kruger! They're gonna shoot ever' last one of us for this!" A flurry ran through the crowd. "I'm transferrin' to tent 5 afore they find him!" another voice said. "Yeah, let's go!"

"No!" another prophet cried. "They won't just shoot tent 3; they'll shoot the *whole fuckin' camp!*" The men backed away, whispering, groaning, their faces grim. "Just when the fuckin' Rooskies're gettin' close, too!" one man yelled. A tall, thin POW next to Lumley stamped his foot. "I find out who killed this Kraut, I'm gonna wring his fuckin' neck and dump his ass in there with 'im!"

As usual, Wilhelm, Lumley, Goldman, and Danzig lined up for *Appell* with the rest of the twenty-eight hundred Americans. A *Leutnant*, their official counter-upper, stood in his usual place before tent #3's formation, the now-infamous latrine behind him.

"The guys seem extra quiet this morning, don't they?" Wilhelm whispered.

"Yeah, Will, they are. Wonder why."

"Our boy, the *Herr Leutnant*, looks tired. Been workin' out with the *Fraüleins* in town, I bet."

"Could be. Maybe he won't even look in the latrine. I bet his don't stink as bad as ourn." Lum grinned.

Suddenly, a shout and one of the guards stood pointing. The officer turned and stared. He waved to the six *Leutnants*. The young officers, probably recently commissioned, put their heads together and decided which of them would break the news to *Der Oberleutnant—Appellmeister*. Hard-faced and silent, they went back to their posts to await his arrival.

The count was completed by the *Obergefreiters* (corporals), who, with much clicking of heels and high-handed salutes, reported it up the chain of command to *Der Oberleutnant-Appellmeister,* who, apparently satisfied with it, stepped aside and waved his *Leutnants* to join him. The group began a low and animated discussion, inaudible to POW ears.

Once dismissed, most of the POWs headed inside for morning tea. Some, however, noticed the men of tent #3 still standing in formation. Shouts of: "Oooh, they musta been naughty!" and "Tch, tch, tch!" and "Tough shit!" followed by loud laughter drifted down the wind. But silence replaced the laughter when a detail of ragged Russians marched through the east gate, stopped next to #3's latrine, and hunkered down around it. Eyebrows rose when, bare-handed, the Russians pulled a body up and out of the hole. Stone-faced, every man in #3s formation watched the body disappear through the gate.

Now *Der Oberleutnant* stepped before them and shouted, "Who hass killt *Feldwebel* Kruger?" His cold gray eyes swept the men before him, an evil smile slowly growing on his broad, pallid face. Silence. "Ach! Ve haff *hier niemand*! uhhh, nobody!" Squinting, he pursed his lips. "Tsuicite! *Ya? Der Feldwebel hat* himzelf gekillt! Ya?" The yellow-toothed grin broadened. "*Gut! Sehr gut!*" Nodding, he turned to *der* Tent *Nummer Drei Leutnant* beside him. "*Zehn!*" he pronounced, "Ve shoot *zehn!*" He waved to the other officers. "*Komm!*" *Der Appellmeister*, with three *Leutnant*s and three *Feldwebel*s in tow, walked along the front rank of the formation, deciding who would and who would not be shot.

Back in the third rank, Goldman, feeling always at the top of every German's death list, mumbled, "Okay, guys, I'll see yooz later." He bent low and drifted away, ending up as far from the German contingent as possible.

"He's gone, Lum," Wilhelm whispered. "Kruger's killer has got away." He slipped in next to Danzig, filling Golman's space.

The tall redhead nodded and said nothing.

The officer's heavy-lidded gray eyes stared into those of each POW. When he nodded, a *Feldwebel* stepped in and pulled the American off. *Der Oberleutnant* passed Danzig, then Wilhelm, but stopped before Lumley. He reached out and felt, then caressed, Lumley's dark red beard. "Ahhh!, he sighed, then shouted, "*Ein Rote Communiste!*" His entourage exploded in laughter. Two *Feldwebel*s immediately grabbed the big man and hauled him off.

The word *No!* formed on Wilhelm's lips. Lumley, of all people, accused of murder! For a second, he considered saying he'd done it. But he had no voice. He couldn't, or wouldn't, say it. Which was it? He was sure Lum would do it for him. Wouldn't he? But Wilhelm couldn't, or wouldn't, do it, not for Lumley, or, for that matter, for anybody else.

"They ain't gonna shoot nobody," Danzig declared. "'Specially now the Rooskies're so close. Don't worry 'bout Lumley, Wilhelm. They ain't gonna shoot 'im."

Minutes later, a line of ten grim-faced Americans stood facing the tent #3 formation. "Zooo, *is' gut, sehr gut!*" A snort, a chuckle, then: "Deese vee shoot!" *Der Appellmeister* grinned. "Who killt *der Feldwebel* ve don't find oudt, den more ve shoot!" At his order, a rank of six guards, rifles in hand, formed before the condemned men. Again, the sharp, clear words: "I done it!" rose in Wilhelm's mind. Lips quivering, he couldn't speak. He just couldn't.

"*Halt! Halt!*"—echoed across the compound. The Germans, recognizing the voice of *Der Hauptmannn*, the *Stalag Kommandant*, snapped to attention. The old man, breathing hard, stopped before *Der Oberleutnant*, flipped a desultory salute, and choked momentarily for air. *Der Kommandant* spoke sharply to his junior officer, stomping his foot and pointing to the east. Shouting something unintelligible, he glowered at the younger man, turned and limped away toward the gate. *Der Oberleutnant*, obviously miffed, threw a salute at the old man's back, swung around and called his *Leutnant*s together. Orders flew. The recently appointed firing squad was posted around the condemned Americans. The POWs, smiling with relief, headed for the tent to wait for morning chow.

"Boy, that was close!" Wilhelm mumbled, looking through the crowd at Lumley. "I just hope...I just...." He saw Goldman and Danzig going around the tent and thought: They don't give a damn about

Lum. He pushed into the crowd gathered near the condemned men just as the guards waved them away. "See, there, Lum," he yelled, standing on tiptoe. "I told you that damn beard would get you in trouble some time!" The big redhead shrugged and forced a smile.

Back inside the tent, Wilhelm sat down and looked at the empty blankets next to his, remembering Belgium and the hill and Lum saying Charko was dead, and Lum in the boxcar mumbling the Lord's prayer over and over, and then Limburg and Lum reading the 23rd Psalm to everybody and—dammit, here we are about to get liberated and he's out there waiting to be shot! Dammit! Damn these Krauts to hell! After all that praying and Bible studying, you'd think God would do something for him!

Wilhelm closed his eyes and breathed deeply, but his mind wouldn't stop. Goldman should've waited till the Russians got here before he killed Kruger. But he never waits. Nooo, *he just does!* Bet he got a real kick outta sticking that Kraut and shoving him in the shithole. Wilhelm slipped into a rolling, tossing half-sleep and didn't wake up until too late for morning tea. He was furious with himself and the whole world. One word—*Goldman*—filled his thoughts. I'm gonna threaten that little bastard with Dad's knife and make him confess. *Then* I'll kill him! Wilhelm got up and, scratching his crotch, trotted down the aisle. Standing behind Goldman, he turned on his meanest look and shouted, "What're you gonna do, Goldman? Sit there and play with yourself while Lum gets shot? Or you gonna admit it like a man?"

"Say what?" Goldman twisted around and looked up.

Squatting, Wilhelm stared narrowly into Goldman's close, dark eyes. "*You* killed Kruger, didn't you? With the screwdriver you stole from Jones' bag." He watched the tic twist the little man's face. "Ain't that right, you little bastard?" He grabbed Goldman by the collar and tried to pull him up, but the Jewish kid was heavier than he thought.

"What the hell you talkin' 'bout, Wilhelm?" Goldman knocked Wilhelm's hand away. "You got a burr up your ass, or somethin'?"

"You did it, you little shit! And I'm gonna kick your ass till you tell the Krauts! Lum ain't gonna die out there 'cause you're too damned yellow to...."

"Look, buddy, I was *plannin'* to get that sumbitch soon's the Rooskies got here. But somebody beat me to it, that's all there is to it. I find out who did it, I'm puttin' 'im in for a medal when we get back."

"You ain't foolin' nobody with that crap!" Wilhelm grabbed Goldman's arm and, standing, pulled the small man to his feet. "C'mon, let's you and me go out and talk to the Krauts. *Now! Right now, dammit!*"

"Hey! Leggo!" Goldman yanked his arm away. "Who the hell you think you are, Wilhelm? You gone off your fuckin' rocker, or somethin'? Get away from me!" The dark eyes flashed around. Where the hell was Danzig? "Look, Wilhelm, really I..." His voice dropped to a whisper. "I didn't have nuttin to do wit' killin' that Kraut. Honest to God, Wilhelm, I didn't do it."

"You got that screwdriver outta Jones' bag the other day. I saw you take it. You loved stickin' it in that Kraut, didn't you?" Wilhelm grabbed Goldman and pulled him into the aisle. "I don't blame you for killin' that sonofabitch, but Lum ain't takin' the rap for you! *Nossir!* You gotta go out there and tell the Krauts you did it!"

Goldman wheeled around and threw up his fists. "Awright, Wilhelm! You want some a me, come on! *Come on!*" When Goldman's right blocked his left jab, Wilhelm realized for the first time that Goldman was left-handed. Back in high school, the "little guy" who had bloodied Wilhelm's nose and cracked one of his ribs had been left-handed, too. Wilhelm stepped in and swung for the solar plexus.

The little man's hard, muscular abdomen twisted away, causing Wilhelm's vicious left uppercut to miss.

"Awright, knock it off! I said *knock it off!*" Sergeant Jones stepped in and shoved the fighters apart. He grabbed Wilhelm, turned him around, and drug him off down the aisle.

"You ain't gonna settle *nothin'* like that, Jimmy." Jones let Wilhelm drop onto his blankets and stood over him. "You ain't no little boy anymore. You oughtta know better!" He grinned. "Ain't much of a boxer, anyways, are ya?"

"That little bastard's gonna let Lum die for somethin' *he* did, Sergeant. I *know* he did it! Lum gets shot, I'm gonna *kill* 'im. You can bet on it!"

Jones shook his head. "Ain't worth it, Jimmy." The sergeant's eyes narrowed. "How's come you're so all-fired sure Goldman did it, anyways?"

"Kruger's the one that got 'im shot! Made 'im clean shit in the sick tent and then dumped his casino in the mud! He hated that *Kraut*. And I was here when he went through your stuff and took your screwdriver. You were gone someplace, and I know he took it."

"You saw him take that screwdriver, did ya? You're crazy, Jimmy. Just plain crazy." Jones sat down and stared up at the canvas. "You're so damn sure, whyn't you go out and tell the Krauts yourself? Save your buddy and let *them* take care a Goldman."

Wilhelm's eyes went wide. He hadn't thought of that. "You mean *rat* on him? Another American? Hell, no! I would never do that!"

Jones smiled. "Awright. Let it go, Jimmy. Just let it play out. And don't do nothin' stupid!" Eyes going to half-mast, he pulled his feet in tight against his thighs and placed his hands palms-up on his knees.

Yeah, sure, Wilhelm thought. It's easy for you. You don't really give a damn about Lum. Poor guy's laying out there in the cold, with nothing to eat since yesterday. But I'm gonna take care of this. Dad's knife'll scare it outta that little Jewboy. Jewboy? I never called him that before, must be in my blood...Or else what? Or else my blade's going in his skinny little gut, that's what else. The thought made him smile.

A strange quiet overlay the East that evening. During *Appell*, the prisoners of tent #3 whispered and shuffled and kept their eyes on the men sitting around the latrine. Back straight, head high above the others, Lumley nodded at Wilhelm as he passed by. After the count, Wilhelm attempted to share his evening chow with him, but the guards kept him away.

After dark, Wilhelm squatted on his blankets. He looked down the tent and watched Goldman and Danzig, laughing and yelling, roll the dice. When the big guy leaves to hit the latrine, I'll go after the little bastard. But the game went on and on and on; Danzig caught Wilhelm's eye off and on. He knows something's up, Wilhelm thought, but he'll still have to check his water level some time. The game finally over, Wilhelm watched the two players, carefully ignoring his hot stare, stroll up, and then down the aisle, going and coming.

The evening gone and Goldman still loose, Wilhelm lay back and covered himself. Come morning, I'll talk *to Der Leutnant* and tell him what I know. I am *not* being a rat. This is different, a matter of life and death. The Krauts'll shoot Goldman, and those ten guys out there can thank me for it. I'd love to do it myself. He was surprised at the thought. Things sure have changed around here. Or is it just me?

# CHAPTER 20

▼

# LIBERATION!

Next morning, Wilhelm, still heavy with sleep, got up and headed out to *Appell*. A dark gray sky hung low over the *Appell* field, a thick white fog obscuring the ground. Nose wrinkled by the stench of the latrine, he noticed the condemned men lying in close for warmth. In the morning fog, he stopped and listened: the chirp and chatter of the spring birds recently arrived and the usual shuffling of men waiting in formation were absent. Strange, he thought, very strange. But I *will not* be distracted! I *will* talk to *der Leutnant*, dammit! Lum *will not* die for Goldman's crime!

As he looked around for the officer, he found the condemned ones on their feet aligning themselves, apparently of their own accord, facing the incipient formation. Lumley's face showed chalk-white against the clouds. An eerie sight, Wilhelm thought. Turning, he found six rifle barrels pointing out of the fog at the chosen men. Then a voice, much like his own, shouted, "Hey! What's goin' on? Where's *der Leutnant?*" A *Feldwebel* standing next to the guns lifted his hand, dropped it into the swirling fog and yelled, "*Fuer!*" The guns fired and three men fell away, a muffled splash confirming their departure. The voice again: "Hey, wait, wait! I know who killed...." But the hand was risen and now it fell again. The rifles fired, and three more Americans fell back into the filthy hole.

Lumley, squinting at the six smoking muzzles, stood at the center of the last three men. The guns, still up and pointing, awaited the order to fire, but something stopped them. Wilhelm suddenly felt a weight on his chest. And a voice, *that* voice, cried, "No! No! Don't shoot! It was Goldman! Goldman killed Kruger! Goldman killed Kruger!" A second voice, close to his ear, whispered, "Will! Will! C'mon, boy, wake up! It's me! Lum! We're *liberated,* boy! The Krauts're gone! We're *liberated,* Will! We're *free!*"

Wilhelm reared up. "Lum! My God! Where did...." He blinked and stared, his jaw slack. "You didn't get...I thought you were...what the hell is goin' on?" Something big and warm wrapped itself around him, and stiff bristles raking his cheek. It *is* Lum! My old buddy! Alive and not shot and.... Tears ran and he smeared them away. "Dammit, Lum, I thought you was a goner!" He grabbed the redhead by the shoulders and held him out at arm's length. "Damn your hide, anyway. I was about to...oh, hell, we're liberated, you say? The Krauts'er gone?"

"Shhhh. It's the middle of the night! You're gonna wake ever'body up."

"Hell, I don't care!" Wilhelm dropped his voice. "These guys *oughtta* know we're liberated, don't you think?" He frowned. "And don't you think they should know you guys didn't get shot." He shook Lumley again. "You mean the Rooskies came and there was no shootin', or anything? How can you...how, how do you know the Krauts're gone?" He patted Lumley's scruffy cheek and decided not to shake him again.

"One of the guys got up to take a leak and saw the guards was gone. Then we saw the fences was empty, so...." He shrugged. "So here Ah am." Lumley put his hands together and, whispering softly, sent a prayer up to his God. "Y'know, Ah never thought Ah'd miss sleepin' on this damn straw, but Ah'd forgot how hard bare ground is. And the stink out there? God, it's awful, just awful! Goes to show a man oughtta 'preciate what he's got no matter how bad it is."

Wilhelm couldn't stop the tears running down his cheeks. Speechless with joy, he sat staring at Lumley, a glow like the one he'd felt at Limburg after the bombing. He couldn't stop thinking: Good ole Lum! Good ole Lum!

Sighing long and deep, Lumley lay down and rolled onto his side. "Gotta get me some shuteye, Will. Ain't had much the last coupla nights." He yawned and slipped away.

"*Liberated!* We're *liberated!* What a beautiful word! Lum's back and…." Wilhelm tried to swallow the lump of joy in his throat. "He's alive and kickin' and…God, we're goin' *home! Home!* Tomorrow, maybe! Maybe *tomorrow!*" His dream took him home, to Indianapolis, the train station and down Madison Avenue past his old school—Manual Training High School—the old blue Plymouth purring softly, Dad driving and Mom, tears rolling down her cheeks, looking back at him, while Fritzie licked his face.

*    *    *    *

A loud bang! Another! Then another! "They're gone! They're gone! The Krauts're gone!" someone outside was yelling. "They're gone! Hooray! Hooray! The Krauts're gone! They done cleared out!" Wilhelm, still half asleep, did not immediately understand the words. Next to him, Lumley's bed lay empty. "Oh, no!" he mumbled, "It was all a dream! Lum is still out there and…hell! The bastards probably shot him already!"

Galapo's broad, black head came through the front flap. "The Krauts're gone!" he screamed. "*The Krauts're gone! Wake up!* We're *free, boys!* We're *liberated!*" Spooning the dixie with all his might, the stocky Italian spun around and went back outside.

The whine and whoosh of shells shook the ground. Oh, oh, Wilhelm thought, jamming on his boots. I knew we wouldn't get out of here without some kinda fight. He bent low, ran outside and into a crowd of prisoners milling around, clapping and shouting. No guns, no firing. Shells must have landed out in the east woods. Feeling foolish, he straightened up and looked around for the redhead. There he was, whooping and waving like all the rest.

"Damn it, Lum, why didn't you holler when you got up? I saw your empty blankets and...." The big soldier grabbed him and danced him around in a circle.

Goldman, smiling, whooeeeing, clapping, limped up to them and shouted, "Hey, Lumley, I see you made it! I knew them yella bastids wasn't gonna shoot nobody." He reached out and tried to hug his two buddies together, but Wilhelm pulled away. With that, Goldman waved his fists in the air and, bad leg and all, stumped away into the crowd yelling, "We're *free! Free! Free!*"

"What's the matter with you, Will? Ain't you excited 'bout gettin' liberated?"

"Sure I'm excited. Excited as anybody could be. But that fuckin' Goldman...he's such a...you came so close to...." Wilhelm had decided not to tell Lumley what he knew but did it anyway. "He's the one that killed Kruger, y'know."

"*Goldman?* You sure?"

"Course I'm sure. Kruger made Goldman carry shit at the sick tent, got him shot at the fence, and then tore up his casino. Nobody hated

Kruger like Goldman did. *Nobody!*" Wilhelm waited for the redhead to agree. "Goldman had the screwdriver, too, y'know. I saw him take it."

Lumley sighed and turned away. "Sure is a lotta shootin' out east there, ain't they? Wonder when the Rooskies is gonna git in here. Cain't be too long."

"Well, dammit, Lum, didn't you hear what I said?" A ragged column of Russian prisoners, bare toes sticking through their shoes, trotted along the other side of the fence. A rash of applause rose from the Americans.

"Wonder how they got loose so quick?"

To hell with it, Wilhelm was thinking. I won't ever speak to the little bastard again. Never. "Rooskies're crazy to join up with their army, I guess." Wilhelm chuckled. "Can't figger it. I sure as hell ain't goin' out there. Nossiree, not me."

"My God, look at that, Will!" Lumley stared intently at the far end of the compound.

Wilhelm turned toward the western fence. "Shakin' hell outta that fence, ain't they?" The tall weeds he used to crawl around in playing Hide 'n Seek came to mind. "Reminds me of how them big ole black-and-yellow spiders that shake their webs when you touch 'em. Ever see one do that, Lum?"

"Yeah, they was a buncha them in the bushes around home. Us kids used to...." The western fence, prisoners and all, crashed down and the men, whooping and hollering, ran out into the field and began throwing lumps of plowed earth at one another. The crowd, staring west, missed the arrival of a tall, gaunt, American officer coming through the eastern fence.

"All right, you men!" he shouted. "Let me have your attention! There's some things you need to know, and I'm here to tell you about 'em!" Hands behind his back, gold bars on his collar gleaming in the morning sun, the lieutenant stood at-ease, waiting for silence. Still talking and laughing, POWs all along the tent row began to saunter toward him, a crude semi-circle slowly forming around him.

"Looks like Regular Army," Wilhelm whispered, "maybe even a West Pointer." His idea of West Pointers came from war movies he had seen.

"All right, now. I'm Lieutenant Carver, One Oh Nine Artillery. Major General Woods, Commander of all American troops in this camp, has appointed me liaison officer for you. From now on, I'll be bringin' you the latest scuttlebutt around here." A rough silence had developed, and the officer waited for his words to soak in.

"As you can see, the Krauts left us during the night (much clapping and shouting), so we're on our own until the Russians get here. Probably some time tomorrow." Shouts and hurrahs—the liberation party threatening to break out again. Lieutenant Carver held up his hands.

"General Woods," he shouted, "has *ordered,* get that, *ordered* that every man will *stay in camp.*" Groans and half-whispered curses brought the lieutenant's brows together. "I know, y'all want to get out and see what you can find (shouts and laughter), but the town's empty, and I don't think we wanta hang around here till the Germans get back" (boos, laughter, a storm of talk). "Besides, it's *dangerous* (a sudden quiet). "Yes, *dangerous!* There's nothing out there worth riskin' your life for. *Absolutely nothing!*"

"How the hell does *he* know what's out there?" Wilhelm's head shook. "I bet he ain't been outside any more'n we have. Just look at 'im, Lum. The man's fresh-shaved, hair's been cut, clothes washed, pants look like they been pressed. I s'pose the Krauts had people waitin' on him while we lived on the ground like a buncha goddam animals."

Wilhelm had hated officers ever since he'd done Officer's KP back at Benning: three days—four-thirty in the morning till nine at night—

kissing ass, taking orders, serving officers their food at the table, and cleaning up after them. He would never, ever forget it.

"So get this straight, men," Lieutenant Carver went on. "You are under *direct orders* from the Commanding Officer to *stay in camp.*" The last three words came slowly and distinctly. "Is that clear? *Stay inside the fences!*" His eyes swept the crowd. "You got it?"

Wilhelm smiled. Good ole Sergeant Dolan: You got it? You got it? How he'd love to be here now and hear this guy mimic him.

"Hey, Lieutenant," a voice from the back shouted. "Is this fuckin' General What's-his-name gonna get us somethin' to *eat?* Some *decent chow* for a change?" An intense silence established the massive weight of the question.

"The German rations left at headquarters will be dispensed as soon as we can get organized." Men began to volunteer to peel potatoes, go rabbit hunting, deer hunting, "cow" hunting, anything to hurry things up. Again laughter took over.

"We may have to take some of y'all up on that," the officer said, grinning. "Okay, now, one more thing. You are to get organized into squads, platoons, and companies. The ranking or tent non-coms will take care of it." The crowd groaned. "And another thing, starting tonight a guard will be posted around the camp. Roving bands of...." Curses and foot-stomping drowned the lieutenant's words. Hard-faced, he raised his hands. "Listen here! There are Krauts carrying *burpguns* out there! Hungry, just like you are. And some may be lookin' for hostages to get 'em through the Russians to the American lines!" Silence, now. "That's why we need guards around here! We must post guard around the camp!"

Up on tiptoe, Lumley waved and shouted, "You from the South, Lieutenant?" Wilhelm grabbed his buddy by the arm and pulled him down. "For God's sake, Lum, don't call 'im *Lieutenant!* Call 'im *Sir.*"

The stint he'd served on garbage detail for committing that terrible offense filled his mind.

Lumley's tall red head brought a smile to the officer's face, but he did not respond.

"Sir!" A tall thin POW raised his hand and yelled, "What're we s'posed to use for weapons, Sir, while we're walkin' this fuckin' guard duty?"

The crowd laughed, but the officer frowned. "Use your imagination, soldier. Get yourself a club or a knife, or whatever you can find. Better we have a guard out there to warn us than to...."

A sharp voice cut through the groans. "Warning? They got burpguns and we got nothin' but sticks and stones?" The speaker looked around for approval. "That's suicide, Sir! *Crazy fuckin' suicide!*"

"How about a piece of that Kraut bread, Lieutenant?" somebody in the front row suggested. "It's hard as a fuckin' rock!" A smattering of laughter, then silence. The crowd was no longer in a laughing mood. The men began to move away.

"All right, all right! Wait a minute! You men! Wait a minute! Your orders are to *stay in camp, get organized,* and *post guard!* I don't care *how* you do it! Just *do* it! You *must* follow orders!" A snappy right-face and the lieutenant headed for the gate.

A high, thin voice stopped him. "Hey, Lieutenant, you s'pose maybe the Krauts're lookin' to carry out Hitler's last order?" The prisoners looked around for the speaker. A blanket of silence fell over them.

The officer stopped and turned back. "Yeah, we heard about that. But the Krauts around here aren't about to kill anybody. They knew it'd be their ass if they did." Before he could get to the gate, another question burst out: "Hell, Lieutenant, if it's only forty miles to our lines, why don't we just pack up and get the hell outta here? Them renegade Krauts ain't gonna take us all hostage, are they?"

"Let's go," one man said. "Fall in," yelled another. Several POWs lined up and marched off toward the western fence. Laughter again.

Lieutenant Carver scowled. "The *General* will decide *what* we do and *when* we do it. Not *you* and not *me*. So don't get any crazy ideas. Just follow orders and we'll all get outta here in one piece!" He stepped quickly through the gate and slammed it shut.

"Well, shit, we shoulda knowed. The same ole chickenshit we had before!" Goldman stared at his buddies. "Tell you what. I ain't stayin' in this fuckin' camp any longer'n I have to. And I ain't gittin' organized, and I *ain't* walkin' no *fuckin' guard duty,* neither! Whatta yooz think a that?" He kicked at the defunct warning-wire with his good leg as he limped along the fences.

That afternoon, the Russians arrived. Tanks—American Shermans with Russian markings—roared through the woods knocking down trees and tearing out underbrush. A ragged phalanx of pale-faced, unshaven men carrying weapons of all kinds slogged along among them. The POWs gathered along the fences, watching, grinning.

Some two hours later, Sergeant Sharkey came into tent #3 with the first Russian communique: "Prisoner register at Headquarters. Not leave camp before register—ing," he added, smiling. "Rooskies don't write English so good."

"Register? What the hell for?" somebody shouted. Sharkey's eyes flashed about, looking for the speaker.

"I hear they're gettin' fifty dollars a head for us. That's what for," Sharkey said.

"Ah, ha," Goldman shouted, "so that's why they been so fuckin' careful. Our ass is worth fifty bucks! Without holes, a course!" The tent roared.

Pretty soon a steaming pot of thick, green pea soup came through the east fence, a stack of black bread right behind it. The men whooped and hollered as they lined up.

"Not bad," Wilhelm said, chewing mightily. "At least, these Rooskies know how to feed."

The redhead dipped the crust of his bread into his soup. "Yeah, but it don't come close to Moon Pie and RC Cola."

"Zagnut bar and a Coke, either." Wilhelm laughed. They got up and joined the mile-long line for seconds.

Three days of pea soup and black bread passed before Sergeant Sharkey brought in a second Russian communique: "When register done, US and England prisoners go Odessa. Take ship home." Hoots filled the tent.

"Odessa? Where the hell is that?" Wilhelm frowned.

"Somewhere down on the Black Sea, Ah think." Lumley squinted. "Seen it on the map once. Down south a here."

"Well, wherever it is, I don't wanta go."

The words *American lines* and *ain't-nobody-gonna-stop-me* bounced around the tent. Some prisoners began to gather up Red Cross leftovers and roll up blankets.

Standing astride the middle aisle like a defensive end, Sharkey's face went hard. "Remember the General's orders to stay in camp? You pull out now, you'll end up in the stockade when you get back. Bread and water, no steak and puddin'! No furloughs and no pussy, either."

The incipient travelers cursed and threw down their makeshift packs. The uproar subsided, but after Sharkey left, serious voices made serious plans to leave.

Wilhelm and Lumley wandered silently around the compound. The American lines were only *forty miles away!* A day's hike, maybe two. Each man felt that same gut-deep force pulling him away from the stench and squalor of the camp. How long would they wait? How long could they stand it?

# CHAPTER 21

▼

# ON THE WAY

"See, this here overlay shows the tracks goin' straight down to the Elbe River where the American lines are at." Goldman traced the route with his finger. "All we gotta do is follow them tracks and we're home free! Couldn't be easier!" Tic jerking his cheek, he looked from Danzig to Wilhelm to Lumley. Wilhelm looked away. *Not with you, you SOB.* I ain't going nowhere with *you!*

"Yeah, but what about the general? And Sharkey talkin' about the stockade and all…and, and the Rooskie registration. How 'bout that?"

"C'mon, Lumley, don't be such a goddam yokel. Fuck the Rooskie registration! And the fuckin' general, too. Ain't nobody gonna put us in the stockade when we get back! We're heroes, boy! We're all *heroes!* Ain't you figgered that out yet?" Goldman stared at the translucent map in his hand. "Well, *I* am, anyways."

POWs? Heroes? That's bullshit, Wilhelm almost said, clamping his mouth shut. He would never again speak to Goldman. More likely, he thought, they'll throw us in the stockade for surrendering.

"You got forty miles in that leg of yourn?" Lumley looked down at Goldman's torn pants leg. "You ain't walkin' as good now as you was a couple a...."

"Hey, don't worry about me. Ain't nuttin gonna keep me away from that fuckin' river, boy. No Krauts, no Rooskies, and this leg neither."

"It ain't smart." Lumley turned and squinted at Wilhelm. "Chances of us gettin' through all them Rooskie troops is mighty slim. They're likely to take us for Krauts and blow us away. Or, like the lieutenant says, some Krauts might get us for hostages and...."

"Always pussyfootin', ain't ya? Nuttin' but a fuckin' redheaded pussycat!" Goldman glared. "Look, Lumley, Danzig here talks the Rooskie lingo like a native." He turned to the big man next to him. "Use ta talk to 'em back home alla time, didn't you, buddy?"

Danzig nodded, pearly-whites flashing. "Understood you perfect, didn't they?" Another nod, a wider grin.

Lumley kept his eyes on Wilhelm, who pursed his lips and turned away.

"Ahh, to hell wit' yooz guys. Stay here and let 'em shove your ass back into Rooskieland someplace! I don't care. *We're* goin' soon's it gets dark, ain't we, Danny?" The small soldier got up, pulled his shoulders back, and limped away. The Polish kid nodded and followed close behind.

The two buddies, minds churning, watched in silence as the little man led the big one down the aisle. Look like Mutt and Jeff, the midget and the monster in the funny papers back home, Wilhelm thought.

"So, whattaya think, Will?"

"Look, I ain't never havin' nothin' to do with that little bastard again. We wanta take off, we can do it without him. Right now, I'm for sittin' tight a while. See how the wind blows."

"Well, I ain't too crazy 'bout him, but walkin' back into Russia don't xackly thrill me, neither." A grimace grew on Lumley's face. "Fact is, we could get lost back in there and never ever git home. Kinda scares me, don't it you?"

"Yeah, it sure does, Lum. It sure does." Hand across his lips, Wilhelm stared into space. "Who knows, some a our guys might come bustin' in here and carry us off." He grinned. "Forty miles is nothin'. Specially in a truck." He looked around at Jones. "You hear what Goldman was sayin', Sergeant? Whatta you think? You stayin' or goin'?"

Jones unwound his legs and stretched his arms over his head. "Hadn't give it much thought, Jimmy. All depends on where you wanta be."

Wilhelm cocked his head. He had to ask, "Where do I wanta *be*? Home, Sergeant, home! Like ever'body else in this fuckin' camp. But that's not what I...."

"But that's the future, Jimmy. You're thinkin' 'bout the future 'steada the here-and-now. The past is gone and the future ain't here yet, don't ya know? There's only *now*, Jimmy. There's only *now*. Live in it, boy. *Live in it*." He stared hard into the corporal's eyes.

Wilhelm turned back to Lumley. "I shoulda known he'd come up with somethin' like that." Then to Jones: "Thanks a helluva lot, Sergeant. You're just bustin' with good advice."

"Hey, c'mon. Didn't you tell me you wasn't gonna have nothin' to do with Goldman again?"

"Yeah. And *you* know why, too. He killed Kruger and was gonna let the Krauts shoot Lum and a buncha other guys. He's a first-class shit."

"Yeah," Jones chuckled, "but you got it all wrong, Jimmy. It was *me* killed that Kraut, *not* Goldman."

Wilhelm's jaw fell. "*You?* You killed Kruger?"

"Yeah! I killed 'at Kraut. Caught 'im pissin' out there that night. Happened to have the screwdriver with me, so I shoved it into him and pushed him in the shit. He had it comin'." He chuckled again. "Too bad Goldman wasn't there. He'd a enjoyed hell out of it." The hurt look on Wilhelm's face seemed to shake Jones. "But, don't worry, Jimmy, I was gonna tell the Krauts before they got around to shootin' anybody." The yellow teeth flashed. "Goldman's got a big mouth, but at least he lives in the here-and-now, and has lotsa ideas, too. I like that."

"Well, I'll be damned," Wilhelm mumbled, his eyes narrowing. "But wait a minute! Goldman had that screwdriver! I saw him with it. Took it outta your bag!" He covered his mouth. "Oh. But maybe you got two screwdrivers and…."

"Nah! I only got one. You made up all that stuff 'bout the screwdriver. You was so damn sure he did it, you couldn't see it no other way." Jones reached for his Sergeant's voice. "So don't tell *me* who killed Kruger, *Corporal*. I *know* who did it!"

Wilhelm lay back, staring. Dust motes danced across his eyes, his thoughts. Why would Jones lie? He's got no reason to. Not when it comes to killing a man. Nobody would claim that, unless he….

Suddenly an explosion, the ground rippling under the tent. A second, and a third. "What the hell's goin' on?" somebody shouted.

"Sounded like 37s," Jones said, softly. "Tank rounds. Some drunk Rooskie's decided to play games with us."

Goldman burst through the front flap, a wide grin splitting his face. "Boy, that was close! Piece of one of them buggers damn near't got me. C'mon out and take a look! 75s, maybe bigger." He stepped across the intervening beds and squatted between Wilhelm and Lumley. "This shit does it, guys. I ain't sittin' around waitin' for some fuckin' Rooskie to drop a bomb on me. Me and Danzig're headin' out tonight! For sure!" He got up and jumped back into the aisle. "Have a nice hike into Rooskieland, guys. I'll be thinkin' 'bout yooz while I'm eatin' my steak, drinkin' beer, and diddlin' my girlfriend." He threw back his head and, as he strutted down the aisle he sang: "Leavin' tonight, I'm leavin' tonight, leavin' on the midnight train...tonight." A sprinkling of applause rose up.

\*      \*      \*      \*

Clouds obscured the moon, the night cool and damp. Bits of green spotted the dark soil, the trees nearby budding. Four men, blanket rolls on their backs, scanned the darkness as they stepped across the downed western fence and headed into the field. Only the crunch of their boots and the sigh of the night breeze broke the silence. Wilhelm bent and loosened his left legging, the anklebone unhappy with the return of his dad's knife.

"Halt! Halt! You guys stop right there!" A soldier of medium size suddenly appeared in the darkness before them. Goldman, motioning for Lumley and Danzig to follow, stepped forward to meet the guard. Wilhelm, ready to take off back to the tent, stepped away.

"You guys ain't s'posed to be out here!" A piece of wood the size of a bed slat from IIIB slapped the guard's palm. He pointed it back the way they'd come. "Go on! Turn around and get back to camp!"

"Okay, buddy, y'done your duty real good." Goldman stepped up to the man and smiled. "Wouldn't want your sergeant to catch yooz standin' out here shootin' the breeze wit' us." Goldman looked around to make sure his backup stood close. "What's your name, anyway? I'm gonna put you in for a medal when I get to the American lines."

"Awright, Corporal, don't give me no shit. You ain't goin' no place. I'll call the sergeant and see what he...."

"Go ahead. Try it, Jack." The little man's eyes narrowed, a finger jabbing at the guard's chest. "You can still talk when he gets here. Tell 'im we left for the good ole U S of A." Goldman brushed the guard back as he limped past him, Lumley and Danzig close behind.

Wilhelm gave the guard a wide berth and slogged along behind the others. They catch us now, the shit'll fly and we'll all end up in the stockade. He hears about it, Dad'll be so damn mad he'll, he'll...I don't know what. I oughtta head back, *now! Right now!* He tagged along, though, not wanting to leave his buddies and be hauled off into Russia alone.

Goldman led them around *Luckenwalde.* They looked for and found the railroad tracks. Almost immediately they came upon a crowd of Russian soldiers sitting around a roaring fire, eating, drinking, laughing. Behind them against the darkening sky stood a low building, round and black, rails leading to and from it. Wilhelm knew instantly what it was. A roundhouse, an honest-to-God German roundhouse. The Krauts use them, too. Gramps—my Mom's dad—was an engineer, and he took me inside one once. Got to see a big, black steam engine go around and head back outside, just like my own little engine did. I was thrilled to death.

"Look at that." Goldman hunkered down and pointed. "Fuckin' Rooskies're all over the place. Down the tracks, too, I bet. We'll hafta keep to the woods and get some shuteye when it gets light." He got up and disappeared into the darker darkness of the woods alongside the tracks. The others followed silently.

Walk all night and sleep all day. It sounded good, but any soldier would tell you it wouldn't be that simple, not in almost total darkness. They fell over logs, stepped into holes, slipped on ice hidden beneath melting snow. The movements of the windblown bushes and small trees sent them onto their bellies on the cold, wet ground. Overcoats held over their heads, they forded one roaring creek after another, their clothing soaked, muscles aching. Cursing through clenched teeth, they stumbled on behind Goldman toward the promised land.

As day broke, they found a clear, dry-looking spot, laid out their blankets, and ate some Red Cross leftovers, augmented somewhat by largess from the defunct casino. "Musta made six or seven miles already, maybe," Goldman muttered. Wilhelm took that *maybe* to be a limp apology for his having to stop and rest so often and for leading them into the deepest part of that last creek. And for being such a general pain-in-the-ass. They split the day's guard duty among themselves and went to sleep.

The second night, they covered even less ground, stopping during a rainstorm. Lumley made Goldman drop his pants so he could examine his leg, dark and swollen from crotch to knee. Goldman said it was fine. Lumley said it needed a fresh bandage. The grumpy one pulled up his pants and turned away.

About dawn on the third day, they came upon a small house, its roof partially collapsed, the single side window broken. "Hey! Look at this!" Goldman stopped at the edge of the woods. "Let's watch a while, and make sure there ain't nobody in there." They sat down, resting, watching. No smoke from the chimney, no sounds of life inside, only the chirp of birds and swish of wind in the trees. "Ain't nobody in there." Goldman declared. "It'll be a good place to hole up and git some sleep." He caught Lumley's eye. "Go on in, buddy, and take a looksee. And, Dannyboy, you go around and check the other side."

As the two men walked off, Wilhelm wondered at the ease with which Goldman had assumed command. Especially of the two big guys, who could make mincemeat of him any time they wanted to. Must be how it's done, he thought. Just take over and see what happens. Probably the same way Hitler and Mussolini and Stalin did it. Done that way all through history, I bet. They just stand up and *do* it.

"Looks okay to me." Lumley stepped into the woods next to Wilhelm. "Nothin' but one room, no beds or nuthin'. They's a ladder stickin' up out of a hole in the floor. Prob'bly a cellar or somethin' underneath."

"No beds? Shit, I was hopin' we'd find somethin' softer'n these fuckin' pine needles."

Danzig came around the house and walked up to Goldman. His hand began to rise as if to salute, but stopped at belt level. "All clear on t'other side. Nothin' but trees and a shithouse over there."

"You check it out?"

"I didn't take a crap in it, if that's what you mean. Was I s'posed to, *Sir?*" Danzig grinned.

"All right. Let's move out." Goldman's voice sounded parade-ground crisp. He walked stiffly to the broken window and peered inside. Wilhelm watched the little man, his limp almost gone: sergeants don't limp; it damages the image. Inside the house, the ladder sticking out of the floor brought memories of that other cellar and the burpgun fire, the thought making the tip of Wilhelm's nose itch.

Goldman looked down into the hole. "Dark down there. Good for sleepin' but prob'bly cold as hell." He turned and pointed into the hole. "Lumley, go down and take a look. Might find somethin' to eat or some guns or somethin'."

Backing down the ladder, the redhead disappeared into the darkness below. "Boy, its *cold* down here awright!" He sounded tired. "And black as pitch! Cain't see my hand before my...anybody got any matches?"

Goldman, back at the window, tossed a matchbox to Danzig, who dropped it in the hole to Lumley. "Don't lose 'em, Lumley," Goldman shouted, remembering he still had some Lucky Strikes. "I get mean when I can't smoke."

Yellow streaks flashed across the ceiling as Lumley moved about in the cellar. "Ain't nothin' much down here. Buncha rags and busted chairs and, oh, hey, a pile a wood. Too bad we cain't build us a fahr." Darkness, then a flash as he lit another match. "Looks like a blanket or somethin' hangin' against the wall behind the woodpile." Lumley was barely audible now. "Oh, wow! They's a little room back here, and there's a, a pile a somethin'…coal, Ah think. Yeah, theys' a pile a coal inside here!" He was shouting now. "And, wait a minute, there's pile a…let's see…potatoes! A *big* pile a potatoes! Hey, guys…." His match went out and he struck another one. "C'mon down! They's boocoo potatoes down here!"

Goldman made a face. "Don't be tellin' us to come down there! Bring 'em up!" Goldman waited for a response, but got none. "C'mon, Lumley!" he shouted, "We ain't goin' down there! I said bring 'em up!"

My God, the whole damn county must know we're here by now, Wilhelm thought. He walked over to the window and looked out. "One of us can keep watch, Goldman, while the rest go down and…."

Lumley, pockets bulging and one arm full of potatoes, struggled up the ladder into the room. Besides the raw vegetables, they ate leftover Spam and black bread for dinner. The sounds of fevered mastication filled the little parlor.

Goldman, the nascent sergeant, sat near the window looking out. Between bites he said, "Danny, you take first guard. Lumley, you go next, then Wilhelm. I'll take the twilight trick." Surprised looks flashed around: the sergeant had volunteered to stand guard!

"We'll cover the guard, Goldman." Wilhelm said, staring hard at the small soldier. "You gotta rest that leg a yours. We need to make some time tomorrow."

Goldman pursed his lips and turned back to the window. He was holding them up. He knew it. But he would never admit it.

# CHAPTER 22

▼

# OH NO! NOT AGAIN!

About dusk, Danzig, taking his stint on guard, decided to sit outside a while. He liked the woods, the smells, the birds and buzzings of the forest. Leaning comfortably against a tree, he was getting drowsy when he heard the soft shift of pinestraw behind him. Somebody was coming! Crouching low, he ran in the house to the window. Some twenty feet away, three men appeared at the edge of the woods: an officer wearing a cap, twin lightning bolts gleaming on his collar; a steel-helmeted enlisted man carrying a burpgun stood on either side of him.

A finger at his lips to indicate silence, Danzig woke his buddies one at a time. Silently, the four Americans gathered in the shadows behind the window and watched the Germans. The SS officer pulled off his cap and hunkered down, while his men moved off a short way and did the same, their weapons trained on the house. Trained combat soldiers, Wilhelm thought. First-class killers.

"Damn! Looks like they might stick around." Goldman whispered. "They're lookin' for a place to rest, for sure. We better get down below." They picked up their blankets and leftovers, tiptoed to the ladder, and followed their leader down into the icy darkness. They waited for their eyes to adjust, but it didn't help much. The small room, its dirt floor littered with rags and broken furniture, remained essentially invisible. What do we do now, Wilhelm wondered, distrusting Goldman's leadership. Suddenly, a pair of boots, then a second, thumped across the floor. They separated and posted themselves at either end of the little parlor. Now a third pair stepped inside and moved to the middle of the room. A mirthless smile crossed Wilhelm's lips: the Kraut's looking through "Goldman's window," he told himself.

Straining into the darkness, Danzig found Goldman's ear. "Ain't no place to hide down here, Izzy. They come down, we're gonners!" They all heard the quiver in the big Hoosier's words.

"Don't worry, they'll be down, awright," Wilhelm whispered. "Krauts check out everything. Always." Being a blood Kraut myself, he thought, I *know* what I'm talking about.

Lumley felt around and caught Wilhelm's arm. "We could git in that potato hole Ah found a while ago. If I can find it again."

"Lead the way, Lum. It's better'n just standin' here doin' nothin'." He waited for Goldman to disagree, but heard nothing.

"Awright. Y'all grab onto Wilhelm. Hold onto me, Will and let's go." Linked together hand-to-shoulder, they tip-toed sightless to a corner, then turned down a crumbling dirt wall until Lumley suddenly stopped, causing much bumping and stepping on heels. He waited and listened for German voices and movements, but heard nothing. "The woodpile's right here, Will." He pointed, knowing very well none of them could see it. "Ah'll slide behind it like Ah did before and hold the cloth back so y'all can git inside. Keep close to the wall, then bend down and scoot on in."

Wilhelm did as he was told. A sliver of light slipped between the floor and the earth, slightly illuminating the small space. He tiptoed down a narrow aisle between barely visible piles of coal and potatoes and dropped into the far corner. Potatoes made a lumpy bed, but the lumps felt good under his exhausted body. Goldman dropped onto the coal pile across from him, a black avalanche skittering down around him. Danzig, always curious, squatted in the coal near the entrance and peeked around the cloth into the cellar's darker darkness. Lumley, last to enter the room, stretched himself between Wilhelm's feet and the doorway. Settling in, the redhead breathed a sigh into the darkness, thinking he had single-handedly saved his buddies from the burpguns upstairs.

Boots thumped over their heads, lights flashing through cracks in the floor overhead. "Oh, hell," Danzig groaned, "they got flashlights! They're gonna find us down here for sure."

"Shut yer trap, Danny!" Goldman ordered. "You're gonna bring 'em down here yourself if you don't shut up!"

A deep, guttural voice speaking unintelligible words sent four boots across the floor of the parlor toward the ladder. Down below, Danzig sat holding aside the cloth. He watched two broad shadows float down the ladder and stop at the bottom. "Here they come!" he whined, a tear in his voice. He held the cloth shut, as a beam of light flashed around the cellar. Words passed quietly between the two Germans, then, from above, a sharp, authoritative voice spoke. Quickly, they mounted the ladder and disappeared upward. "Damn, that was close!" Danzig mumbled. "*Damn* close!" On guard, as always, he resumed his grip on the cloth and relaxed into the coal pile.

The Americans sighed and stretched themselves. "Yeah, it was, Danny. It sure was. Maybe they'll just rest up some and move on. Let's keep very quiet. We might as well get some shuteye." Coal rippled past him, as Goldman leaned into the coal pile.

Wilhelm lay back and closed his eyes. "Nah. They're movin' at night and sleepin' durin' the day, just like we are. Prob'bly followin' the tracks, too. They'll move on tonight, then we can go. I just hope they ain't stayin' more'n one day."

Sounds of eating and settling in came from above. Wilhelm wanted to say 'See, what'd I tell you,' but he didn't. Danzig continued to keep watch, tirelessly holding aside the cloth at the entranceway. Lumley nestled into the potato pile next to Wilhelm and went to sleep. Goldman sank deeper into the black pile across from Wilhelm and shut his eyes. Except for the sporadic tread of a single pair of boots overhead, silence reigned. In his mind's eye, Wilhelm saw the guard, burpgun across his shoulder, stepping with care past *der Hauptmann*, the officer sleeping *across* from, but not *next* to, the other man. *American* officers would do the same thing. Damned officers are all alike, no matter what army you're in.

Suddenly Wilhelm heard rushing water. An underground stream somewhere? He found Goldman, up on his knees, penis in hand, pissing straight up the coal pile behind Danzig, the dark yellow stream pouring down the black hill and under the cloth out into the cellar.

Danzig grabbed the peeing man's arm, something Wilhelm had never seen him do before. "Jeez, Izzy, squeeze it off! They're li'ble to hear you upstairs and...."

"Dammit, Danny, it ain't gonna wake nobody up!" Goldman jerked his arm away. "When I gotta go, I gotta go!" He did, however, pinch it off as best he could.

They all heard the guard's boots slow and stop. Now a deep voice said something, and four boots headed for the ladder.

As the Germans dropped off the ladder, Danzig, two fingers barely holding the cloth away, watched them flash their lights around. Hearts thumping, the Americans sat upright, breathing short and shallow.

"*Wasser!*" one man kept saying. "*Ich habe wasser gehört!*" The two men separated and, flashing their lights and kicking anything they came to, thoroughly examined the room. Neither man, however, saw fit to dismantle the woodpile. That deep-throated voice, louder, more vehement than ever, startled everybody. The searchers stiffened visibly and trotted across the room to *der Hauptmann*, coming down the ladder. After listening to his tirade, they separated again and started a more thorough search of the walls and corners. "*Wasser!*" they kept whispering, "*Wasser!*" "*Wasser!*"

The Americans all but ceased to breathe.

This time around, they kicked the woodpile apart and one man examined the floor beneath it. "*Hier!*" he shouted, "*Herr Hauptmann! Hier! Hier ist wasser!*" Danzig let go of the cloth, bent and covered his face with his hands.

The officer ran across to his men, dipped a finger into the "*Wasser*" and held it to his nose and tasted it, stiffened and tasted it again. Smiling, he grabbed a torch, fixed its beam on the puddle, and followed the little stream to the hanging cloth. "Ahh!" the officer breathed. "*Was haben wir hier?*" He jerked to his feet, grabbed a burpgun from one of his men and fired into the cloth. The curtain fluttered and fell, Danzig's scream, loud and shrill, cutting across the reverberating blast. *Der Hauptmann*, *Luger* in hand, waved his men into the little room and followed them. On their left, four wide eyes glittered, uplifted palms gray-white in the torch's beam. Goldman's coal-spattered face jutted from beneath Danzig's bleeding body on their right. Mouth red in the sleeve of light, the small soldier kept shouting, "*Bitte! Bitte! Nicht schiessen! Nicht schiessen!*"

Wilhelm tried to think where he'd heard those words before.

# CHAPTER 23

▼

# FREE AT LAST?

Silhouetted against the twilight sky in the doorway, the SS officer stood speaking to the *Obergefreiter*, the enlisted man with two upside-down stripes on his sleeve. Goldman, watching the officer's lips in the fading light, tried to translate. "Bugger's got a funny look about 'im, ain't he? Cheeks twitch and his eyes keep flittin' around like he sees somethin' in the air," he whispered. "Other two ain't 'zackly Einsteins, neither."

Wilhelm, sitting next to Goldman against the parlor wall, was thinking about Danzig lying dead in the hole below, how strangers would find it, shake their heads and say, "Another dead American. Let's get him outta here." He shook the thought away and turned to Goldman. "Well, lucky us, caught by some nutty SS captain and two loonies. I knew I shoulda stayed in camp. I just *knew* it! I never shoulda listened to you."

"That Kraut thinks he knows where we're at," Goldman slowly translated. "Says it's about twenty-five miles to the river." Goldman's eyebrows jumped and his ears wiggled. "Why, the dirty...."

"What's he sayin'?" Lumley leaned in close. The third German, a *Gefreiter* with one upside-down stripe on his sleeve, stepped in and jabbed his *Schmeisser* at the hostages. They stared up at him and clamped their mouths shut.

When the guard withdrew, Goldman went back to translating. "Bastid says only one of us is necessary." His lips barely moved. "Likes the redhead, likes his color, I think, and, wait…his man says they need all of us because…shit, he talks funny…got a funny dialect."

"Cover your face," Wilhelm hissed. "Your tic's rollin' like mad. The guard'll know you're translatin'." Both Americans smiled, as if something funny had been said.

"Yeah." Goldman ducked his head and twisted his eyes around, but *der Hauptmann* had turned away.

When darkness fell they lined up and moved out, the two-striper on point, the officer, followed by the prisoners, the *Gefreiter* bringing up the rear. Lumley and Wilhelm, wishing Danzig were there, helped Goldman keep up with the Germans' rapid pace. It would be a long night. Since the Germans had devoured all their food; the Americans suffered the pains of starvation alone. Several hours passed before they stopped to rest. Goldman dropped to the ground, his left pants leg dark with blood. Lumley tore a strip off the bottom of his shirt, tied it around his leg, and twisted it tight with a stick. "Let it go ever' so often, buddy, or it'll go dead on you."

"Yeah, yeah, I know," Goldman said testily, sick of hearing those words. The look on the redhead's face said Goldman would never make it to the river.

*Der Hauptmann,* standing over the two men, shoved Lumley aside and squinted down at the little American. "*Steh auf! Aufsteh'n!* Up! Up! Schtandt up!" Goldman, glaring, struggled to his feet. "*Vit us du* vill moof, *oder du ich schiess!*" The officer fingered the butt of his *Luger.*

"Move with us or I shoot you!" Goldman understood those words very well. "Don't worry, *Sir*," he shot back. "I can go anyplace you can—you rotten sumbitch!" The appended phrase hung almost inaudibly in the cold, wet air. As Goldman turned and limped away, the officer's scowl softened, seeming, to Wilhelm at least, to admire the little Jew's spunk.

The column set off again at a faster pace. They stopped to rest only two more times before the sky began to brighten. As they slogged along, the words *one hostage* hung in Wilhelm's thoughts. *I gotta be the one. I can talk to der Hauptmannn and tell him mein Grossvater ist von Deutschland gekommen, von Mühlenberg, or Meckmühl,* or someplace around there. Hell, maybe he's from around there himself. One thing I do know, a man's gotta put himself first. Down deep, though, he wondered if Lum would compete with him somehow. He didn't think he would, but he couldn't bring himself to care what he did. He *knew* what he had to do and would do it, come what may.

As the first light of morning filtered through the trees, the six men stopped in a little clearing. The Americans dropped to the ground, exhausted. Wilhelm could hear engines on his right, tanks and trucks on the other side of the railroad tracks. Must be a road over there, he decided. From his left came a gurgling sound—*wasser,* he thought, maybe a creek emptying into the Elbe. My kingdom for a canoe, a raft, anything that floats. I'd be behind our lines in nothing flat. He settled onto wet, cold pinestraw and loosened his leggings, the left anklebone raw under the knife's scabbard.

Lumley said Goldman's leg looked better, less bloody, more color now in his calf. "Ah cain't believe it," he whispered to Wilhelm. "Tell that li'l bugger he *cain't* do somethin', and he'll *do* it no matter what." Lumley rolled up one of his blankets and placed it under Goldman's knee to keep the injured thigh up off the ground. Once a medic, always a medic, Wilhelm mused. *A rare bird, if I ever saw one.*

The day passed, the Americans sleeping fitfully without interruption. The SS officer slept, too, one of his men on guard at all times. Just before sundown, Wilhelm awoke to the sound of voices. Some distance away, *der Hauptmannn* and *der Obergefreiter* conferred quietly. *Planning which one of us they're going to kill first*, he surmised, looking around. The dark blue eyes of the *Gefreiter* stared down the barrel of his *Schmeisser* at him.

Suddenly, the guard looked up and stiffened. He gave a low whistle and pointed. The officer and the *Obergefreiter* ducked low and came running. A rough line of a dozen or more Russian soldiers came down off the tracks and approached the woods. *Luger* in hand, *der Hauptmann* woke Lumley and Goldman, and, seeing Wilhelm's wide eyes, waved him and the guard to join them. The Germans, their captives before them, duck-walked deeper into the woods. Stopping, *der Hauptmann* positioned his men behind trees on either side and herded the Americans further back. The sounds of rushing water came more clearly now, the presumed creek closer but still out of sight.

"Why are we hiding?" Wilhelm muttered. "Thought they grabbed us so they could get through the Rooskies to the American lines. Why don't they just stand up, parlay and take us through?"

Lumley shook his head.

The officer stuck his *Luger* into Goldman's side, threw his arm around his neck, and pulled him in tight. To Wilhelm's surprise, the German and the Jew—an unlikely couple, he thought—took cover behind a large, nearly leafless bush. The German waved Lumley and Wilhelm to trees on either side and muttered something into Goldman's ear. Wilhelm saw the small one's cheek squeeze in a knot.

By now the Russians had found themselves a place to stop, their helmets and rifles just visible to the onlookers. Loud voices and laughter echoed though the woods. Breakfast time, Wilhelm thought, licking his lips. He looked across at Lumley, some ten feet the other side of their captor and saw the redhead licking his lips, too. Wonder what *der Kraut* would do if I ran out there and grabbed some breakfast with them? Shoot me? Be dumb, wouldn't it? Maybe I should…nah.

The SS officer was shouting at Goldman now. "Zey see us, Jew, *du bist tot! Versteh?*" Goldman's head moved slightly. Wilhelm knew what *tot* meant. *Dead. Very dead.* The German looked over at Wilhelm. "*Und du! Du bist auch tot!*" Me too! Nice of the bastard to let me know. The wild blue eyes danced around toward Lumley: "*Aber du, Rotkopf! Du kommt mit mir!*"

So! Goldman was right: he wants to take the redhead but not us! Look how he's holding Goldman! The bugger's a goddamn fairy! And he prefers redheads! The German's wild eyes bounced back to Wilhelm, then back to the *Luger* digging into Goldman's temple. The bastard never intended to let us go. We've been dead men from the start. A broad guffaw bounced among the trees, Rooskies laughing. So close and so goddamn far away. I oughtta run out there and holler, "*Amerikanski! Amerikanski!*" They'd probably get me before the Krauts did.

Wilhelm eased against the tree and studied the distance between himself and the SS man. Suddenly, a crackle of underbrush and a Russian helmet bounced toward them among the trees. The man stopped near the *Gefreiter's* tree and his head disappeared. The splash of the man's urine was barely audible above the distant rush of the stream. He's taking a leak, Wilhelm decided. The Russian turned to go but stopped and turned back. A belt buckle tinkled and the helmet dropped out of sight again. Now he's decided to take a shit. Could this be his last one, ever?

Wilhelm felt into his left legging. The knife seemed to reach out and push his fingers. Like Fritzie, he thought, wanting to be petted. That solemn vow never to use the knife to kill flashed across his mind. He thought of Volitch and how close he'd come to using it that time. A smile twisted his lips. He would not have recognized his own face in a mirror.

Wilhelm almost dropped the knife when the burpgun fired. The Russian's helmet leapt straight up and dropped out of sight. "What the hell?" Wilhelm muttered. "They've done it now!" A stunned silence, then Russian shouts and wild firing in all directions. Both *Schmeissers* opened up and all hell broke loose. Bullets whined, snapped, and ricocheted. Wilhelm and Lumley hugged the ground. *Der Hauptmannn*, however, still behind the leafless bush, only hugged his Jewish shield more tightly.

Amidst the roar of the guns, a voice came up in Wilhelm's ear: *This is it, Jimmy! You gotta do somethin'! Now!* His dad. He'd heard it a million times: *Do something, boy! Do something!* He shifted his weight to one foot and decided it was now or never, bullets or no bullets.

In three low, wide steps, Wilhelm was behind the German. He slammed his left forearm across the man's eyes, yanked his head back, and plunged the knife into his exposed throat. Blood, German blood like his own, spurted through his fingers into Goldman's hair. The *Luger*, firing wildly, swung up toward Wilhelm, but Goldman's hand came up with it and pulled it down. The bullets meant for Wilhelm drilled holes between Goldman's legs. Wilhelm held the jerking, twisting man until Goldman could slip away. Gurgling, the knife still deep in his throat, *Der Hauptmann* fell forward on his face, blood pooling around him. The incubus on his back held him down with all his might. In seconds the SS officer stopped struggling and lay still. I've killed another Kraut from behind, Wilhelm thought. Always from behind. But this time it was *right*. *Very right*.

"He's dead, Will. C'mon! Let 'im go!" Bullets from the Russian guns snapped past as Lumley grabbed Wilhelm's shoulders. "We gotta git outta here before the Rooskies…." Seeing Wilhelm's wild look, he gave him a mighty pull and leaned close. "C'mon, Will! Let's go! Let's go!" The redhead turned and crawled away toward the sounds of rushing water. Goldman, on his belly, the *Luger* in hand, appeared from nowhere behind him.

Wilhelm, elated, crawled behind a tree and began to clean the knife on his overcoat. "Might need you again, old buddy," he whispered. "Never know, do you? Nossir! You *never* know." The crash of three Russians in the bushes brought him around. The point man, bayonet up, hit the ground and took aim at Lumley.

Goldman reared up, raised his hands and dropped the *Luger*. "Don't shoot! *Amerikanisch!* Uhhhh, *Amerikanski!* Uhhhh, prisoners! *Krieg*ies! POWs!" Russian bullets from behind snapped around him. He dropped back into the prone position. "Don't shoot! Don't shoot!" He shouted over and over.

The lead Russian turned, waved at his leader and lowered his rifle. The man in charge crawled past and stopped before Lumley. He said something unintelligible, then motioned his men forward. Wilhelm smelled their rotten breath and filthy pants as they moved past him. He smiled, silently wishing them luck. Some day, he told himself, I'll come back and find that Rooskie and buy him the biggest damn steak he ever saw.

The Americans watched their rescuers slip in behind the burp-gun-wielding Germans and shoot them in the back. Wilhelm looked back at the SS man's body. Cowboys don't sneak up behind people and kill them, he mused, but soldiers do. Guess that makes me a soldier, a real soldier. Just what I always wanted to be. Ha! Like hell!

# CHAPTER 24

▼

# I LOVE MEATBALLS!

"Dammit, now's when we need Danzig." Goldman got up and limped over to the nearest Russian. "*Sprechen Sie Deutsch?*" The man cocked his head and stared. "*Deutsch? Sprechen Sie Deutsch?*" The Russian mumbled something and turned away. Head shaking, the American limped back and sat down between his buddies. "Bastid probably knows what I said...just won't talk." He kneaded his sore thigh with both hands.

Some of the Russians carried their dead out of the woods; others dressed wounds and checked weapons, but most of them sat and finished their lunch. The Germans were left to rot where they lay. Just another day in the war.

"Sumbitches don't offer *us* nuttin', do they? Do we look fat, or somethin'?" Goldman struggled to get up.

"Hey, sit tight, buddy. These killers don't look too damn friendly to me. I wouldn't be pushin' at them." Wilhelm noticed one of the Russians beckoning. They got Goldman up and followed the man out of the woods and over the tracks to a truck full of soldiers. The three

- 242 -

Americans squeezed in next to the driver. When the starter squealed, Wilhelm said, gleefully, "Hey, you hear that? This is a GI three-quarter-ton just like ole Kratus! Wonder what ever happened to her, anyway." His senses filled with the sound of the engine. "I can't believe we're finally pullin' outta this mess! We're goin' home, guys! Goin' home!" He wanted to thank somebody—God, or somebody—but he didn't know how. Watching the driver shift into third gear, he heard himself say, "You oughtta double-clutch it, buddy. You're gonna ruin the transmission if you don't." The driver, eyes on the road, ignored him.

Goldman sighed. "Y'know, Wilhelm, there ain't no place I'd druther bleed to deat' than in that fuckin' truck a yours." He sucked air and lifted the bloody pants leg away from his wound. "Fuckin' leg's gonna kill me yet."

"Hey! Listen!" Lumley leaned out the side of the truck. "Hear that? They's water a gurglin' over there! Ah bet it's the river!" Hand behind his ear, he leaned further out. "Yeah! It's over there! Ah can see it through the trees!" The truck dropped into a hole, and he almost fell out.

"Yeah, I hear it, awright. But is it *die Elbe*?" Goldman stared across Lumley at the woods.

The driver wheeled the truck around a sharp turn and suddenly there it was: *Die Elbe! The River!* A pontoon bridge rolled and yawed in the current, inviting the truck to go across. Pup tents populated the woods, a row of GIs standing in line before a big tent on the other side. "The *American lines!* My God, I never thought I'd see 'em again." Wilhelm had tears in his eyes. "We're here, guys! We're finally here!"

"Yeah. A sight for sore eyes, huh." Voice thick, Lumley sounded almost sad.

"I'll believe it when I git over there." Goldman said, squinting at the line of GIs.

The truck stopped hard, and the men in back scrambled out into the road. An officer, medals glinting in the sunshine, came out of a little house next to the bridge and spoke to the driver. The Americans understood only one word: "*Nyet!*" It came, not once but many times. Meanwhile, the men in the road had marched away.

"C'mon, you fuckin' Rooskie, what's the holdup?" Goldman, cheek twitching, yelled across Wilhelm at the officer, who coolly ignored him. The officer stepped away, and the driver turned the truck off the road toward a copse of trees near the river. "What the hell we goin' over here for?" Goldman shouted. Without a word, the driver stopped the truck, dropped out, and walked away. Two Russians, rifles in hand, came up and escorted the ex-POWs toward the trees, pointed at the ground, and took up positions on either side of them. Annoyed, frustrated, furious, the Americans found trees to lean against and sat down. If a soldier knows anything, he knows how to wait.

"Pup tents look real good, don't they? Never thought Ah'd see the day one a them'd look so good." Lumley grinned.

"Yeah, ain't it da troot?" Goldman groaned. "We're here, and dey're over dere. I don't git it! Don't they see us over here? Still hurtin' and starvin' and bleedin'?" Closing his eyes, he slid down the tree and lay flat. "Once a fuckin' POW, *always* a fuckin' POW!"

All morning they watched Russian trucks come and go, some crossing the bridge, some not. About midday, meat, bread, and drink were delivered to their guards, who sat down and ate. The Americans licked their lips and made motions. They got nothing.

"Y'know, for some reason my ole girlfriend, Lucy, keeps jumpin' up." Goldman scratched his chin. "Usta hang around the poolroom alla time, she did, watchin' me take moola off the suckers. Wonder if she's still...."

"Girlfriend? C'mon, Goldman, you never mentioned any girlfriends before." Wilhelm grinned at Lumley. "In fact, you ain't never mentioned any kinda females before. I was beginnin' to think maybe you might be a, you know, a...."

Goldman glared at him.

"Hey, that reminds me, Will, you ain't never finished that story you was tellin' me. Remember? 'Bout the time you was in that ho-house deliverin' Cokes. And this girl—what's her name?—come after you? Whyn't you go on and finish it up while we're sittin' here killin' time?"

"Naaah. I'm too damn hungry to be talkin' 'bout sex. Nothin' happened anyway. We ever get across this damn river, I'll tell you sometime." Wilhelm frowned at the river.

"A ho-house, huh?" Goldman reared up. "I ain't heard nuttin' 'bout no ho-house before! C'mon, boy, let's hear it!"

Lumley chuckled. "Actually, Ah just wanted to find out if you was still a virgin, that's all. You never did say, y'know."

"A *virgin!* Shit, Wilhelm, don't tell me you ain't lost your cherry yet!" A nasty smile broke across Goldman's dirty face.

"Don't tell me you *ain't* lost it!" Wilhelm shouted, still looking at the waves.

The guards were staring at both of them.

"Go on, quit lookin' like that. We're jus' plannin' to take your rifles and kill bot' a yuz, 'at's all." Goldman turned back to Wilhelm. "Course I lost it, dummy. Long time ago. In fift' grade, us guys had a eight'-grader 'at let us have it any time we wanted. Sloppy seconds ain't da best, but, hell, y'gotta take what you can git." He snickered. "You prob'bly don't even know what sloppies are, do ya?"

That did it. Feeling weak and a little sick, Wilhelm got up and walked over to the river. One guard got up and followed but said nothing. He hunkered down on the bank and squeezed his belly tight. Sometimes that slowed the hunger pains. An old POW trick. He stared into the swirling water, wondering if he could swim it, but he knew he couldn't. A poor swimmer, he'd hardly made it across the pool at Garfield Park. "Prob'bly end up feeding the sharks out in the Baltic," he muttered.

He looked down at his hands. Traces of reddish-black lines still webbed his right palm, a black solid, packed tightly around the nails. Charko's blood. From the hill on that first day. *My God, will it never leave me? No, it can't be Charko's blood. That's SS blood. It felt so good to kill that sonofabitch.* He took a deep, pensive breath. *Never could've done that before—kill a man with my bare hands like that. The war has made a killer out of me. But I hope there's still a difference—be kind to yourself, Mom always said. I'm a soldier, and my job is to kill people. Never thought of soldiering that way before, but we're all killers, hired to kill the enemies of our country.*

Wilhelm remembered Belgium and the black, deadly hole in the muzzle of that young Kraut's burpgun and his fingers on his privates. *An enemy, for sure. Wonder if he lived to be the hero he figured he was.*

The tinkle and slap of mess gear came softly across the water. *They've eaten over there, the buggers, and now they're washing up. Their bellies are full. Hey, what's that? Smells like* tomato sauce! *They had* spaghetti *for lunch! Jesus H. Christ!* He wanted to yell something, anything. He got up, took a deep breath, and cupped his hands around his mouth. Something inside said don't bring attention to yourself—a long-time rule since capture—never bring attention to yourself. He didn't make a sound. He sat down again and watched some GIs amble through the woods and crawl into their pup tents. Hitting the sack. Must be nice.

A question suddenly popped into his mind: these Rooskies ain't planning on taking us from here to *Odessa*, are they? Would they bring us all the way over here and...he squinted up into the sunshine and shouted, "Hell, I wouldn't put it past 'em."

A sudden roar and a column of topless, five-ton trucks burst around the curve in the road, dust flying all around. It slammed to a stop at the guardhouse next to the bridge. Russians quickly surrounded the lead truck, the bridge officer, fat legs pumping, waddling out and waving them away. Wilhelm marveled at the rippling of the pines along the road behind the column. He hadn't seen heat waves like those since he left the states.

Lumley jumped up. "Hey! They's *stars* on them trucks! They're American! And look at all the guys standin' in 'em. Must be hundreds of 'em! Wonder who...."

"Look like GIs to me! But, but, they couldn't be...unless...." Wilhelm's jaw dropped. Could it be?

"Look like a buncha fuckin' *Krieg*ies to me!" Goldman was up now, too. "Hey, wait a minute! Yeah! There's what's-his-name from tent 4! Well, I'll be damned!" Rifles up, the guards stepped before the three Americans, blocking their view.

"Them trucks're ours!" Goldman, pointing, shouted in the guards' faces. "Them guys come from our camp!" The Russians didn't move. "They're from Camp Three A! Our camp! They go across the river, dammit, we're 'sposed to go with 'em!" The bigger, tougher-looking guard shoved Goldman back with the butt of his rifle. "Damn you! Them's are our guys over there!" Goldman screamed. "Them's *POWs*! *Americanski! Krieg*ies!" Lumley grabbed Goldman and held him back.

Now the bridge officer came out, handed some papers to the lead driver, and waved him on. Water poured onto the roadway, splashing the sides of the trucks, as the column moved across the yawing, swaying bridge. The newly repatriated Americans clapped, yelled, waved, and stomped their feet.

Wilhelm stiffened. "Oh, my God, look! It's Jones! In that last truck! That big guy there! See?" The tall, gaunt American smiled broadly as he passed across the bridge.

"Yeah, 'Ah see 'im, Will. At's him, awright. That bunch is from IIIA, sure as hell." Lumley's lips formed a hard, straight line.

"Yeah. I'd know that ugly sucker anywhere. Seein' his mug makes me wanta puke. But I ain't got nothin' to puke with."

The gleeful shouts of their erstwhile companions rose above the river's gush and died away as the convoy disappeared into the woods. "Yeah, go on, you bastids, celebrate! Celebrate while you can!" Goldman's fist slammed into his palm. "They *ride* alla way over here and go straight on across, and we walk t'ree, four days and damn near't get our ass shot off and here we are sittin' on our butts waitin'! And for what? When are these fuckin' Rooskies gonna do somthin'?" Goldman stamped a frustrated foot. "Danny was here, we could talk to dese dumb bastids. Hell, I give up!" He looked up at the sky and began to sing: "Oh, Danny boy, oh where are you, my Danny boy? We need you, Danny boy, we need you now, my Danny boy." He dropped against a tree and closed his eyes.

*     *     *     *

Just after sundown, a Russian officer, his broad, bemedaled chest glittering, arrived at the bridge. He and a contingent of men debarked from a truck, formed a column, and, with the officer at the head, stood waiting at the bridge.

On the American side, a lieutenant led a platoon of men out of the woods onto the bridge, halting them about half way across. He turned to his men and shouted, "At Ease!"

At those familiar words, Wilhelm and his buddies sat up. "Hey, what's that all about?"

Lumley grinned. "Maybe they're gonna rassle and see who gits to keep us for the rest of the year."

"Well, I don't give a damn what they do, just so they git on with it. I'm starvin'!"

"Hey, what's goin' on?" Goldman, blinking, wiped his eyes.

The Russian detail marched onto the bridge to meet the Americans, the officers saluting. With their interpreter, they proceeded to parlay.

"Look how they stand back away from each other. Wonder if there's a line across the middle out there. One they ain't s'posed to cross."

"Ah thought we was all on the same side, but they sure ain't actin' like it."

Suddenly, the American officer saluted, about-faced, and led his men off the bridge. The American unit did a column-right, halted, turned and stood at attention facing the river. The Russian unit came back east, and the commanding officer went into the little guardhouse.

"What the hell're they doin' now? Havin' a shot a wadka'r, somethin'?" Goldman groaned. "I can see the headlines back home now: 'Officers Talk Shit While Hero Bleeds to Deat'!'" Wilhelm snickered. Lumley covered his mouth.

It was dark when the guards kicked the three ex-POWs awake. The bridge was a blur, lighted at both ends with lights the size of buckets. With the wounded man supported between the other two, the Americans were escorted to the rear of a Russian unit standing at the bridge. The Russians came to attention, shouldered arms and, on command, started forward. Grinning, Wilhelm thought he could hear *Semper*

*Fidelis* playing, as they hobbled along behind the Russians. Barely on the bridge, the unit stopped. The Americans craned their necks to see up ahead.

An American colonel with a platoon of men stood waiting at the center of the bridge. Wilhelm's heart thumped so hard he could hardly breathe. Is this it? Are we going across? Twisting sideways, he saw a flash of paper, saw the colonel scribble something on it and hand it to the Russian officer. Boots shuffling, the Russian column opened down the center, the officers, Russian and American, coming into view. Without being told to, Wilhelm stumbled forward, one hand supporting Goldman, skipping twice to match Lumley's step. As the bridge rose beneath his feet, he floated along, head swimming. Russian soldiers slid past him, moving east, he thought, going the wrong way. Go West, young man, go West, somebody had said. Yes, sir, *I'm going West!* Wait! Who's that? The Rooskie officer! Look at all those medals! Now the American officer, a *full colonel!* And I can't salute him! Damn! Goldman's got my arm! He'll be mad! No! He's *smiling!* The Colonel's smiling at me! GIs pass by now. And they're smiling, too! They love me and I love them. God, how I love them! But, hey, you guys're at Attention. You ain't s'posed to smile! My arm! I think it's paralyzed!

He staggered off the bridge, pulling Goldman and Lumley with him. Lumley's long arms pulled Wilhelm and Goldman in tight, his red beard scratching their cheeks. Suddenly Goldman was gone. A couple of medics had him on a stretcher, hauling him off. Wilhelm and Lumley stared at each other, whooped and hollered and clapped. The colonel came up, shook hands, and congratulated each of them. His words sounded important, extremely important, but Wilhelm understood none of them. He just stood there, his eyes streaming, not believing where he was: *The American lines!* He was across the Elbe and behind *the American lines!*

Now that the colonel was gone, he wished he'd asked why the Rooskies let truckloads of *Krieg*ies cross over but held the three of them back. Did they think we were heroes because we killed some *Kraut*s? That's crazy! A typical military snafu. How stupid can you get? Danzig and Charko and Dolan—wouldn't it be great if they were here, too? Why did *we* make it and they didn't? Who or what decided? I think we're just plain lucky. And, right now, *I*'m the luckiest guy in the whole damned world.

A first sergeant beckoned and Wilhelm and Lumley followed him into the big tent. The air was warm inside and smelled of disinfectant. He hadn't been in a lighted room for so long, the electric lights made him squint. "Pure heaven," he muttered, "light and heat at last, pure heaven."

Goldman lay spread-eagled, bare-bellied, and pants-less on a table, white-coats hovering over him. "Doin' okay over there, buddy?" Wilhelm shouted. The little man's head came up. He grinned and nodded, that notorious tic out of action.

A GI walked up to Wilhelm with a big, black bellows in his hand. He blew a white powder into his hair, pulled his pants away, and squirted it down inside. "Hey! What the hell you doin'? What's that stuff?"

"DDT, buddy, it won't hurt ya. Kills bugs. Makes 'em quit chewin' your balls." The medic chuckled. "All you stinkin' POWs get it. Okay, raise your arms. Gotta git 'em outta there, too."

"Your hair's done gone white, Will." Lumley snickered. "Krauts treat you that bad, did they?" His dirty, red beard and bushy head were already white. They laughed and began to dance around, shaking the powder out of their shorts. The medic pointed them to a row of chairs and told them to wait there for the doctor.

Wilhelm stared at the small folding chairs. A long time since I've seen a chair, he thought. What simple little things they are, so comfortable and up off the ground. Sitting down, he looked across at Goldman, still besieged by the medics. He felt guilty for being so healthy and thought again what a lucky guy he was.

A tall captain in a long white coat bustled into the tent. "All right, you men," he said, "get undressed." The two "men" looked at each other, chuckled, and took off their clothes. Wilhelm was surprised by the dirt clinging to his overcoat, the greasy feel of his beloved field jacket, the terrible stench rising from his wool sweater and shirt, and the appalling filth in his crotch. When he tossed his pants, now slick with dirt both front and back, on a trash pile, they stood up a moment by themselves before collapsing. In the bright light, he saw his thin, narrow thighs and wasted calves were wrapped in loose, gray skin. My God, he thought, look what's happened to me. The folks'll think I'm some kind of ghost!

The doctor checked their hearts, ears, eyes, noses and throats, held their testicles and told them to cough, examined their hands, and asked if their feet had been frozen. Both men said no, then maybe. Lumley finally said yes, his were. "You're in pretty good shape. A little undernourished, perhaps, but that's to be expected." He smiled. Wilhelm laughed aloud. Lumley smiled into his hand.

"All right! Sergeant!" The doctor turned to the first sergeant next to him. "Get these men a shower and some clothes. And something to eat, toot sweet!"

The sergeant pointed to a pile of fatigue uniforms in the corner of the tent. He turned and followed the doctor out of the tent. Wilhelm smiled through his tears. *Toot sweet! Sergeant Dolan always said that.*

Minutes later, a short, squat staff sergeant with an apron across his ample waist came in. "Yooz the ones 'at jus' come in?" A voice like a grinder.

The two men, now in stiff new fatigues, looked at each other. They recognized this round little man with the sweaty face, the forever obscene and unforgiving martinet who exercised absolute power over poor unfortunates called Kitchen Police. He was a *mess sergeant through and through.* Right now they *loved* him.

"Yeah, Sarge, we're the ones, awright." Wilhelm sniffed and unconsciously brought his heels together.

The sergeant looked them up and down. "Yeah, yooz look like alla the rest of 'em. Dirty as hell." It was his turn to sniff. "T'ink dere's some sketti left. Yooz want it, come and get it." He executed a half-hearted about-face and, thighs rubbing, ambled out of the tent.

Lumley clapped Wilhelm on the back: "How about it, Will? Spaghetti okay with you?"

Wilhelm shouted, "Hey, Sarge! You got any meatballs with that? I love meatballs!"

# EPILOGUE

▼

After a ride on a C-47, in those days called a "Gooney Bird," across bombed-out Germany, I ended up in Camp Lucky Strike on the coast of France. Between bouts of sleeping, eating, and standing in chow line, I sent my folks a telegram, courtesy of the American Red Cross, telling them I was okay and to expect me home soon. I felt this was completely unnecessary, since I had written them more than once from the camps, explaining that I was a prisoner and unhurt.

After a twelve-day ship-trip across the placid, gently rolling North Atlantic, as opposed to the same wild pitching sea of the previous November, our so-called "Victory Ship" entered New York harbor and slipped past the Statue of Liberty amid a myriad of small ships with horns hooting, their fountains of water saluting us. An unforgettable sight. I joined many a tough, seasoned soldier in shedding a tear that day.

It was a warm, humid June evening when, after a long, boring ride, the train pulled into Union Station in downtown Indianapolis. I called home immediately. My mother answered, saying my folks had heard nothing from or about me since a War Department telegram designating me Missing In Action. They had been over-joyed to receive my "unnecessary" telegram from Lucky Strike. Again, I was furious with those "rotten *Krauts*" who had failed to forward my letters.

When the old blue '39 Plymouth pulled up before the station, I tossed my duffle bag in the back and dived in beside it. Fritzie, my half-beagle, half-dachshund buddy of many years, licked my face so vigorously I could hardly speak to my folks. The car rolled quietly down South Meridian street past Manual Training High School— my *alma mater*—past Garfield Park, the scenes of many a baseball game I played in, and swung into the alley behind the house. Nothing had changed. My room, Fritzie, my mother and dad, all felt the same. With Germany, the POW camps, and the war behind me, the future now ahead lay bright and promising.

The GI Bill paid for my undergraduate and graduate education at Indiana University and the University of Wisconsin, respec-tively. What a lucky guy I was to have the United States of America waiting to welcome me back! There are no words to express the feelings I have for this great country of ours. I just hope my chil-dren, presently middle-aged, will enjoy the rights and privileges my generation has enjoyed so much.

*        *        *        *

Wars have been fought since the beginning of time. Why? Is there no other way to solve disputes among men, among nations? Our present record would indicate that there is not. Men (and I use the word generically) have, it seems, always been willing to die for a cause, the origin and the importance of which, they poorly under-stand.

I have, in *Wilhelm's War,* an amateur effort at best, tried to portray the lives of young men trapped in that idiocy. I hope at least a few readers will gain from it some insight into what combat, capture, and the life of a prisoner is like.

I still wonder why men—why I—willingly joined the armed services, organizations dedicated to killing other men. Is this a rational decision? Is it because their buddies have joined, because of a sincere desire to support their leaders, their country, or just to avoid criticism by, even ostracism from, their society? Or perhaps it is the result of some deep-seated, testosterone-driven lust for blood, a hidden desire for the lawlessness, the chaos and absence of morality present in combat. Perhaps this wild, unfettered desire to kill the "enemy" is forever embedded in our genes. A possibility, I think, rarely considered.

The question that filled my mind, as I sat starving in the frozen waste of that German POW camp during the winter of 1944–45 was this: Is all this suffering really necessary?

Charles H. Stammer
October 2004

0-595-33609-4

Printed in the United States
24431LVS00002B/154-186